Broken Lands

Roxy Leigh

Book Cover by Wingfield Designs

Formatting by Lukas and Leigh Literary Services

Proofreading by Scarlet Le Clair

For anyone who ever used a fantasy world as an escape. I see you.

Content Warnings

- Open Door Spice

- Kidnapping

- Violence

- Cliffhanger

- Why Choose (FMC ends up with multiple partners)

Contents

CHAPTER ONE

Riley

"Time's up," I yelled as I clapped my hands together to grab the children's attention. "Clean up quickly and meet Miss Hatley in the mudroom. She'll escort you to the ceremony." I smiled at the group I'd been working with this morning before turning to gather some gloves, pots, and shears to put away.

A small sob, barely audible above the sound of chattering, caught my attention and I spun around to find Nora still in her seat, crying quietly.

I put down the items I'd still been holding and walked to her, squatting down in front of her and lifting her chin to see her face.

"What's wrong, sweetheart?" I asked softly. Her short black hair framed her pale face, the effect making her bright blue eyes seem larger than normal. Tears poured freely down her cheeks as her gaze met mine.

"I'm sorry," she sobbed. "I didn't mean to. It slipped from my hand."

"What are you... Oh."

Behind her chair, half underneath the table, was a scattering of dirt. The pot itself had rolled a few desks down while the seedling had landed underneath her chair.

"Please don't punish me. It was an accident. I'm so sorry."

"Shh." I stood up from my crouch and wrapped my arms around her, holding her close. The poor child was terrified she'd be in trouble for knocking over the plant.

"You've done nothing wrong." I guess there'd be some people that would, but I couldn't imagine punishing a child for such a simple mistake myself. Just the thought of it set my nerves on edge.

Earth changed during the Last War. We damaged the land and soil with the weapons we wielded against each other. Our history books—those that survived—show lush green fields and flourishing crops. I've never seen anything like those photos. What little grass we have now is dry and brittle, our fields dusty and barren. Our crops struggle. We struggle. Every single plant is a precious, treasured resource.

I pull back from Nora, wiping the tears from her cheeks and offering her a gentle smile.

"Why don't we see if we can save it? We can add some of my special compost to the pot, maybe some worm castings too.

That might give the seedling a chance to grow. What do you think?"

Good crops are scarce, and they require constant attention. Even then, we barely grow enough to feed the children and staff at the orphanage. We often can't afford to buy extra food at the local market, either. It breaks my heart when we don't have enough. That's why I took on this role in the garden. I'd been blessed with a green thumb and enjoyed the peace that gardening bought me. I enjoyed knowing I was doing the best I could for my community, too.

Nora sniffled and then nodded, wiping her cheeks with the sleeves of her dress. Moving toward the front of the room, I grabbed a couple of trowels and a small container of compost.

I returned to Nora and together we set about scooping the spilled dirt back into the pot, mixing in the compost and gently resettling the seedling.

"How about I keep a special eye on this one, okay? You need to meet Miss Hatley and the rest of the children before they leave without you, but you can come back and check on it later."

She smiled at me. Her tears were long gone now that she knew I wasn't going to punish her for knocking over her potted seedling.

"Okay. Thanks Riley. I'll see you later." She turned for the door before pausing and turning to face me again. "Have you heard from James yet?"

Pain spread through my chest at the mention of my older brother. We'd grown up here at Sommer's orphanage. Miss

Hatley had taken us in when she'd found us wandering the streets together, wet and starving, the day the Last War ended fifteen years ago.

No one had come forward to claim us, so here we'd stayed—or at least I'd stayed. James left two years ago. He was lucky enough to be chosen to ascend.

I blinked back the tears threatening to fall as my heart ached with the need to know what had happened to him. I stifled a sob as I answered her, "No. Not a peep. I'm sure he'll write to me soon." Forcing a smile, I waved her on her way and put away the last of the tools, my hands shaking as I worked.

I hadn't heard from my brother in over a year. The fae had chosen him to ascend, and he'd moved to Danann a little under two years ago. He'd promised to write, and he had to start with. Six months later and his letters had stopped coming. No one knew what happened to him. Nor did they seem to care. His disappearance left me with a bad feeling swirling in my gut. It nagged at me and kept me up at night. Something wasn't right. He wouldn't just cut me out. It had always been the two of us against the world. We only had each other.

I desperately needed to find him.

Sighing to myself, I turned to lift the heavy tray of seedlings, and started out towards the greenhouse. It was time to check on the tomatoes I'd transferred yesterday. I breathed in deeply, the scent of fresh earth filling my nose as I passed Mr Cole, the caretaker, puttering around in the garden.

His contribution was small these days. The arthritis in his hands didn't allow him the range of motion and dexterity he needed to contribute in any meaningful way. He was good company, though, often spouting stories of life before the Last War.

I could hear the children chattering in the distance as they made their way to the main house. They were excited about the ceremony today. It was the first time for some of them. Most of the town got excited. Once a year, applications for ascension were open for anyone eighteen and above. It was a chance to leave the struggle of our community behind and join the fae in their city in hopes of a better life.

The only requirements were to undergo the required testing and pay the modest application fee.

Maybe it was modest to the fae from Danann, but here... it was more than most families earned in a month. Most of those who wanted to apply couldn't afford to. It wasn't really an inclusive process.

It had taken me almost two years to save the application fee. Two years of working my ass off, but I'd saved enough and applied this year. It was only one way into the city. It was the last place James had been and therefore the first place I should look. So, I'd completed all the test requirements, paid the application fee, given my blood sample, and had heard absolutely nothing back. Zip. Zilch. Zero. Nada.

Feeling a renewed sense of disappointment, I nudged open the greenhouse door with my foot, placing the tray of seedlings on a worktable to my right, and made a beeline for my tomatoes.

They were my pride and joy. I was the only one in the community who had grown any seedlings this year. If I was lucky, I'd have extra to trade in the markets. A bit of wishful thinking, for sure. The harvests grew smaller each year, a major concern for the three human communities surrounding Danann. We were all worried about the soil quality, particularly how it continued to deteriorate, but for the moment, we had no answers.

Humans had fought war after war after war, damaging the land as they went. Before we reached the point of no return, a group of fae had traveled from Faerie to Earth. They fought against our kind for control of the Earth and won. They promised to heal our planet. To make the lands bountiful again. They promised us luscious green rainforests, clear skies and fresh air.

Nothing has changed. In the last fifteen years, they've delivered on exactly zero of their promises.

Lifting my fingers, I run my hand along the fragile vines, slowly winding their way up the trellis. My fingers tingled at the touch. I had always felt at one with nature. I felt a sense of calm surrounded by these living things I didn't feel anywhere else. The greenhouse was my happy place.

Bending down, I grabbed the large watering can kept under the wooden garden table.

"Riley!" someone shouted, and I startled, narrowly avoiding bumping my head. "Riley, come quick!"

I straightened and started for the door. Who needed me so urgently? And what for? Miss Hatley should have left with the children by now. The whole town was expected to gather at the ascension ceremony today. It was a big show, followed by a celebration of the fae's generosity. I rolled my eyes at the thought just as Sarie came barrelling through the door. She was a sight, her cheeks flushed, auburn hair falling free from her bun, her apron twisted to the side.

"What is it? Is everyone okay?" I asked, panic rising in my chest as I took in her disheveled appearance.

"Everyone is fine," she puffed, catching her breath. "You need to read this, Riley. It just came today. I've run from town to catch you in time." She handed me a heavy parchment envelope.

My name, Riley Embers, was scrawled across the front in fancy writing, fancier than anything I'd ever seen before. The ink was dark, indented against the thick cream paper. I traced my finger along the looping scroll, wondering at who could have sent this to me.

"Don't just stare at it, Riley. Open the damn thing. I didn't run all the way here for you to keep me in suspense." Sarie sat herself down on the stool, pulling her wild curls back from her face. She looked at the letter pointedly and I had to bite back a laugh. Sarie was another orphan of war, a few years older than me. She'd also been raised in the orphanage and now worked as a kitchen hand and maid. She was exuberant and dramatic and the closest thing I had to a friend.

"Alright, alright, keep your panties on." I said, caving and opening the envelope. I was curious about what was inside, nervous too. Maybe it was connected to James? I'd written to a few fae in the city, pleading for help to find him. So far, no one had responded.

The letter inside was made of the same heavy parchment that spoke of wealth and waste. Unfolding it, I began to read.

My mouth fell open as I read and reread the words written on the page before me. My heart began to beat at a frantic pace as I realized this was the opportunity I'd been waiting for.

"Shit. Shit. Shit. I have to go. I have to go now." Dropping the letter, I sprinted from the greenhouse, leaving Sarie staring after me in bewilderment. She'd work it out soon enough. There wasn't a second to spare.

My stomach churned as I raced through the grounds, worried that I wouldn't make it in time. I had to get to town, needed to get to the ceremony as quickly as possible.

I'd been offered a chance, a pathway, to find my brother and make sure he was okay. There was no way I could miss it. No, I needed to make it in time and check in.

I'd been chosen as a candidate. But that was only the first hurdle. Now I had to make the fae believe I'd be a valuable addition to their community. Make them choose me as the candidate to ascend today. Then I could continue my search for James from the inside.

Time slowed as I ran. I had a feeling that making it to the ceremony in time might be the difference between never knowing what happened to my brother or saving his life.

The deafening clang of the ascension gong rang through the air and vibrated up my legs as I sprinted through the empty cobblestone streets of Sommers. Every year it was struck five times, a minute apart, signaling the start of the ceremony. On the fifth strike, the candidates presented themselves to the judges as the entire town looked on.

I am so fucking late.

I pushed myself harder, pumping my arms and legs as fast as I could, my muscles screaming in protest. Racing past the familiar shop fronts, my breaths came in quick gasps, my lungs burning as I struggled to maintain speed.

The markets were deserted, the usual smells of fresh bread, fruit and vegetables missing. Stalls were empty of their usual wares, with nobody out selling this morning. Everyone must have made their way to the ceremony. I started to panic, my heart beating frantically in my chest.

I can't be the last to arrive. What if I'm late for presentation? It's not an option.

The town square loomed just around the corner. I had to make it in time. I had no idea why the letter advising that I'd been made a candidate had only just arrived. Others had known for weeks.

Shit, I hope I'm not too late.

Another strike rings out, louder than the first, the crash of it shaking the cobblestone road beneath my feet. I skidded around the corner and spotted the green candidate tent up ahead.

Relief flooded through me at the sight and realization that I might actually make it in time.

I stopped a few feet short of the door and leant forward, resting my hands on my knees, and took a moment to catch my breath and gather my thoughts. I let my breathing slow before I straightened and entered the tent, holding my head high.

I don't feel the least bit confident, but I need to pretend I do. Pretend I belong here. There are butterflies fluttering up a storm in my stomach. As far as I know, no one has ever been late to the ascension ceremony before. It's too big of an opportunity to risk. Too much of a life changer.

I needed to pull it together. This was it. I had to be chosen to ascend. It's the only way to find James. The only way I might be able to figure out what happened to him and where he is.

You've got this, Riley.

I plastered on my sweetest smile, choosing to ignore the erratic beat of my heart as I approached the nearest fae at what I assumed to be the check-in desk.

"We aren't ready for transportation yet," he said, not bothering to look up from the screen in front of him. "Please wait outside."

Most of the fae I'd met in my eighteen years had the same arrogant demeanor, like they thought they were better than the rest of us, and we should be honored by their presence.

I was glad we only had to put up with their shit once a year. Though, if I'm chosen, it'll be a lot more often.

I groaned inwardly at that thought, rolling my eyes and clearing my throat to pull his attention to me.

"Riley Embers, reporting for presentation." I said, just as the third gong sounded.

That caught his attention. He looked up from his tablet and quickly scanned me from head to toe.

"You're cutting it very close, Riley. We have barely enough time to fix you up." He stood and rounded the table as he approached me. "But I do love a challenge. I'm Stefan." He held his hand out to me and I took it.

His grip was powerful, the muscles of his forearms lean, matching the rest of his body—or at least what I could see of it. He was taller than me and I tilted my head back to look more closely at his face. A sharp angular jaw, high cheekbones, and plump lips grinned down at me. He was gorgeous, his bright silver eyes sparkling with mischief. And they weren't even the most unusual thing about him.

Most of the fae who conducted these ceremonies looked the same as the humans in our community. Healthier. But the same. There weren't any physical features that distinguished our kinds from one another. One possessed magic; the other did not.

But Stefan... There was something about him that screamed he wasn't from here. His hair was a bright shade of pink, shaved along the sides and spiked a little on top. The color was unusual, but it was his aura, the feeling I had standing in his presence that made him seem... other.

My breath caught in my throat as he reached for me, twirling his fingers through my hair before I had a chance to protest. I couldn't bring myself to be offended by his comment. I was definitely a mess. I cringed as he gathered more of the sweaty strands in his hands.

A wave of warmth ran down from my head to the ends of my hair, as soft golden curls fell to my shoulders. His fingers brushed my flushed cheeks, and I felt the heat from my sprint leave, a different heat beginning to build in my lower stomach as the touch of his hand lingered. Finally, he pulled back and, with a click of his fingers, a warm breeze circled around me.

I looked down at myself and found I was no longer wearing my jeans and tank. In their place was a soft white maxi dress, the skirts flowing around my legs, the lace bodice fitted perfectly to my body.

I glanced up at Stefan as my jaw dropped in awe. This was too much. I'd never witnessed magic before. The fae didn't use it when they visited.

I had so many questions. How? What? Where did my clothes go? But I was speechless as I stared at him.

Stefan grinned wickedly at me. "First time witnessing magic, little dove? Better get used to it." He winked at me as he took my arm, hurrying me past a few empty tables towards the back where I could see another door.

I was too shocked to respond immediately, and I let him drag me along as the fourth gong sounded. I knew magic existed, but all fae lived in Danann, and I had never seen it wielded before.

The fae had no reason to venture into the human communities, and only those humans chosen to ascend could enter their city.

I could feel every inch of where Stefan's hand gripped my arm as he pulled me along, something electric shooting through me from the contact. My eyes roamed over the sharp lines of his face again as we moved. He was magnificent, and I felt drawn to him, felt a pull like I'd never experienced before. There was a feeling of comfort and safety that I couldn't quite explain to myself.

Despite his cocky demeanor, despite the fact that he was fae, I wanted to know him better. Maybe I'd have that chance if I ascended.

We reached the end of the tent, and Stefan pushed me through the billowing flaps with a final wink as the fourth gong sounded.

"Thank you," I shouted after him, a little delayed as I found myself in line with the other candidates. Shaking my head to clear it; I couldn't believe I'd made it in time. I would have to thank Sarie for hauling ass to get the letter to me in time.

It struck me then that my life could be about to change. It was out of my hands now, and come what may, I would have to hold on for the ride.

CHAPTER TWO

Riley

Nervously, I ran my hands down the front of the dress Stefan had conjured for me. It was beautiful, even if it wasn't my usual style. I'd never worn anything so delicate, so beautiful. Miss Hatley had given up clothing me in anything other than jeans and a shirt when I was around four years old after I'd repeatedly returned home covered in mud and dried leaves from exploring the Dead Forest.

Not much had changed since then. I was often covered in dirt from the gardens. James would die of laughter if he could see me now. Still, it was nice to wear something that made me feel pretty.

The final gong sounded, drawing me back to the present. This was my moment, my chance to ascend. It was the only way to be accepted into the Fae city and the only way I knew to find my brother. Most of the human population would give their right arm to ascend, but the idea had never really appealed to me until James had gone missing. I didn't want to hand control of my future to someone else. Or spend my life serving the Fae and then be expected to feel privileged for it. No, thank you. Count me out.

Taking a slow, deep breath, I tried to steady my nerves as I followed the other candidates forward. A few of them were familiar, maybe from when I attended school. Other's I recognized from the markets. Not that I was friendly with any of them. I preferred to keep to myself. I didn't need or want the pity and sympathy that others often gave the orphans of war. My brother and Sarie were all I had and were all I needed.

They all looked as nervous as I felt, some fidgeting, some biting nails, others repeatedly smoothing their clothing, and I thanked my lucky stars I wasn't first in line.

We filed up onto the makeshift stage set in the middle of the town square, a presenter announcing each candidate as we took our place in line. The crowd gathered around us was large, children running around as the adults watched the ceremony.

It wasn't unusual for most of the town to gather here on Ascension Day; it was a welcome break from the monotony of our daily lives. An excitement we rarely got to experience. Most of the town would give anything to be accepted in Danann. I'd never really wanted to ascend, and the only reason I was here was to find James.

As the presenter called my name, I heard a cheer come from the back of the crowd. I squinted, spotting Sarie elbowing her way through the throngs of people. She must have been right on my tail as I ran into town. My heart swelled with love for her. Sarie hated any form of physical activity, and she'd run to town and back for me today. If today were my last day in Sommers, she might be the only person I'd truly miss.

Swallowing the lump in my throat, I brought my attention back to the presenter. He had finished introducing the candidates and had moved on to today's judges. My focus turned to the small table facing the stage where two stoic figures stood. The presenter introduced the first as the Fae Army General, Colin Brand.

I did a double take as I took him in. Standing at about six and a half feet, he had to be the tallest man I'd ever seen, towering above his colleagues. His face was clean shaven, hair dark and short, shaved close to his scalp. I shivered as his gaze fell on me, his stare cold and calculating. His face was youthful, younger than I would have expected a General to be. As far as I knew, the fae aged similarly to humans, meaning he'd have to be in his early twenties. He wore a formal army uniform, the same green as the candidate's tent. I swallowed hard as I spotted the thick, muscular arms straining against the fabric of his short sleeves.

I raked my eyes over his tall frame, a warmth spreading from my core as I examined him more closely. He was magnificent.

He was assessing me—assessing all of us with those eyes. Eyes that were a shade of brown so light that they almost looked golden in the morning sun. I could lose myself easily in those eyes. Was losing myself as he continued weighing us against one another. His gaze shifted from mine, and I was left wanting, with no way to tell if I'd passed or failed his assessment.

I turned my attention to his colleague, who the presenter was introducing as the Fae Academy Dean. Professor Darmon was shorter than the Army General, though not lacking in height by any means. He was older, his short hair beginning to gray. He had a kind smile as he looked toward us, giving a little wave that caused my body to relax as he took his seat, leaving the General standing beside him.

"Welcome," General Brand's deep voice boomed through the town square, amplified by some form of magic. He turned to face the crowd gathered behind him. "Thank you for coming to support your candidates." The crowd clapped and cheered. I shuffled my feet, growing more and more uncomfortable the longer I stood up here on display.

"This year's ceremony will proceed a little differently," he continued. "There will be no need for the candidates to present themselves to the Judges. We will not be making any further assessment of your skills, or what benefit you bring to Danann. The successful candidate has already been chosen. They have been chosen for a very specific reason."

He paused, letting the news sink in, and my curiosity piqued. So, I didn't have to stand here and sell myself to them? We weren't usually given reasons why any one individual was chosen to ascend. Usually, the candidates presented themselves and tried to sell the fae on why they would be valuable to the community. Those considered the worthiest were chosen by the judges. They left for Danann the following day and, as far as any of us knew, were assigned roles in the community there and lived happily ever after.

"Each candidate before us has undergone the testing we required with the application. As you know, usually each candidate would have an equal chance of ascension. However, this year the criteria is much more difficult to meet. It is not one any of you could have prepared for." Facing the candidates, his face was grim. A pit of dread settled in my stomach. What was the new criteria? And why couldn't we prepare for it?

Beside me, the other candidates fidgeted, the news clearly upsetting them. A few had resigned looks on their faces, accepting that they likely wouldn't make it this year. Many people built their lives around being the most skilled at their trade and based their application on it, hoping it would be something the fae would value. I had been planning to sell myself as a green thumb, able to nurture and grow more crops than the average farmer. That would count for nothing now, just like the other candidates' skills would not matter. I could almost smell the disappointment radiating off of those standing with me.

Movement to the side of the stage together with a flash of pink caught my eye. I watched as Stefan joined the outskirts of the crowd. A surprised laugh caught in my throat as he waved at me, excitement clear on his beautiful face.

I took a moment to study his features again, admiring the almost aristocratic look he had, with high cheekbones and a chiseled jaw. Sensing my gaze, he turned to catch my eye, winking as the silver in his eyes sparkled with joy. He was something to look at. Flushing, I turned my attention back to General Brand, who had continued with his speech.

"There will only be one successful candidate today. That person possesses blood markers that suggest they are a descendant of fae or some other magical being. They will be given a place at Danann Academy, where we will work with them to awaken any magical skill, be that elemental or Origin in form, and teach them to control it." His expression was serious, as though he didn't quite agree with this decision.

Muffled gasps rang through the crowd as they processed this information. The community whispered among themselves, many looking toward the stage, studying the candidates before them, trying to work out which one of us may be descended from fae.

We were likely all asking the same questions. How was this possible? What other magical beings existed? I had never heard of anyone in the human communities having access to magic before. Magic hadn't existed on earth before the fae traveled from the Origin, and all fae lived in Danann. There was no deserting fae, or at least none that I had ever heard of.

It hit me like a punch in the chest then. I would not ascend today. I was an orphan of the Last War. There was zero chance I was a descendant of the fae, or these other magical beings the

General so casually mentioned. What even were they? It didn't matter. Today was not my day. I'd have to find some other way to find my brother. There was no other way into Danann that I knew of. I buried my head in my hands as hot tears burned behind my eyes.

This was not the plan. I was so screwed.

CHAPTER THREE

Riley

The sound of my name being called drew me out of my pity party and back to the present. Alarm ran through me as I realized the General had continued speaking. I lowered my hands from my face and looked back towards the judges.

"Riley Emmett, please step forward," General Brand repeated, the lack of patience clear in his rumbling voice, his brown eyes dark and narrowing on me.

Why was he calling my name? Were they eliminating us one by one? Honestly, I wouldn't put it past the Fae to torture us like that. They kept us humans segregated from their community, only allowing a special few to share in their wealth and leaving the rest of us to just scrape by. They took control of us, of our land, and made promises they had yet to keep. A little humiliation pales compared to what they're capable of.

My cheeks heated as I forced myself to step forward. I clenched my fists, nails biting into my palms. My emotions were all over the place. I was mourning the loss of my brother, and the last chance I had to find him. That there was no other way into the Fae community, and that no one had seemed interested in helping me so far, made my blood boil with anger. I didn't feel like being put on display for whatever reason the General had.

I took a deep breath, clenching my jaw in an attempt to calm myself. The morning sun began warming my back as I stepped to the front of the stage where General Brand had been pointing.

Once I was in position, the General climbed on to the stage and stood to my right. He seemed even larger this close, the bulk of him dwarfing my five-foot frame. The smell of freshly chopped wood combined with the finest whiskey assaulted my senses, drawing me in. My favorite things. The sudden urge to get closer to him, to touch him, and run my hands all over that large muscular frame hit me like a punch to the chest. I froze, clenching my fists even tighter as I worked to keep my hands to myself.

What was happening to me? That's two men—two fae men—that have made me feel *things* today.

General Brand's eyes locked with mine, a flicker of some emotion crossing them briefly before he shut that shit down and fixed his expression again, his face void of emotion. He was shutting me out for some reason I couldn't begin to understand.

I had the impression that he didn't care much for today's ceremony.

Facing the community again, he gestured in my direction. "We know you must have many questions. The main being how this might be possible. We understand that magic was considered make-believe before we arrived here. The thought of a human possessing magic is new to all of us. We will work to find answers and share them with you all. In the meantime, please join me in congratulating Riley, the first of your kind to possess magical markers, earning her a place at the Fae Academy."

My mouth fell open, and I took a step backward as disbelief coursed through me. The community began to clap and cheer, the noise fading to a muffled cacophony as I processed the news.

No. Fucking. Way.

I was chosen. Me. Riley.

There had to be a mistake. I had no magical ability. I wracked my memory for some kind of sign, some event where I'd done something unexplainable.

There was nothing. They must have the wrong person. Maybe these tests got mixed up.

I'd let them work that out on their own, though. This was my chance to get into Danann. Life would be easier at the very least, and maybe I could find James. I would not fuck it up. There was no point denying the opportunity when I needed every single moment I could steal to search for my brother.

Suddenly I was surrounded by the other candidates, all of them shaking my hand and offering me well wishes. Their disappointment was clear, though they seemed genuinely happy for me. Once they'd all said their congratulations, they filed off of the stage, leaving me alone with the General and the Professor.

"Congratulations, Riley." Professor Darmon said, clasping my hand with both of his. "I am really excited to work with you at the Academy." The smile on his face was kind, no hint of a lie in his words. He was genuinely excited. As a scholar, he was more than likely excited about the chance to study the anomaly that I apparently was than to really get to know me. Still, he seemed to mean no harm.

"Thank you," I said, returning his smile, trying my best to remain calm and dispassionate. The fae had all but abandoned the humans, leaving us to make our way on a land that was dying, and I didn't hold them in very high regard. "I am very grateful to be chosen for ascension. I'm even more grateful for the further honor of a place at your Fae Academy."

"You are most welcome, dear," he said, patting the top of our clasped hands. "You are one of a kind, unique, and I, for one, am interested to see what type of magic will awaken in you. That may also give us clues to your origins." With a wink, he let go of my hands then and headed back to the candidate tent, leaving me alone with General Brand.

"Congratulations," he said, his voice devoid of emotion. He was robotic, or at least trying to be. Looking up at him, our eyes locking, I again felt the draw to move closer to him. What was going on with me?

Head in the game, Riley.

"We leave at midnight, celebrate with your people and say your goodbyes before we head directly back to Danann. Discovering your latent magic has meant no others will ascend this year. We will focus on you alone. The King and Queen are eager to meet with you. We will provide further details regarding the awakening of your magic and your enrolment at Danann Academy once we arrive there. Do you have any questions?"

Did I have questions? Yes, sir, I did. Was this for real? Why me? How was this latent magic discovered? What did it mean? And most importantly, would he help me find my brother?

I didn't think he'd appreciate the barrage of the thousand questions I wanted to ask, least of all that last one. So, I decided to keep it simple.

"Why are we leaving at midnight?" In the past, the successful candidates had left in the morning. James had been able to have breakfast with me before he left. That last meal together was one I'd treasured and always remembered fondly.

"Is there anything I need to bring?" I continued. I didn't own many possessions, just a few changes of clothes, really. There was only one thing I wouldn't leave behind. A small, tarnished locket I'd had for as long as I could remember. I'd never been able to open it, no matter how hard I tried. But I liked to imagine it had belonged to my mother, and that I held a little piece of her with me wherever I went. I never took the necklace off, preferring to always keep it close to me.

I reached for it then, my fingers rubbing over the intricate carvings on the front.

"Everything will be provided for you. There is nothing you need to bring. You are not forbidden from bringing any personal items." His eyes fell to my hold on the locket. I let it drop, not wanting to draw attention to the one thing that held sentimental value to me. "We leave at midnight because it is safer, less predictable. You are an unknown. We do not know how your kind will react to this news. I want to ensure you reach Danann safely." Brand kept his feelings pretty well locked down, but I caught a minute tightening in his brows.

Despite his cold front so far, he was concerned for my welfare and committed to getting me to Danann. I hadn't expected him to be so honest with me. My surprise dulled some of the anxiety rising because of his words. Not all the anxiety, though. Was I at risk of being targeted?

"It kind of sounds like you expect an attack, General. Am I in danger?" It didn't matter if I thought they'd made a mistake. Many of the community had believed them. Unrest and dissension had been growing in the human communities. It wouldn't take much to set them off.

There had been rumors of a group wanting to stand against the fae. They were calling themselves The Resistance, and they seemed to be gaining numbers. They were angry. Angry that the Fae had failed to heal the earth. That they were stuck trying to survive on a desolate land and that the Fae city seemed to be thriving amongst the wastelands.

There wasn't anywhere else for us humans to go. The communities surrounding Danann encompassed the only truly inhabitable area left in the world as far as we knew. The dead forest lay behind us, the sea in front, the rest of the lands destroyed in the Last War. Nuclear and chemical warfare had all but killed our planet.

Brand stared at me for a moment, his eyes darkening. Taking a deep breath, he wiped a hand through his short hair. "I don't know. And that makes me uncomfortable," he growled. "Be alert. Stefan will stay with you until we depart." With those final words, he turned and followed Professor Darmon's path towards the candidate tent.

A hand dropped on my shoulder, and I jumped, spinning around quickly to find it was only Stefan. He was grinning from ear to ear, joy lighting up his eyes as he embraced me.

Taken aback by his familiarity, I stiffened. Something about him screamed kind, safe. Before I knew it, I relaxed, hugging him back as he congratulated me.

"What do you know, little dove," he said, placing me back on my feet. I hadn't even realized he'd picked me up. "Soon you won't be watching others use magic with your bottom jaw sitting on the floor. You'll be casting it yourself!" He covered his mouth in mock disbelief, then put his arm around my shoulders and led me from the stage.

"We're going to be the best of friends. I'm calling it now." He declared, pulling me tight against him.

I laughed at his declaration, but I really couldn't disagree with him. It wasn't like I could turn down the offer of a friend; I was going into Danann blind after all, and I liked Stefan's energy. I didn't know what to expect or how the other Fae may treat me. It wouldn't be hard for them to dismiss the freak human.

Something tugged inside my chest and screamed for more. It was not satisfied with the title of friend. It wanted far more from Stefan.

I smothered the feeling, deciding to deal with it another day as Stefan led me out of the town square, towards the main street. There was always a party held after the ceremony to say farewell to those who were ascending. The community went all out, everyone bringing whatever they could spare; be that food, drink, or just their time and talent.

"How do you feel about coming to Danann, little dove? You don't seem overly excited?" He was looking down at me under his arm, his eyebrow raised as he studied my expression.

I sighed. I'd known Stefan an entire three and a half minutes, but despite that, and despite his rude greeting in the candidate tent, I felt as though I could trust him. He bore no ill intention and seemed genuinely curious as to my lack of excitement. Even so, I wasn't sure I was ready to reveal all my secrets.

"Most candidates enter Danann a bundle of nerves and nearly bursting with excitement," he continued. "They can barely contain it. They want to see what kind of future Danann holds for them, hope it will be better than what awaits them here in Sommers. They are amicable and happily take whatever role is given to them in the city. And even though many leave some form of friends and family behind, they thrive inside the walls and make new lives for themselves."

He stopped suddenly, spinning me around to face him, grasping me by both shoulders. Usually someone putting their hands on me would trigger the animal instinct within me and that person would regret their decision quickly.

Stefan didn't trigger that reflex in me. I trusted him. Maybe that made me a fool. He was Fae, after all.

I looked up at him, biting my bottom lip as I tried to decide how to explain myself. I couldn't tell him I felt this was a mistake, but could I tell him I had applied for ascension for reasons that had nothing to do with the opportunity that was on offer? Could I tell him I held a low opinion of his kind and the way they segregated our community?

His silver eyes sparkled at me as he waited for my response. Come what may, I decided to tell him some of my truth.

"You've made a mistake," I said, my voice shaking and just above a whisper. "I have no magic. I'm an orphan; with nothing to my name. My most prized skill is that I can grow a decent crop of tomatoes. I'm not a lost descendant of the Fae—or other magical being, as Brand put it. What other magical beings even exist?"

I'd started rambling, the stress and surprise of the day flowing out of me in a torrent of word vomit.

"Sorry, I'm just... I'm overwhelmed."

Stefan grinned; his teeth were so white I was sure they must be bleached with magic.

"Don't apologize, Riley. I'm sure it's a lot to take in." He wrapped his arm around my shoulders and led us again towards the party. I leaned into him, soaking up the comfort his warm embrace and the closeness of him offered. "Your life and your future as you know it have changed considerably in a few brief hours. That's enough to overwhelm anyone."

I nearly tripped over my own feet as he continued, the shock of his next statement stunning me into silence.

"No mistake has been made, little dove. There is powerful magic in you. I sensed it the moment you entered the tent. Why do you think I mistook you for one of our own?"

CHAPTER FOUR

Riley

Wait, what?

I tried and failed to wrap my head around his words. When did he mistake me as one of his own?

Somehow sensing my unasked question, Stefan continued. "When you ran into the tent, I sensed your power and mistook you for one of our guards. I never meant to dismiss you." He explained, shrugging his shoulders like it wasn't a big deal. "Honestly, I shouldn't have mistaken you. Your power differs from any I've ever felt before."

I shook my head in disbelief. It was a big deal, actually; it changed everything I thought I'd ever known about myself. Stefan was telling me I wasn't the person I thought I was, that my whole life so far was a lie.

If I possessed magic, did that mean James did too?

My heart clenched, my chest restricting painfully as I considered the alternative. No. I wouldn't believe it. James was my brother. I just needed time to prove it.

Letting the subject drop for now, we moved into the crowd gathering in the street. There were tables set up with food and drink, and a little stage set up for anyone who wanted to perform. Troy—the town blacksmith—and his brothers were up there now and likely would be for most of the night. They had somehow commissioned instruments from before the Last War and were well known for making the best music in town.

Stefan stayed by my side as I made the rounds through the crowd. He was a social butterfly, fitting in comfortably with the community, quietly poking holes in my view of the fae as arrogant, unapproachable creatures.

It seemed like everyone wanted to congratulate me. People I barely knew came to say goodbye and wish me luck, as well as those I'd barely seen since I left school. I guessed that was probably my fault. Keeping to myself, I never left the orphanage unless I was sent to town to run errands. Even then, I kept to myself, not one to stop for idle chitchat.

Sarie joined us as the sun began to set, linking her arm through mine, a quiet sadness sitting underneath the brilliant smile she plastered on her face. We ate, we drank, and we danced, but the smile never quite reached her eyes. The sadness lurking there caused tears to threaten.

"Are you okay?" I asked her as we moved off the dance floor for another drink. Someone had brewed cider specifically for today's celebration, and the town was getting rowdier as the sun started to set. I couldn't help but smile and delight in the way everyone was letting their hair down. Life was harsh out here. There wasn't always much to celebrate. It made for a pleasant change.

"I... I guess I'm not," she said, her eyes glistening with unshed tears. "I'm so happy for you Riley, but I'm worried about you, and I'm going to miss the fuck out of you."

"I'll miss you too, Sarie. You're the best friend I've ever had. I hate leaving you behind." I pulled her in and held her close, my throat tightening as I fought back my own tears. Sarie was usually so bright and bubbly. It was hard seeing her this way, so emotional.

"I'll be back," I whispered quietly enough that Stefan couldn't hear. "I'm going to find James and then I'll be back for you."

She sniffled, squeezing my arms as she pulled back, her eyes catching my own. "I know you truly believe that Riley and I love you for it. But I'm scared I'll never see you again. That one day you'll stop writing, just like James did."

Tears flowed freely down her cheeks now, and I swallowed hard, trying to hold myself back from sobbing with her. I couldn't deny the ring of truth in her words. Who knew what Danann held, or how long it would take me to find James. There was no predicting what would happen on that journey. Sarie was family too. I wouldn't—couldn't—leave her behind.

Taking both her hands, I looked her directly in the eye. "I promise, Sarie, that I'll do everything in my power to come home, to come back to you with James." She looked so vulnerable. The heaviness of this moment was weighing on me. I needed a reprieve. Something to break the growing tension in the air and lighten the moment. "Don't let Mr. Cole touch my tomatoes. Take care of them for me?"

A snort of laughter escaped her, and she smiled at me as she wiped away her tears. "I'll look after your tomatoes, Riley, I swear." With that, she took my arm and led me back out to dance.

After what felt like a few minutes—but must have been a few hours—Stefan waved me off the dance floor.

"It's time to say your last goodbyes. Transport is ready." Butterflies danced in my belly as he squeezed my hand reassuringly. Somehow this guy got me and understood I was feeling all kinds of nervous about leaving.

The crowd had thinned, most of the community having gone home to bed by now. Those that were left must have sensed it was time for me to leave and were making their way over to where we stood.

Murray, the baker, had disappeared for a while but returned now with a few tears in his eyes and a bag full of warm cheesy scrolls—my absolute favorite.

"Be careful now, girl," he said, his voice thick with emotion. "Don't let them good for nothin' egotistical fae take advantage of you. No offense meant, sir." He briefly glanced at Stefan, then pulled me in for a hug before he pivoted and walked away.

A startled laugh escaped me. Murray had always been a little strange, but he cared in his own way. Stefan seemed easy-going, but Murray had just insulted his entire race. I didn't know him well enough to gauge his reaction.

Before I could worry myself about it, Ms. Hatley pulled me into her embrace. I froze. The Directress was usually very formal, rarely giving any of the orphans any physical affection. This was new. And strange. Her hug was comforting though, in a way I'd never expected, and I sank into her hold, letting myself relax just a fraction.

"Good luck Riley. I hope you find what you're looking for. Please, keep me updated?" She didn't come out and say it directly, but she must have known I was looking for James. It warmed my heart to know she cared about what had happened to him.

She stepped back, allowing Sarie to come forward. Silently, we wrapped our arms around each other, holding on tight. We'd said our goodbyes earlier, and after a long moment, she stepped back, turning and starting back to the orphanage with Ms. Hatley, with a small wave and a sad smile on her face.

I watched them leave until I could no longer see them in the darkness. It felt as though I was watching my life as I knew it walk away from me and I couldn't help but let a few tears escape. My hands shook as I willed myself not to chase them. My heart bled in my chest as I wondered if I'd ever see them again. Finding

James was something I needed to do to calm my soul. But I would miss the family I was leaving behind.

Stefan took my hand and silently led me back to the candidate tent. I needed a few moments to gather myself and I was grateful that he seemed to sense that, not rushing me as I wandered slowly next to him.

Today had been overwhelming. Being the chosen candidate and ascending just like I'd wanted didn't make it any easier to process. Knowing I would have my opportunity to find James helped a little, though it would not come without challenges. I was new to these people, and their assertion that I held some kind of magic in my veins meant they would be watching me closely. I had to be careful. Any mistake could cost me my chance to find my brother.

Breathing deeply and closing my eyes briefly, I found my center. I was more than ready for this.

Let's go.

CHAPTER FIVE

Riley

"Are they horses?" I asked Stefan, my voice hushed in awe as we approached the candidate's tent. In front of it was a long, dark carriage, two massive creatures harnessed to the front of it.

I'd never seen a horse before. I'd learnt about them in school, and I knew the fae used them for transport instead of the old technology. Things like cars and airplanes had been destroyed in the war, and what hadn't simply didn't work around fae magic.

The fae monopolized the horses, though. Our community barely had enough food for ourselves and our livestock. We just couldn't afford the resources to feed these majestic creatures.

I approached the mare harnessed to the front left of the painted navy carriage. She was magnificent. Chestnut in coloring, a bright white strip marked her snout, her mane almost glowing in the low light of the carriage torches.

"She's beautiful." I whispered, raising a hand to press it against her nose. Her eyes were dark and depthless, seeming to go on for eternity. She chuffed happily, nuzzling into my hand. I closed my eyes, resting my face against her cheek, taking a moment to indulge in the connection I could feel thrumming between myself and this beautiful creature. Something in my heart told me we'd met before, though I could not recall when or how.

"That's Annie," a gruff voice said, interrupting my bonding time with the horse.

Looking up, I saw General Brand rounding the back of the carriage, followed closely by Professor Darmon, four guards, and two coachmen. "It's time to return to Danann. Are you ready?" He opened the carriage door and gestured for us to climb inside.

The carriage itself was elegant and understated. The outside was painted midnight blue with some light gold markings in the corners. There was only one window recessed into the door on the left side of the carriage. There were exterior seats on both sides, one behind the front wheel, another in front of the rear wheel. I assumed these were for the guards.

I stroked Annie's nose once more, before moving towards the carriage door. "I'm as ready as I'll ever be." I said, grasping Stefan's offered hand to help me climb inside.

The interior seats were covered with midnight blue velvet, gold accents continuing the theme from the exterior. There were two benches to the front and back of the carriage, leaving a space in the middle to climb in and out. The walls were again painted a midnight blue with the same gold accent. I was starting to think the colors were a fae thing.

"This is a royal carriage," Stefan said, reading my mind. Again. "Midnight blue and gold are the chosen colors of King Ronan and Queen Ciara. They rule the water elementals back in Faerie and lead the fae who crossed to Earth in the attempt to save your world."

"How's that working out for you?" I asked sweetly, a hint of bitterness seeping through. "It's been what, 15 years now? Earth is fading faster every year." I took a seat next to him, already feeling a little guilty for my words.

I knew it wasn't Stefan's fault, but the fae kept us at arm's length. We were struggling to survive whilst they seemed to thrive and live with everything they needed at their fingertips. Really, it appeared they were doing nothing at all to save our world, despite their promises to save it and return to Faerie.

General Brand appeared in the doorframe, his enormous frame blocking the view of outside momentarily before he climbed into the seat directly opposite me. He stared at me for a moment, his eyes dark, a frown lining his forehead. "There's a lot you don't know about us, Riley. A lot that you are going to have to learn in a short space of time."

"We hope that you'll be able to help us," Professor Darmon revealed, taking the last seat next to General Brand, who shot him a warning look.

"That's enough. We can discuss this further in the city." General Brand closed the door and knocked on the window, signaling that we were ready to go.

The carriage began to pull forward then, and silence stretched between the four of us. There would be plenty of time to gather information later, I supposed. Leaning forward in my seat, I stared out the window, watching as the only home I'd ever known slowly faded into the night. Silently, I said goodbye. I didn't know when—or even if—I would come back here.

Swallowing the lump that had formed in my throat and blinking back the tears burning my eyes, I continued to watch the scenery pass as we entered the dead forest. The men spoke amongst themselves, but I tuned them out. I wanted to take it all in. I had never traveled this far outside Sommers before.

It was so dark, the only light coming from the moon above and the small torches lit at the front of the carriage. Shadows blanketed the surrounding area, dancing in the lowlight. The silence was almost deafening and created an eerie and ominous feel to the land.

True to its name, much of the forest was withered and dry. Even on a sunny day, it felt as though no color existed here. No life either. Not much had survived the years of chemical and nuclear warfare the Last War had brought upon the world.

I had spent a lot of time on the edge of the forest as a child. It surrounded our community, keeping us walled in. No one ever ventured further than a few feet inside.

Always drawn to nature, I had shadowed Mr Cole in the garden almost as soon as I could walk. I felt at peace tending to the crops, nourishing the seedlings, and encouraging new life. I had naively tried time and time again to tend to the forest. In my child's mind I had thought that if I only gave the hollow trees and the dried shrubbery enough attention soon enough, they'd flourish, bringing back color and life to the barren lands.

Of course, I could never revive a single plant and I was eventually disheartened enough to leave the forest be and concentrate on our crops.

It had always saddened me that I'd been unsuccessful in bringing any life back to the forest, and I think that was why I held such animosity toward the fae. They were in power. They had promised to restore our land and had so far failed. They had not kept their word.

A swift double knock on the wall pulled me from my thoughts, and I realized the carriage had slowed. I pulled back from the window, looking at General Brand and Stefan in question.

"Why are we stop..." My question was cut off by a curt shush from Stefan. He was hard to make out in the darkness of the carriage, but I felt him tense beside me, his fists clenching at his sides and worry painted across his moonlit face.

The General had leant forward, looking out the window. He shook his head as he pointed to the Professor and I. "Stay here and get down."

Command filled his tone, leaving no room for argument. Professor Darmon nodded as the General opened the door, and silently slipped out, gesturing for Stefan to follow.

I swallowed hard. Fear coursed through my veins, making my heart race and my throat dry. General Brand had hinted that an attack was possible, but I hadn't really believed there was a threat. I was a nobody.

Following the General, Stefan shuffled past me toward the door. My hand shot out, grabbing his shirt to stop him. He grabbed it and squeezed tightly for a moment. "Please stay with the Dean, Riley. It's our job to protect you." He said, before letting go and slipping out the door.

My stomach dropped as he closed the door behind him. What if something happened to him? Something tethered me to Stefan. Something deep, instinctual, and like nothing I had felt before. Losing him had already become an unfathomable thought.

Professor Darmon swiftly locked the door behind them and laid down flat on his side of the carriage, gesturing for me to do the same. I scrambled down quickly, trying to calm my breathing and listen to what might be happening outside. All was quiet for a moment, the light of the torches outside flickering through the small window.

Suddenly, we were plunged into darkness. The air inside thickened, like the oxygen had been stolen from it. I couldn't hear or see anything outside the carriage, except for a small sliver of the moon peeking through the thick covering of tree branches. My heart was beating a wild pace, knocking against my ribs as the bitter taste of fear coasted my tongue. What was happening? What should I do? Were the boys okay?

Fumbling through the darkness, my hands swiped through the empty air in front of me as a bright orange light flared outside, bringing an intense heat with it. Flames burst past the window, scaring the shit out of me and I screamed in both surprise and fear.

The Professor reached over, resting his hand lightly on my shoulder. "Shhh, dear. It's okay. The fire will be from General Brand. It's his element. He has excellent control." He whispered, patting me on the back as he tried to calm me.

My palm began to sweat as I held it against my mouth, physically preventing myself from screaming any more, and willing my heart rate to settle. That was the second time someone had mentioned the elements. I knew little about fae or their magic, and I made a mental note to ask about it later. When we weren't under attack and hiding from unknown assailants on the carriage floor.

Shouts rang out around us, more fire lighting up the space beyond our small window. It felt like a storm was coming to life outside as a strong wind rocked the carriage, something thudding hard into the sides every now and then.

A pained whinny rang out and my mind emptied as I realized it was Annie. Without a thought, I leapt to my feet, unbolting the door and jumping from the carriage.

Instinct had me keeping low as I landed on my feet, my gaze darting around and assessing the fight around me, searching out any immediate threat. Annie was hurt. I needed to make sure she was okay.

An arrow whistled past me, and I rolled to the side just in time to avoid contact. Arrows. Shit. That explained the thudding I had heard inside the carriage.

Movement behind a large fallen trunk caught my eye, and I spotted an archer about to nock another arrow in his bow. A powerful beam of fire was sent in his direction, and my gaze landed on the General a little way to the left. He hadn't noticed me yet—probably for the best. I didn't want to distract him. But I couldn't leave Annie when she sounded injured. Who the fuck shoots an innocent creature?

Not waiting to see what happened to the attacker, I crept up to the front, where Annie was still harnessed. She was tossing her head from side to side, trying to dislodge an arrow buried towards the base of her neck.

"Oh girl, it's okay, let me help you." I whispered, rising from my crouch to stroke her nose. To my shock, she calmed, giving me a chance to assess her injury. There was blood, but not as much as I had expected. The arrow didn't look as though it was buried deep.

"Looks like you got lucky, girl," I murmured, still patting her nose with one hand while I reached down and tore a strip of cotton from the bottom of my dress. I didn't want to remove the arrow. I didn't think it had hit anything important, but I was far from an expert and now was not the time to take the risk. Snapping the arrow so that it wasn't jutting out of her, I wadded up the strip of cotton and pressed it firmly around the wound.

The heat of fire flared behind me, followed by a large gust of wind that would have knocked me off my feet if I hadn't been anchored firmly against Annie.

Now that the horse was taken care of, I took a moment to really assess my surroundings. General Brand was still to my left, shooting beams of fire from his palms out into the trees surrounding us, aimed at assailants I couldn't make out in the shadows beyond the tree line.

The two coachmen and guards were scattered around the clearing, some sending their own beams of fire around, others seemed to be shooting water or throwing balls of wind. Professor Darmon had joined in the fight—he must have followed me out of the carriage—but I couldn't see Stefan anywhere.

Logically, I knew we were under attack, and now was not the time to gawk at the display of magic in front of me. But I couldn't seem to stop myself.

It looked like we were gaining the upper hand, pushing the attackers back into the trees. A shrill whistle rang through the clearing. It must have been some kind of call to retreat, those that were still fighting turning and running into the shelter of the dead forest.

General Brand waved to the others to pursue, and they obeyed, taking chase deeper into the forest. I was suddenly alone with the horses—I'd have to ask the other mares' names—the sudden quiet of the clearing unnerving.

The crack of a twig had me whipping my head toward the tree line behind me. My heart thundered in my chest as I scanned the direction the sound had come from. The light of the carriage torches allowed me to make out two large shadows stepping out from the forest.

They were both dressed completely in black, some kind of emblem printed on the right-hand side of their black shirts. Each had a bow and quiver strapped to their back. Their hoods were drawn up, their faces covered by shadows.

"Grab her." One of them commanded as the other moved toward me at a rapid pace. There was no time, no chance to run. I was still holding pressure on Annie's wound, the carriage blocking any other possible escape route.

I kicked out at the man advancing on me, aiming low, with no other option. He dodged my attack, grabbing my ankle and pulling me down, forcing me to let go of Annie. I screamed as he hauled me up, tossing me over his shoulder.

I kicked and punched, battering his back to no avail. He was a lot bigger than I was, tightening his hold, making it harder for me to thrash about.

He turned, heading back towards his partner as Annie let out a loud neigh that echoed through the clearing. Despite her injury, she bucked, tearing herself free of her harness.

The bastard holding me ran, but he was no match for the furious horse. She barreled into him, breaking his grip on me, and I was flung far across the clearing. The world blurred, whirling past in shades of gray and black, my head slamming against the dead trunk of an old oak tree. My vision darkened, unconsciousness claiming me.

But before the world went black, I could have sworn a flash of pink fell from the sky.

CHAPTER SIX

Riley

S omething bumped against my cheek rousing me from unconsciousness. Once. Twice. A loud snort, followed by hot
air blowing on my face, broke through the fuzziness of my mind
and woke me enough that I opened my eyes.

Annie was there, nudging me awake. There was an awareness
about this horse that went beyond what I'd learnt about them.
Maybe she wasn't a regular horse at all.

The sound of fighting, of men grunting and shifting as they
battled against one another reminded me of where I was. Looking past Annie, my eyes locked on Stefan amid a fight against the
two men who had tried to take me. He was a sight to behold,
moving so fast he was a blur, weaving his way between the two,
ducking and dodging their attacks and landing a few of his own.

Move. Help him.

Not sure how I'd do that, I pushed to my feet anyway, my head throbbing where I had smacked it against the tree. On instinct, I reached up to touch the wound, finding my hair matted with blood, a trickle running down my neck.

Wobbling on my feet, I took a step forward. Then another, my limbs shaking with the effort as my body tried to get its bearings and fight the fear constricting the breath in my lungs.

I needed to get to Stefan, to help my friend and do what I could to make sure the fae, whose soul mine seemed to know, was safe. Clenching my teeth, I willed my body to listen, to stay upright, but I tripped over my own feet, collapsing back onto the forest floor on my hands and knees.

A deep voice shouted my name from afar, and I lifted my head to see the rest of our party returning to the clearing, General Brand leading the way. Muttering a curse, my knees buckled, and I fell against the floor beneath me in relief. The General muttered directions at the others, directing them to help Stefan, seconds before I felt him sink to his knees by my side.

Large hands gripped my chin, turning my face to look at him. His brow creased in concern as his gaze scraped over me, assessing my injuries, lingering on the blood trickling from my head wound.

"What happened, Riley? Why did you leave the carriage?" He asked, tempering his tone. There was anger there, and a sense of something else... protectiveness? That couldn't be right? I must have hit my head harder than I thought.

"Annie was hurt, I could hear her pain. Felt it. I couldn't keep hiding knowing she needed help, and I was right there!" My voice was little more than a whisper, my skull throbbing, the pain keeping me from explaining any further.

General Brand's jaw was tight, his lips pressed into a thin line as he inspected my head. He must have decided not to push me any further for the moment. I was sure the questions would come, though; he didn't seem like the type to just let it drop. I'd defied his orders to keep me safe. I was in for a grilling.

For now, though, I was lucky to be holding on to consciousness. My vision was blurring, black spots dancing across the General's face as I looked up at him.

"I'm going to heal your head, Riley. Can you turn your face the other way and keep still for me?" I nodded slightly, grimacing as a sharp pain lanced through my head at the movement. He helped me turn my head, cupping it in one of his large hands, his hold much gentler than I had imagined him capable of. He placed his other hand above the wound.

A gentle warmth spread across the side of my head, surrounding the injury, and after a few moments my vision cleared, the pain lessening. Stefan, Professor Darmon, and the rest of our party were in the center of the clearing, still fighting our attackers. One of the guards was standing behind the General, watching out for us as he focused on healing me.

He should be out there. Fighting with his men. Not here with me.

"Go, help them. I can wait."

"No." His tone was clear, firm, no room for argument.

The two men who'd attempted to take me had been joined by more of their people, and we were looking seriously outnumbered. Stefan was a machine, though, and as I watched him cut down two of the black-clad men in one complicated move, I felt confident we might make it out.

My vision cleared completely, the persistent pounding in my skull easing, as General Brand continued to heal me. It hadn't escaped my attention that as the General he was probably a better fighter than the rest of our party. He really should be out there. Instead, he'd run directly to me. Why? What was that about?

"Please. Go." I urged him, trying to pull free from his hold. His grip tightened around my jaw, not enough to hurt, but enough to let me know he'd be having none of this.

"They'll be fine. You, on the other hand, are not healed yet. Stay still." He growled at me, forcing me to lie back. I hated lying here, watching the others fight, and not doing anything to help. Not that I could do much anyway if I were being honest with myself.

Slowly, we gained the upper hand. Stefan cut down the last attacker in a blur of limbs. What type of weapon did he have? I'd have to ask him, ask him to teach me to move like that. Our men fell back, scanning the area as they made their way to where General Brand was still working to heal my head.

Professor Darmon was the first to reach us, followed closely by Stefan. The coachmen immediately went to the horses, one heading to the gray dappled mare, still harnessed to the carriage, the other heading to Annie. She had made her way to the side of the clearing and had seemed to watch as General Brand worked his healing magic into me.

"I think that's all of them," Stefan said, his breathing labored as he fought to catch his breath. "They wanted Riley." His gaze narrowed in on me, like he was trying to figure out what it was they wanted.

General Brand cleared his throat, pulling his hands away from my face and helping me sit up. "I've done what I can, your body will continue to heal you at its regular pace, and you will need to rest as much as possible once we return to the city," wiping his bloodied hands on his pants, he stood to his full height, his large figure towering over me. "I'm only going to ask you this once and I expect you to be completely honest with me. Do you have any ties to The Resistance?" His eyes were hard as he waited for my response.

A lump formed in my throat, and I swallowed against the flicker of hurt in my chest that his accusation bought. His question was fair. He didn't know me. Didn't know if he could trust me. I didn't know why that mistrust pained me.

"No, I don't." I shot at him, crossing my hands across my chest. I might not love the fae, or hold a very high opinion of them, but I wasn't radical. Yeah, I might be hiding my true intentions from them, but I wasn't going to hurt anybody. Unless they'd hurt my brother—then I might get a little stabby.

Some of this must have shown on my face, and Stefan snorted. "Your face just got all murdery, little dove. Not the best way
to convince the Army General you aren't a threat." He clapped
Brand on the shoulder before offering a hand to help me up.
"You are going to be trouble." He predicted, putting his arm
around my waist to support me as he led us back to the carriage.

Scoffing at this assessment, General Brand followed as we
crossed the clearing. He must have believed there was some
truth to my words to let it drop. Something in my chest loosened.

As we walked, I could see the second coachman leading Annie back to the carriage. She was no longer actively bleeding, and
I assumed he had used his own magic to heal her. She was no
longer in pain, though how it was possible for me to know that
was beyond me.

"Do all fae have the ability to heal?" I asked Stefan, my curiosity getting the better of me.

"Yes. Healing is magic that all Fae draw from the origin. It is
one of the first things taught at the Academy, but that's because
it takes a long time to master. Magic drawn from the origin is
more advanced than accessing our elements."

That was interesting. I hadn't completed my schooling,
meaning I had little knowledge of the fae and their abilities. I
had always felt indifferent, if not resentful, toward them. Humans were isolated from their kind. Our worlds didn't mesh,
and that was by their design. I hadn't really felt it necessary to
know more.

When James went missing and none of them would help me, I was even more inclined to distance myself from them. Probably a stupid move given I was now on my way to integrate into their community, told that I was possibly one of them, but it was too late for would haves and regrets. I'd wing it.

It'd be fine. Right?

We arrived at the carriage as I was mulling over that thought. The coachmen checked the horses were harnessed in correctly, as two of the guards circled around the back to take their exterior seats. Glancing around the clearing, I saw it was littered with bodies. A shudder ran down my spine at the sight; I'd never seen so much death. It was unsettling. The hairs on the back of my neck stood on edge, like someone was watching us.

Instinctively, I whipped my head around, trailing my eyes along the tree line. Almost in slow motion, a shadowy figure emerged, an arrow notched in his bow. The figure stood tall and steady, taking aim. I shouted a warning at the same time as Stefan did, though not before the figure released his arrow, turning and disappearing into the woods as it sailed through the air.

General Brand leapt into action immediately, his long legs crossing the clearing at great speed, and he too disappeared into the trees. In the same moment, Stefan pulled me to the ground, covering my body with his.

Only a yell for help allowed me to wiggle out from under him as we both rose to the call.

I was not prepared for what we found behind the carriage. Of everything I had seen tonight, the magic I had witnessed, I just could not wrap my mind around it.

One of the guards was on his knees, hands pressed flat to the dirt, kneeling before what could only be described as an explosion of life.

A patch of long grass had risen out of the dead forest floor. It was a vibrant, healthy green with wildflowers scattered here and there. Such a stark contrast to the lifeless forest around us that I thought I might be hallucinating. Shaking my head to clear it, I wondered if I was still injured. But it was still there.

What the fuck?

Sticking out of the middle of the tiny oasis, the arrow caught my eye. There was something attached to it. I reached over and pulled it out of the earth. It was a note, folded neatly in half. Opening it, I read aloud, instantly regretting it as the words fell from my lips.

We will not stop.

We will do what the Fae have not.

We will save the Earth.

Choose the winning side, Riley. Or we'll choose for you.

The Resistance

A wave of panic tore through my body, my blood turning to ice in my veins as I sunk to my knees, dropping the note. It fluttered to the ground, and I watched as it landed in the center of the life before me. It took me a beat to realize Stefan was also on his knees, his head bent forward, the surviving guard falling into a similar pose. Stefan reached over, giving my shaking hand a reassuring squeeze.

"When we die, our body and energy return to the land we stand on. In a land as depleted as this, that energy causes a recognizable change, like you see before us. Let us show Henry our respects." His silver eyes locked with mine, shadows and pain dancing in them before he let go of my hand and lowered his forehead to the ground.

Henry. It was harder, knowing his name. The shot he'd taken had caused instant death. From what Stefan just said, it was Henry's energy that created this patch of life we were kneeling before.

I briefly notice the rest of our party gathering around, falling into the same pose. This must be how the Fae show their respect to the fallen. Copying, I lowered my palms to the ground and rested my forehead on the ground.

Only a few hours into my time with the Fae and already a life had been lost. I didn't understand the depths of what was happening, and I had about a thousand questions that needed answering. But for now, I prayed that this was not how my new life would continue.

CHAPTER SEVEN

Riley

We stayed like that for what felt like hours but couldn't have been more than a few minutes. Exhaustion was settling in my body, my limbs heavy and sluggish, but I forced myself to rise with the others as General Brand returned to the clearing.

The General's shoulders were hunched forward, his gaze glassy and unfocused as he stared at the site of Henry's demise. There was no other word for it. He looked defeated. Silent for a moment, he knelt down and began his own prayers for our fallen companion.

As he rose, he seemed to pull himself together, shoulders straightening as he stood to his full height, his eyes bright and alert, a serious expression firmly in place. He crossed his arms in front of him, and I watched as his shirt strained across his muscles, the buttons seemingly about to pop at any moment. Not that I'd complain. An image of him shirtless flashed through my mind, and I swallowed hard, shaking my head to clear my treacherous thoughts.

Not the time, Riley.

The General shook his head as he turned to address us. "The last attacker got away. He disappeared up into the canopy of the dead forest. We should go before they have time to regroup. We need to get the fuck out of this forest." He spun and marched back to the carriage, the set of his broad shoulders all business and leaving no room for debate.

Stefan wrapped his arm around my waist again, and I leant into the warmth of him, letting it comfort me as we followed silently, climbing in after Professor Darmon. General Brand had taken the guards' empty space on the exterior seating, leaving just the three of us inside the carriage. The silence was heavy, the weight of what had just happened settling over all of us.

I rested my head against Stefan's shoulder with an easy familiarity as the carriage lurched forward. It shouldn't be so easy to trust him, to find comfort in his presence, but it was.

None of us spoke as we began to move. There was nothing important enough to say, as the loss of one of their own kept both Stefan and Professor Darmon in a quiet, thoughtful reprieve.

I hadn't thought I'd be able to sleep after what we'd just been through. The fear of further attack was weighing heavily on my mind. My muscles tensed, ready to fight should the need to call for it. Surprisingly, it wasn't long before the rhythmic swaying of the carriage and beat of the horses' hooves on the dry dead earth pulled me under and I drifted into a restless sleep.

Waking with a start a few hours later, I found I'd shifted in my sleep, my head resting on Stefan's lap. It wasn't long after dawn, a gentle orange light flowing through the small window in the carriage door.

Stefan was still asleep, snoring lightly, his head resting against the side of the carriage, his bright pink hair contrasting sharply against the dark navy of the interior cabin walls. The Professor was also asleep, having lain out on the bench across from us, his glasses hanging crookedly on his nose, his mouth hanging open slightly.

Suppressing a giggle, I rose gently, careful not to disturb Stefan, and moved toward the window. The scenery had changed, and I blew out a breath of relief as I realized that we'd made it through the dead forest without further incident. My eyes widened as I studied the new land around us, land I'd never ventured far enough to see.

The carriage was trundling through what must have been old farmland, though there was absolutely no sign of life here now. Broken gates and fences made of rusty criss-crossed wire littered the ground. Grass that had once surely thrived in these paddocks, feeding the livestock, had long since died, leaving a dry and hard floor of dirt stretching out around us.

My heart ached at the state of the land here. It was dryer, deader, than the land in Sommers. Sommers was one of very few areas left on earth with enough life left to sustain a small community, and that was a stretch. Seeing just how desolate some of the earth really was made something ache deep in my chest.

I slid the window open and stuck my head out, twisting slightly to peer in the direction we were travelling. The morning air was fresh and cool on my face, the smell of it ... salty? That was new. I liked it. Something coiled tightly in my gut unraveled as I inhaled deeply. It kind of smelt like hope.

A large stone wall loomed in the distance, standing taller than any man and stretching across the wide expanse of dead fields. Two massive hardwood gates stood directly in front of us, an ornate D for Danann carved in the center of both. We would reach them in a matter of minutes.

Pulling my head back inside the cabin, I sat back down next to Stefan—still sound asleep—my stomach tying itself up in knots as I wondered what I'd find through those gates. He was still sound asleep, Professor Darmon too.

What an imposter I'd become. I felt responsible for the guard we had lost last night. No one had said anything that implied they blamed me, but I couldn't be the only one who thought it. They'd been transporting me. I'd left the cabin when I shouldn't have. The Resistance was after me.

Closing my eyes and rubbing my slick hands on my skirt, I tried to calm my racing heart. All I could see was Henry's face, and the strange meadow he had somehow turned into at the end. My breath started coming faster and shallower. There wasn't enough air.

"Hey, hey, hey, shhhhh, little dove," Stefan rubbed my back with the palm of his hand in a soothing motion. Realizing I was no closer to calming, he continued. "Riley, little dove, we're safe now. We've almost arrived at Danann. We'll be protected behind the walls in no time at all."

For the first time since I'd met him, Stefan had misread my emotions and the reasons behind them. My panic rose from the fact that we were about to enter Danann. Not that I felt unsafe outside the walls. I was terrified of what I was about to face, the way my life was about to change.

Riley. I was just Riley, an orphan girl in search of the only family she'd ever known. My only goal was to find James, and I feared the fae were going to distract me or keep me from that goal in some way. They had such high expectations; believed I might be one of them. Me! Riley Emmett! fae? It couldn't be true.

"I think that's what's causing her panic, Stefan. Riley, dear, look at me." Professor Darmon had woken and was kneeling before me, reaching for my hands reassuringly, his eyes gentle and kind.

"You have nothing to fear. We are here only to help you. Yes, you are an anomaly. Yes, we are curious how you came to be, and what power you may possess, but you do not need to be afraid of us. Like any other who has ascended, we will help you settle into our society. There are no great expectations upon you."

His words were sincere and had an instantaneous calming effect. With the way he spoke, and the speckle of grey through his dark hair, he reminded me of a father. He'd known I was afraid of what their plans for me might be. Knowing there was none was reassuring, even if I didn't completely believe him.

Despite that, his words had reminded me of my true goal, the reason I had applied for ascension. I needed to be accepted into their society. Needed to build relationships with the fae and be trusted in a way that would allow me to discover what happened to James. And find out how to get my brother back.

Straightening, I took a moment to find my center, breathing in and out until my heart rate settled and I felt like I could talk again. "I'm sorry. I don't know what came over me. Thank you."

"Nothing to apologize for. I can't imagine how overwhelmed you must feel given the events of the last 24hours." He smiled at me and let go of my hands, pushing to his feet just as the carriage drew to a halt.

"Come on, little dove," Stefan said, as he pushed to his feet and offered me his hand. "Let's get your first look at your new home."

Professor Darmon opened the carriage door and stepped outside, moving immediately to General Brand's side at the front of the carriage. The General was speaking to a couple of guards in front of the gates. They nodded at him, confirming his instructions as he turned to approach us.

As the two of them moved toward us, one of the guards they'd been speaking to strode towards the gate. There was no mechanism I could see with which it could be opened, but as he stretched his arms out wide, a loud creaking and clanging rang out across the barren fields and the gate swung open of its own accord.

My jaw dropped as I watched it open, amazed at yet another display of magic. Less than a day ago, I'd never witnessed any magic in action. It amazed me each time. I wasn't sure I'd ever get used to it.

The second guard had joined us by the carriage and was directing the coachmen inside. I made a mental note to find the stables later so I could check on Annie. There was no way to explain it, but I felt connected to the mare and even though I was sure she'd been healed, I needed to ensure she was okay following her injury in the dead forest.

"Let's not linger out here," General Brand said, his deep voice rumbling with thinly veiled anger. Or maybe it was frustration? His eyes caught mine as I studied him, and he shuttered them, crushing any hint of emotion or clue what was running through his mind as he looked at me. "The Academy is a short walk inside Danann. The Professor and Stefan will escort you inside and show you to your accommodations." Breaking eye contact with me, he turned to the others, addressing them directly as he continued. "We will then need to debrief. I expect you both at Headquarters in an hour."

With that he turned and marched away, his dismissal of us clear. I watched as he went, my attention drawn to him in a way I could not explain. My attraction to him was fierce, and that scared me. I'd been with other men before, but they'd all been a distraction from the harsh realities of life in Sommers. None of them had been anything serious or raised any feelings within me. Allowing myself to be distracted by General Brand would be a mistake. I had a mission. My focus must remain on finding James.

⇶ ⇜

Trailing behind them, I followed as Stefan and Professor Darmon led me inside the gates of Danann City. The further I wandered in, the more I questioned whether I had stepped through a portal of some sort. Behind me had been old paddocks, the land so barren that the only sign of life were the old gates and fences, half destroyed with time.

Once upon a time, these fields would have been luscious and green with livestock feeding on the fresh grass. Now they were just dirt. Hard, dry, soil lacking any nutrients to support the growth of flora.

The bleak, muddy coloring of the fields contrasted sharply with the bright greenery hidden just behind the gates of Danann.

There was grass! Not just small patches of dry yellow straws poking out amongst the dirt that would be better be described as hay, but actual bright green healthy-looking grass that was soft beneath my feet.

Wildflowers were sprinkled through the lush green grass, the colors of the rainbow more vivid than I had ever seen. Green vines climbed the buildings scattered in the distance, spots of color showing that those too were flowering. A cobblestone path lead through the grass towards the city center, trees lining the sides creating soft patches of shade, many fae resting underneath them in the distance.

Kneeling down, I trailed my fingers through the grass, the tips of them tingling at the touch. Picking a few flowers and bringing them to my nose, I inhaled deeply, the floral scent of them awakening something within me and I startled. Inside my chest, a well opened, cavernous and deep, and utterly empty.

The fresh salty smell I'd caught earlier wrapped around me, joined with the perfume of roses, jasmine and lavender floating on the breeze. Brushing off the strange feeling as a reaction to beauty I'd never seen before, I took another deep breath, reveling in all the wonderful smells around me. I'd always been drawn to nature, and it felt as though my soul was awakening with the wonders around me.

Glancing around, I noticed a fork off the main path curving to the left. It led toward a green pasture, where a couple of horses nibbled on the grass. Stables sat behind the field, and I grinned, knowing where I'd have to go to visit Annie when I had the chance.

A little further along, a fork to the right led a short path off toward a tall wrought-iron fence that reached back towards the wall surrounding the city and around into the distance. A large arching gate was set at the end of the path, the words Danann Academy built into the iron across the middle of the gate. On each side of the gate seemed to be a large lit torch, the fire flickering in the gentle morning breeze. The area beyond was thick with green leafy trees, hiding any view of the Academy I had been hoping to glimpse.

Realizing I'd fallen behind whilst taking in my first taste of Danann, I hurried to catch up. Joining Stefan and the Professor just as they reached the gates into Danann Academy, I watched as they swung open, allowing us entry as we approached.

"That's the second set of gates to open on their own and admit us," I said, as we entered the Academy grounds. Heat bloomed in my chest as I passed the torches and through the gates. "How do they know to open? Is there someone in a guard house somewhere watching us on hidden cameras?" Hidden cameras were probably unlikely. The fae had some technology they had developed, like the tablet Stefan was using back in the candidate tent, but old school tech from before the war was scrambled by their power.

Stefan laughed lightly as he threw his arm over my shoulders again, his overt display of familiarity oddly comforting. "They sense our magical signature and allow entry to the teaching staff, students and senior members of the Fae Army."

"I guess it's recognizing me as a student, then?" I asked, glancing back at the gates as we continued down a path between the trees. As the words came out of my mouth, I wondered how that could be. I had no magic, or if I were to believe the fae around me, no access to my magic. A pulsing in my chest drew my attention, making me wonder if maybe they were onto something. Swallowing against the feeling of unease rising in my throat, I turned my head back to the path in front of us.

In response to my question, Professor Darmon stopped and turned towards me. "You might not believe us, Riley, but you belong to our community. You are fae. The magical signature you emanate is strong, if a little foreign." His brow furrowed; the questions clear in his eyes, wondering where I came from. "Have some faith. We will prove to you that you belong here."

"And continue to remind you until there is no doubt in your mind," Stefan added, a reassuring smile dancing on his lips, his pink hair catching the sun through the leaves above us and even brighter than it had in the wasteland outside these walls.

"I don't know how you can be so sure." I said, shaking my head as we started down the path once more. Just ahead, it appeared to curve a little, and despite myself, I was excited about my first glimpse of the academy. "I have never done anything even remotely extraordinary in my life."

"You might be surprised. Our magic can present in subtle ways before we come of age and its full force is unleashed. A small talent or quirk, something that seems insignificant, can be an early indication of what element a fae may possess. I, for one, never felt the cold. Later, I emerged as a fire elemental. The heat of my fire always kept me warm."

Stefan chuckled. "I was always a little faster than everyone else, using wind to help me as I ran." Gardening had always been something I excelled at, despite the state of our lands. If they were right, if there was magic in me, maybe it was earth.

If I thought my soul was waking earlier, it was nothing compared to the way I felt as I took in the academy grounds ahead of us. I halted, staring as the trees thinned around us, and my gaze was immediately drawn to a small lake on our right, the large outer wall of Danann at its back. A few wooden rowing boats were tied to a small dock, others floating out on the clear blue water, students lazing in the morning sun. A rainbow of gardens was spread through the rest of the space, various benches and gazebos scattered amongst the flowers, more fae making the most of the warm sunny morning.

As I took in the flourishing life around me, each breath I drew began to fill that deep well inside of me that seemed like it had stood empty and barren my entire life, hidden and denied. Energy flooded my veins, my skin tingling with electricity as an unknown power spread from my core, throughout my arms, my legs, to the very tips of my fingers and toes.

Wind whipped around me, bringing with it that salty ocean smell again and my arms sprang wide as that well overflowed. My back arched as the tingling on my skin transformed into a burn, fire bursting forth from my skin, the flames electric blue with their heat. My limbs locked as those flames flickered all around me, my feet rising from the stone path beneath me.

My heart pounded and tears poured down my cheeks as terror took hold of me. I was frozen, locked inside myself with no control of my body as the intense heat surrounded me, consumed me, and blocked everything and everyone else from view. The heat was enough that I felt like I should be melting. It continued to build as fire spewed forth from the very core of me. Somehow my flesh was spared, though my clothing wasn't so lucky.

The heat began to die down as the flames changed from blue to red to orange. They flickered wildly before guttering out. A moment passed where my surroundings came into view again, a wrenching sob bursting from my throat, the rest of my body still at the mercy of whatever power was exploding out of me. Stefan was shouting, but I couldn't hear him, could only watch as he tried to get close enough to me to help while the Professor was ushering the crowd of students who'd appeared further away, for their safety or my privacy. I wasn't really sure. Didn't really care.

The well inside of me was filling again, and I felt a second wave of power crash over the lip before a wild wind burst from my skin. It surrounded me, my golden curls whipping side to side through the air as green vines rose from the grass beneath me, reaching up and up until they grasped my ankles and wound themselves up my legs. Their grip was gentle, as though they were greeting me, welcoming me home, covering my body almost entirely for the briefest of moments before retreating once more. The touch was soothing, easing some of the terror, allowing me to suck in a breath to my starving lungs.

A tempest built around me, locking me within as the vines retreated, their welcome done, as they slunk back to the floor below me. Howling wind was all that I could hear as lightning burst through the darkening sky overhead, followed by a large crack of thunder and a downpour unlike any I had ever experienced.

The moment the rain touched me, the wild winds around me stilled, before exploding from my body in every direction. Fissures in the earth appeared at my feet, splintering outwards away from me. The magic holding me broke, and I crumpled, falling to the ground in a heap. My body was weakened, the outpouring of power having taken everything from me. The well inside me settled, near empty but slowly beginning to fill again as I lay unmoving against the stone. Slower this time, without the same potency as before.

Stefan reached me, the force-field around me having shattered with the blast. He gathered me into his arms, his silver eyes dark with concern. His mouth was moving, but I still couldn't hear him, my ears ringing, darkness peppering my vision. I let the soothing calmness of his presence wash over me, as an exhaustion so deep it seemed to come from my very soul took a hold of me. My eyelids were heavy, and they closed of their own accord, blocking out the view of the damage surrounding me.

There was no more denying it. I was fae, or some other preternatural creature. A powerful one at that.

As the mercy of unconsciousness came for me, I swore to myself that I would do everything I could to learn to control the power within me quickly so that it might help me find my brother.

CHAPTER EIGHT

Riley

"Give her to me." A deep, demanding voice cut through the blanket of oblivion smothering me and I began to rouse. I was in a space of semi-consciousness, my body feeling heavy and all but disconnected from my mind. The exhaustion I felt was deep, but I clung to consciousness like it was a lifeboat in a tumultuous sea.

The arms holding me gripped a little tighter, as though they had no intention of handing me over. Warm and safe, the smell of rosewood and cinnamon surrounded me, and I knew Stefan held me. I was still surprised at how instantly he had become my friend. James had always been at me to let my walls down a little more. He'd like that I'd finally managed to do just that. I trusted Stefan, even though I didn't trust the fae.

"Keep your voice down," someone else hissed. "She needs rest, not to be passed around like a rag doll. That explosion was unlike any other wakening of power I've witnessed in my life. Her energy will be completely drained. Come on. Her room is just up here."

Stefan jostled me a little as he upped his pace, following the voice I recognized as Professor Darmon's. I tried to open my eyes, wanting to know where we were, but my lids were heavy and unresponsive. Comfortable enough that they weren't planning to hurt me, I settled for listening as they carried me along.

"She is more impressive than we expected. Such raw power. King Ronan sent word that he felt it on the opposite side of Danann. That's no small feat." There was that deep, rumbling voice again, sending a small shiver down my spine. Having woken a little more, I recognized it as General Brand.

"She displayed all four elements in her release. What do you make of that?" Stefan asked quietly.

"If I'm being perfectly honest, I'm not sure what I make of it," Professor Darmon replied. "The chance that she is one of us is slim. We do not possess control over more than one element. I have never heard of any exceptions. There is no creature in our world, or her own, that wields control over all four elements."

Silence fell for a moment as the gravity of that statement hit me like a punch to the gut. It didn't just strike me, but the men, too. What was I? Clearly, I was more than human, but not fae? What other options were there?

"What do we know of her family, her history?" Stefan asked, his thoughts mirroring my own. An orphan of the Last War, James was the only family I had ever known.

"There isn't much. She was found wandering around with an older male child they assumed to be her brother at the end of The Last War." General Brand answered, succinctly summing up my past in a single sentence.

"She hasn't mentioned a brother." Stefan said, the question clear in his voice. I held my breath as a wave of guilt hit me. No, I hadn't mentioned a brother. Not because I didn't trust him, but because I had been keeping my reason for coming to Danann close to my chest. There had been so many walls, so many roadblocks, trying to track down James already that I wasn't sure who to trust. I had considered telling Stefan my real motivation, but I hadn't been able to yet. I hoped this wouldn't come between us. In the very short time I'd known him, I had come to really value his friendship, and wondered if it could grow into something more.

"I suspect she may be searching for him and that's the reason she applied to ascend this year. He is an active missing person." General Brand said, hitting the nail on the head. Turns out I wasn't harboring as big a secret as I thought. I had to wonder whether the General had access to any more information about James' disappearance. Was the Fae Army in charge of missing people? That seemed like something that would be allocated to them.

"Do you know much about his case?" Stefan asked lightly, curiosity painting his tone.

"Not a lot. I was unaware of the connection until I investigated the orphanage records yesterday. It will become a priority investigation now. James was older than she was when they were found. He may provide valuable information about where they come from and what they may be. He may possess a similar power to Riley. At the very least, we can't have that kind of power missing; or falling into the wrong hands."

He was referring to The Resistance. There wasn't any other group or faction that he could mean. Sure, the idea that James had left Danann on his own two feet and joined the enemy faction had crossed my mind. I just couldn't bring myself to believe that he would join them. He had never expressed similar thoughts or ideals. And I believed, with all my heart, that he would not have gone dark on me by his own choice. It just wasn't him.

We drew to a halt and a loud knock sounded, startling me a little, my whole-body twitching in response. Wondering if I might have some control back, I tried opening my eyes. The world surrounding me was bright and blurry at first, but after a few blinks, things began to clear.

Stefan's face swam into view as my eyes focused, a knowing smirk and twinkle in his eye. He leant down a little to whisper in my ear as both the General and Professor entered the room ahead of us. "Your breathing changed when you woke, little dove. I hope you overheard something that might help you." He winked at me as he followed the others inside, and I smiled to myself. It seemed I had someone on my side now, and that felt amazing.

Stefan strode into the room, aiming directly for one of two giant four-poster beds against the wall opposite us. Leaning forward, he drew the white covers back and placed me gently in the middle of the bed. I sank into the mattress a little, feeling as though I was being supported by nothing more than a fluffy cloud. I glanced around, spotting a large open window. The sky outside had cleared, no trace of the storm clouds that had surrounded us earlier. The day was once again bright and cheery.

I was so comfortable that I had to fight against sleep as it threatened to take hold of me and drag me back into unconsciousness. The well inside me was prominent, its energy both familiar and foreign as it slowly filled back up. My eyelids began to droop and fall closed of their own accord.

The mattress dipped as Stefan sat on the end of the bed, speaking with General Brand and Professor Darmon again. There was an unfamiliar voice in the mix now. One that was soft and musical; pulling me in and making me want to know its owner. I tried to focus on their words, willing myself to stay conscious for just a little longer, wanting to find out if there was anything else these men knew about me and what had just happened. I needed to know about this newcomer; but I was fighting a losing battle and my body drifted off to sleep despite my best efforts.

⇝⇝⇝ ⇜⇜⇜

When I woke again, the sun was setting; the room cast in shades of burnt orange and pink. Someone had opened the window, a cool evening breeze making the white sheers flutter softly. The room was quiet, empty, and I took the opportunity to examine myself and my surroundings.

I was lying in one of two four-poster beds made of a dark mahogany stained wood were separated by matching nightstands with the open window set above them. The walls were a soft cream, the floors hardwood with a simple cream rug between the beds. Matching desks sat against the wall opposite me, one on each side of the door. The desk opposite me was bare, while the one on the other side of the room was piled high with books and pens.

Instead of canopies, a type of ivy winds itself around the bed frames, tendrils draping lazily over the wood with lilac flowers scattered here and there amongst the vivid green vines. Other plants were scattered throughout the room. The energy in my chest purred, the life around us keeping it fed and calm.

Pulling the sheets back, I sat up to check myself over. I was no longer wearing the white dress Stefan had conjured for me for the ceremony. Instead, I was dressed in an oversized army green shirt that smelt suspiciously like General Brand. Not sure how I felt about someone dressing me while I was unconscious, I was at least grateful my nudity had been covered.

The door suddenly flew open, and I startled, shrieking in alarm and jumping to my feet, my flight or fight response thoroughly activated.

"Woah, little dove can fly!" Stefan teased, laughing as he sauntered into the room, a shit-eating grin on his face. The bastard knew he just scared the shit out of me. I rolled my eyes at him, my heart returning to a normal rhythm now could be sure I wasn't under attack. Sitting down on the edge of the bed, I realized Stefan wasn't alone. Following behind him was a girl I hadn't met yet. Short like me, her skin was unblemished, smooth porcelain; her wavy blonde hair cropped just above her shoulders.

"Hi, I'm Bee, your new roommate." Her voice was soft and calming and I felt the tension bleed from me as she instantly put me at ease. She approached the bed, flopping down next to me and I wonder if it might have been her I heard speaking before I passed out a second time.

"I'm glad to see you up. You freaked everyone out, you know? We are all scheduled to be awoken on our eighteenth birthday so that there aren't any surprises and releases like yours." Bee snorted, then continued, "Not that anyone is like you. How the heck do you have all four elements? What are you? Where do you come from?"

Stefan jumped in before I could answer any of the questions she was firing at me.

"Geez, Bee, give the girl a minute!" His tone was light and playful, his affection for Bee clear in the teasing smile set on his face. Crossing the room in two quick strides, he jumped on the bed, landing between Bee and me, patting the space next to him in a clear request for me to lie down with them. I did so softly, flinching slightly as I went. Whatever had happened earlier had my muscles aching and my bones weary from exhaustion.

"Oh, I'm sorry. I didn't even think. You must be exhausted and here I am peppering you with questions you probably don't even know the answer to!" She reached across Stefan, patting my arm apologetically.

"No, no, it's okay," I smiled gently at her, hoping to offer her some reassurance. I didn't mind her questions. James had been similar, always searching for answers, gaining as much knowledge as he possibly could. "I wish I had the answers for you, for myself, too. I honestly thought someone had made a mistake. I didn't believe I was preternatural. I had only had one goal when I applied to ascend, and that goal led me to play along when General Brand announced I was the lucky one." Right, lucky. My whole life had been turned on its head in a single day. I wasn't sure that counted as lucky.

"You came to find your brother, didn't you?" Stefan asked softly, his usual teasing tone absent. It wasn't exactly new information for him. General Brand had worked it out back in Sommers when I was still trying to hide my motives. I felt somewhat guilty that I hadn't confided in Stefan immediately. I didn't trust people easily. However, Stefan was breaking through my walls at record speed.

"Your brother?" Bee asked, her brow creasing in confusion.

"He ascended a couple of years ago. After six months, he stopped writing. If he could, he would still be writing to me. I know he would." I explained to Bee, quickly glancing at Stefan, then looking up at the ceiling before he could catch my eye and notice the tears building in them. Taking a deep breath, I continued. "He isn't here. General Brand confirmed my suspicions when he told you James was listed as a missing person. I thought ascending might give me an opportunity to investigate a little, maybe find some kind of lead as to where I might find him. So far, I only have more questions." I groaned with frustration.

"Why don't we go get some dinner and see if any answers or ideas present themselves?" Stefan suggested, rising off the bed, grabbing my hand and pulling me up as he went. "Go. Bathroom and closet are through there," he said, pointing at a door to the left of my bed. "It should be stocked with the essentials. Shower and change out of that fugly shirt." His nose wrinkled in jest as he laughed and nudged me towards the door.

No way would I admit it, but I felt warm and safe wrapped up in General Brand's shirt. The scent of freshly chopped wood surrounded me. Despite his front being cold and impersonal, I wasn't really in a hurry to change and lose that sense of comfort. The contrast wasn't lost on me. I could definitely use a shower, though; I was filthy from the journey here and the attack along the way and probably didn't smell as good as the shirt I was wearing.

"We'll wait here and take you down to the dining hall when you're ready." Bee said, sitting up with a smile.

Smiling back at her, I found I was glad to have made another new friend. These fae were really challenging my view of them. So far, most them were kind, caring, and thoughtful. Being

able to reconcile that with their inaction to save our planet was
something I just couldn't do.

Maybe I should add that to my list of questions.

I had a feeling I may not like the answer.

Chapter Nine

Riley

Entering the bathroom, I closed the door quickly behind me and flipped the light switch on. The room was simple, but cozy. Light gray tiles covered the floor and walls. There was a toilet and basin, as well as a claw foot bath and walk-in shower. In the corner were a couple of potted plants, vibrant and green. Maybe Bee was an earth elemental. There was a lot I needed to learn about her.

Next to the bath, I found a small wooden table, towels neatly folded on the bottom shelf, an array of soaps, shampoos and conditioners on the top. Grabbing a few bottles and a towel, my eyes grazed over the deep set bath as I made a beeline for the shower. Stefan and Bee were waiting for me, so I needed to be quick today, but plans for a long luxurious soak were forming in my mind.

Placing my chosen items in easy reach, I turned on the water and stepped back, pulling General Brand's shirt over my head and tossing it in a wash basket. Steam built around me, but I immediately missed the warmth and smell of fine whiskey.

Gods, I had to get it together. There was no reason to keep crushing on the stone-cold General. I couldn't help the way my body responded to him, but I sure as hell could make sure he wasn't my focus. James had to remain front and center in my mind.

Shaking my head in an effort to clear it, I stepped into the shower. The hot water felt like heaven on my sore and tired body, bringing life back to my limbs and easing some of the ache in them. Lingering too long, I briefly forgot that Stefan and Bee were waiting for me. Using the products I chose, I quickly washed my hair and body, a hint of orange blossom drifting in the air.

Shutting off the shower and stepping out, I wrapped myself in the fluffy towel. I quickly dried off before opening a door next to the sink, which had to be the closet. Stefan had said there should be essentials waiting for me, but what I found was more clothing than I had ever owned in my life.

My mouth fell open as I sorted through the multitude of garments in front of me. On the hangers were multiple sets of what I assumed to be the official uniforms, crisp white shirts with navy pleated skirts and ruby red blazer jackets, as well as a variety of dresses ranging from casual cotton dresses to formal gowns. An array of jeans, leggings, shorts, and various tops were folded neatly on the shelves. There was even a section for shoes! I owned one pair of shoes. Or at least I had until my magic had exploded out of me. One pair of boots that had cracked soles and peeling leather.

The injustice of it froze me in place. We had so little in our community, particularly those of us raised in the orphanage. The whole town did the best they could to support each other, but our lives were hard, we worked for everything we had, and our belongings all served a purpose. It was such a stark contrast to the luxury the fae had appeared to live in. I couldn't fathom a reason why we must live in poverty when there appeared to be enough to go around. I clenched my fists as anger swelled within me.

Another question for the list, Riley.

My stomach growled loudly, pulling me out of my furious musings, and forcing me to get a move on. I grabbed a pair of black jeans, a fitted white crop top, and some combat boots, throwing them on and quickly braiding my hair loosely to the side. I shot a glance in the mirror as I passed, glad to find myself looking calm and refreshed, the turmoil inside of me only showing in how bright the green in my hazel eyes shone.

I left the bathroom, finding Bee seated at her desk, her nose buried in a book. Stefan was lounging on my bed, propped up on one elbow. He held the other hand open, twisting it slightly from side to side. My eyes traced his line of sight to find a small ball hovering in the air above him, rotating clockwise, then counterclockwise. I continued to watch as the ball fell, stopping inches from the floor, before flying back up.

Suddenly, the ball shot right for me, hurtling at break-neck speed. A high-pitched squeal escaped me as I threw my hands up to protect my face. A burst of power leapt from my hands, hitting the ball and sending it flying across the room, where it bounced off the wall and rolled along the floor. Startled, Bee jumped out of her chair, leaving her book laying open, forgotten on the desk.

Did I just do that? I stared down at my hands, turning them over and back again, examining them as if there may be some sign, some evidence, or some explanation for what had just happened.

Stefan barked a laugh, jumping up from my bed and retrieving his ball, jolting me out of my shock and I dropped my hands to my sides, staring at him. "What was that? What did I just do?" I asked, looking between him and Bee. I hadn't had time to process everything that had happened in the last few days, let alone the last few hours. So much of this was new. There were parts of me I'd never met before.

"I think your self-preservation instinct just kicked in, Riley." Stefan said, a teasing grin spread across his oh-so-smackable face. Seriously, his self-preservation instinct needed to kick in and tell him to lay off the teasing—just for a little while.

"I think you probably let out a burst of air to stop the ball from hitting you," Bee said, glaring at Stefan while she picked up her book, placing a bookmark in it and closing it gently.

She smoothed down the cover and stacked it neatly in her pile before continuing. "It was instinct, self-preservation as Stefan put it, though he really shouldn't be testing you so soon after your powers wakened of their own accord. We don't know what you're capable of or what control you'll have." She continued to glare at Stefan, and he threw his hands up in surrender.

"My apologies ladies, I'll be more careful." His chest shook with silent laughter, his head tilted to the side, a cocky grin on his face. He clearly had no intention of being more careful. I couldn't find it in me to stay mad at him, though. He'd been the joker since I'd met him, and I had to admit I liked it. It made me feel carefree too, something I needed to feel more often. My life had been so full of worry and stress that I barely knew how to relax.

Bee couldn't hold a grudge against him either, her glare morphing into a grin as she watched him. Glancing at me, she shrugged as though to say, 'What can you do?' I grinned back, letting her know I was fine.

"Let's get you fed." Stefan approached me, throwing one arm over my shoulders and pulling me towards the door. He pulled Bee under his other arm as we exited our room. He paused while Bee locked the door, then pulled us back in close and led us towards the dining room. I couldn't help but lean into him, needing the comfort I felt in his arms as we walked through the unfamiliar hallway.

I had seen none of the interior of the Academy, having been mostly unconscious when they brought me in. Come to think of it, I wasn't sure I'd even seen the exterior before my power had overflowed its well.

The hallway was long and wide; the walls were cream just like our room, the floor a dark mahogany. There were no windows, just rows of doors along the walls. The space between doors was filled with so many different things. There were mismatched tables with potted plants and flower arrangements on them, large paintings of a colorful land that bore no resemblance to this one; large trees in pots almost reaching the high ceiling, and most surprising of all, some water features with continuous running water, small fish seeming to live in the space.

Looking up, I noticed the hall was lit by large crystal chandeliers spaced evenly overhead. The light they threw was golden and flickering, each of them holding a dozen candles.

"Why do you use candles to light the space?" I asked. Electricity still worked amongst the fae, even if much of the manmade technology did not. It seemed inconvenient to ensure that many candles remained lit.

"Our elemental magic reserves are refreshed by exposure to the element itself," Bee started, leaning her head forward, peeking at me past Stefan's wide chest, lickable chest. Wow! Talk about intrusive thoughts. "We try to surround ourselves with the elements at all times, so that we remain at peak power as often as possible."

It seemed obvious when stated so simply. The excessive gardens outside and the abundance of indoor plants, as well as the lake and indoor water features, made more sense. It even somewhat explained what had happened to me upon entry into Danann. I'd been surrounded by all the elements in a way I never had been before, and that caused my power reserve to fill. I'd felt it, even if I didn't know that was what was happening.

"What about air elementals?" I asked, genuinely curious. Were their reserves constantly full to the brim just from breathing, or did they need to be amongst tumultuous winds to refuel?

"The strength of the wind determines how fast our reserves refuel. A stagnant room will fill our wells, as there is still air around us. However, it will do so slowly, at a snail's pace as the air is inactive, unmoving. An intense storm with gale winds will see them fill to the brim in less than an hour." Stefan explained, drawing to a stop as we approached the end of the hall and a large set of wooden doors.

"Look up at the chandelier. It's crystal and lit by candles, but what else can you see?" Stefan asked, reaching for my chin, and tilting it up so that I was looking at the ceiling.

I examined the chandelier closer than I had before. The very center, the part hanging from the roof, was an orb. White, almost opaque, it looked like it was filled with a shimmering, moving force. They were strangely beautiful and otherworldly. Extending off the central orb were four crystal arms, each with their own smaller sphere resembling the central orb and three candle holders attached.

"Each sphere is filled with the energy of a storm that raged back home in Faerie. The winds are powerful, though not destructive in nature. They are difficult to harness and were one of the few items we bought with us from The Origin, from Faerie. They fill our halls and there is at least one sphere in every single room, in every house inside Danann."

"Wow." I said, unable to come up with a more intelligent response as I gaped up at the chandelier. It really was beautiful; I'd never seen anything quite like it.

Better get used to it. You're pretty much living in an alternate universe now.

"Come on, the dining hall is just through here and down the stairs." Bee said, interrupting my internal monologue and turning to open the wide double doors in front of us. I followed her through them onto a somewhat circular landing set in front of enormous floor to ceiling windows. To our right was a staircase leading to the floor below us; to our left, three further corridors leading to who knows where, another staircase leading down at the other end of the landing.

I was going to need a map.

Ornate cream balustrades curved around the edge of the landing; a couple of couches scattered across the space. Small tables sat next to the couches, lanterns and flowers spread randomly across them. I moved forward, reaching the handrail and gazing out the giant windows. Spread before me was the ocean; a place I had only ever read about but had never ventured far enough to see in person. A small flat of grass led from the back of the building, quickly shifting into sand. Blue waves crashed gently into the sand, only to be pulled quickly back out. It was mesmerizing. I felt as though I could sit here all day and just watch this massive beast of nature do its thing.

I felt Bee approaching. She stood next to me, staring at the sea with the same reverence mirrored on her face. "They say the sea back home is pink and gold, and that whilst this ocean is majestic, it cannot hold a candle to the pure beauty of our homeland. I am not sure I believe them, but I pray every night I can one day find out."

I pulled my eyes away from the ocean, turning to Bee in surprise. "You've never been to the Faerie?" I asked softly.

"I was there when I was a girl, but I was too little to re-member much of anything" She sighed heavily, leading me to believe there was more weighing on her. I wouldn't push her. She would tell me when she was ready. Hopefully, we would be friends and she would trust me enough to confide in me one day. If I were around long enough.

After a moment, she turned away, grabbing my hand as she went and leading me to the stairs. I followed her down, realizing Stefan was already waiting at the bottom. Stefan smiled as we reached him, stretching out his arm in the direction we needed to go. We turned from the bottom of the stairs to face another set of wide double doors underneath the landing we've just come down from, a plaque on it that simply read 'Dining Hall'.

As Bee opened the door, I braced myself. I was almost positive I was about to be the center of attention, the new shiny new toy to be gawked at. I hadn't seen anyone on our walk down here and I had to assume that was because all the other students were inside.

As expected, the moment I stepped inside all eyes were on me. Swallowing the lump in my throat, I straightened, holding my head high and refusing to be intimidated. I most definitely was, but I wouldn't let anyone see.

I forced myself to look beyond the sea of faces—though there really weren't as many as I had assumed. The floors and walls were much the same as what I'd seen so far. Fae must like their surroundings clean and simple. The room was long, the opposite end mirroring the floor to ceiling windows behind us. They looked out at the lake and gardens I had glimpsed upon my entry here. There were a couple of rows of tables and benches, each one with eclectic centerpieces that seemed to include a little of each element.

Along one side of the room ran a buffet style, serve yourself, canteen. The options seemed endless, from roast meats to salads, to stews and pastas. My mouth watered in anticipation. Our meals at the orphanage were small, sometimes few and far between. I had never truly eaten well. As much as it irked me, at this moment, I was going to take what was on offer and indulge myself.

Following Stefan to the buffet, I grabbed a plate and piled it high with a wide assortment of food. The smells were tantalizing, and I rushed to the table Bee had claimed and began shoveling down my food, no longer caring that all eyes were on me. I was starving. I couldn't remember the last time I'd eaten.

When the edge of my hunger had eased a little, I slowed, looking up from my plate to find Bee and Stefan staring at me, laughter shining in both their eyes. I shrugged, taking another bite of the roast potatoes I was currently devouring. Bee grinned even wider before offering me a glass of lemonade. Offering her a smile of thanks, I took it gratefully. The sweet bubbly drink was heavenly—it might be my new favorite.

Just then, a young waiter arrived at the table. He cleared his throat gently before speaking. "Are you Riley Emmett?" he almost whispered, nerves clearly getting the better of him.

I smiled at him, trying to reassure him I wouldn't bite. "Yes, I am. Can I help you?"

"I've been asked to give you this letter. It's from Professor Darmon." He handed me a letter on the same heavy parchment that had informed me I was a candidate not two days ago.

"Thank you." I said, glancing up to find he was already hurrying away. I turned to my new friends, my brow creasing in confusion. "Why is he scared of me?" I asked them. I wasn't sure there was anything scary about me. In fact, I thought of myself as a mother hen. I'd always cared for and taught the younger children back home. Thinking of them made me miss home and caused my bottom lip to drop a little.

Stefan frowned as he noticed the change in my expression. He reached for my hand on top of the table, offering me comfort once again. "You are powerful, and we don't quite know what you are or where you've come from. That makes people uneasy. Particularly those that already feel vulnerable in this land, like

Mark. His power has not yet woken, despite him coming of age a few months ago."

"Does that happen often? I left school young to work in the gardens at home, and I was never very interested in learning much about the fae." I didn't mean to offend anyone, but it was the god's honest truth. I'd always been angry at the way the world was and the lack of any change. It had never sat right with me.

Bee quirked an eyebrow at me. Her gaze was assessing like she was trying to work me out, to see what made me tick, why I thought the way I did. She didn't seem offended, just curious. I shot her a small smile, hoping to appease her for now. I'm sure we'd have time to get to know each other on that level.

"More and more often." Stefan answered. "We think it's tied to the land and our broken bonds with Earth."

What a curious statement! Earth was dying. Maybe that meant the fae's link to their magic wasn't as strong here. I was about to ask him to explain further when he stood suddenly, someone by the door catching his eye.

Looking in that direction, I found General Brand standing there, waiting. His eyes locked with mine, chocolate brown tonight, lighter than I'd seen them. A flush crept up my chest, spreading to my cheeks as the intensity of his stare increased. I felt both uncomfortable and warm. My stomach fluttered as his stare lingered.

Snap out of it, Riley!

As Stefan mumbled something about having to go and got up to leave, I broke my eyes away from the General's, missing the connection almost immediately.

I bit my lip as I waved goodbye to Stefan, wondering what the fuck had just happened. Why did I always have to like the unavailable guys?

"Wow. Talk about chemistry." Bee said, bringing me back to the table. She laughed as I stared at her. I groaned loudly and buried my face in my hands. That made her laugh even harder. "Here," she said, tapping my hand. "Open this. It might distract you from the train wreck you are clearly heading for. I mean, General Brand, for god's sake, you couldn't have picked anyone more unavailable. I mean, you do you girl, but damn, you've got your work cut out for you." Her laughter was contagious, and I couldn't help joining in.

I sat up, taking the letter from her and scanning the content. "He's arranged a meeting with me first thing in the morning. To discuss my schedule and theories around my abilities." Sighing heavily, I sat the paper down. "I wish I knew more about you and your world, Bee. Maybe then I'd have a working theory about what the hell is happening to me." I was being a little dramatic, but to say I was overwhelmed would be the understatement of the century.

"I can't help with a working theory; I don't have one yet. I am going to spend tomorrow in the library to see if I can come up with one, though. Not knowing irks me." She frowned a little at her admission. "I can tell you more about myself and our community. What would you like to know?"

It was time to pull out my mental list of questions. I really should start carrying around a notebook. "What type of element do you control?" I ask, my mind flicking back to the ivy in our dorm. I wasn't surprised to learn she was an earth elemental.

"Both my mother and father control the element of earth, so it was almost guaranteed I would, too." Her eyes glazed over a little, as though she were remembering something far in the past. "I used to play in the flower fields, and never left without a braided crown of wildflowers." She chuckles softly before continuing. "The only memory I have of our homeland is of leaving two flower crowns on an old oaken table. One large for my mother, the other tiny, for my baby sister about to be born. Dad and I never met her." Her green eyes misted, tears welling, one escaping and tracking a single line down her cheek.

"I'm so sorry." I reached for her hand, giving it a gentle squeeze. "That must be really difficult. Are you able to speak with them at all?"

She shakes her head, sniffling softly as she swipes her free hand across her cheek, the other still holding mine. "No, the crossing was difficult, more difficult than had been predicted. We haven't been able to cross back at all, and as far as we know, our reinforcements never made it."

My curiosity piqued. We'd never been taught about how the fae came to be here, what they might have been through to cross the void between our worlds. I had never cared that much, assuming I would live out my days in Sommers and never really cross paths with them. For the first time in my life, I wanted to know all there was about the fae, their world, and what drove them to ours.

CHAPTER TEN

Riley

Bee and I spent the rest of the night in our dorm getting to know each other. I told her all about James and she told me all about her father, the only family she had here on this plane. The unrelenting drive to be reunited with our families helped us to bond. We were closer because of it, even if both of us were miles away from ever achieving it.

Morning came quickly, and I woke feeling more whole than I had felt at any previous point in my life. The well in my chest was full to the brim, though thankfully felt less wild and less likely to spill over like it had yesterday. I wandered into my bathroom, quickly showering and throwing my hair up, before dressing in a pair of denim shorts and an oversize white shirt.

Pulling on the same boots I'd worn last night, I smiled to myself, ready to face my first full day in Danann, whatever it may bring. A renewed sense of hope bloomed in my chest at being here, one step closer to James. When I returned to the bedroom, I found Bee up and waiting for me.

"I'll walk you to the Dean's office. It's on the way to the library." She said, opening the door and heading out into the hall.

"Thanks." I threw her a smile and followed her through the door, falling in step beside her as we made our way downstairs. "Classes start tomorrow, don't they? What classes are you taking?" I really had no idea what to expect when classes began. I was a little nervous about ending up in a class without Stefan or Bee, and of being the center of attention. Amidst the nerves, though, a tiny part of me was excited. Okay, maybe a big part of me. My power thrummed in my chest and I was eager to learn how to take control of it.

I'd decided last night, whilst listening to Bee snore softly, that blending in and making the most of the opportunities being handed to me was my best course of action. Someone had to know something; I just had to get close enough to the right someone and hope they revealed some kind of clue as to where my brother had disappeared to.

"We'll be in all the same classes," she said, grinning at me as she walked. "There are five core subjects for each year level. Stefan is a second year, so you'll only have Physical Combat with him. We all train together. Then there are the elemental classes, two for each element, wielding, and combat. I'm not sure how that will work. They are all usually scheduled at the same time, which will be a major clash for you." She frowned as she considered it.

"Maybe that's what Professor Darmon wants to discuss with me." We made our way out of the hall and out onto the landing. We'd just made our way down the stairs when footsteps sounded behind us, and Stefan yelled for us to wait.

I glanced over my shoulder to see him coming through a second set of doors on the other side of the landing. He disregarded the staircase next to him, instead crossing the common space quickly, his long stride making it seem easy.

"Good morning, little dove, morning Bee," he said with a grin, leaning down and planting a kiss on top of both our heads. His easy affection and familiarity heated something inside of me, and I willed myself not to blush.

"We were just discussing Riley's schedule." Bee explained, as we continued down the stairs. "You're close to Professor Darmon. Do you have any idea how she's going to manage classes for all four elements?"

"I do. It's going to be interesting. You'll love it." His full lips tipped up in a devastating grin, his silver eyes sparkling with laughter. He refused to reveal more as we passed by the dining hall. My meeting with Professor Darmon was early, so Bee and I had agreed to meet back here for brunch.

We continued across the room, past the staircase leading down from what I now knew to be more dorm rooms. We headed down another hallway leading to the teaching wing of the Academy and stopped outside a door with a simple plaque reading 'Academy Dean'. I bid farewell to Stefan and Bee as they turned back in the direction we came.

Taking a deep breath, I smoothed my hands down the front of my shorts, composing myself before knocking to announce my arrival.

"Come in." Professor Darmon called, his voice slightly muffled through the door.

I entered slowly and found myself in a light, airy office space. A large wooden desk sat in the center of the room, in front of a large arched window. The window had been cracked open, letting in a cool breeze, the briny smell I caught yesterday still tainting the air. Bookshelves lined the walls, filled to the brim with more books than I even knew existed, many of them old and worn.

Professor Darmon rose from his chair, gesturing for me to take a seat in one of the two cream armchairs placed in front of his desk.

"It's nice to see you up and about, Riley. How are you feeling?" He asked, his brow slightly furrowed, concern etched into his features. He had every right to be concerned, I supposed. The last he'd seen of me, I'd been barely conscious and completely drained of energy after experiencing an unscheduled wakening of power. From what Bee had told me, that just didn't happen.

"I feel much better today, thank you." I said, offering a reassuring smile.

"I'm glad to hear it. We have a lot to discuss this morning. General Brand will join us shortly. I'm sure you must have a lot of questions for me and I'm hoping we'll answer them with the information we cover today. If you don't mind, we'll go through any that may linger at the end of our meeting." I nodded my agreement, my thoughts scattering a little, distracted by the mention of General Brand.

"Fantastic." He clapped his hand together enthusiastically, before shuffling some papers in front of him. "Let's start with your enrollment at this academy. We think it's best you be enrolled as a First-Year student, just like any other fae who've come of age and had their powers woken. There is just one minor issue."

"Let me hazard a guess. I possess too many elements?" Bee had been forthright about it being a problem. The downside of being an unknown factor, I suppose.

"Yes, though I believe we've found a solution. As you may or may not know, we schedule both general and combat classes for each element. Our wielding classes teach you how to control your element, and how to use it to assist in your everyday life and what roles you can take in the community. Our combat classes teach you how to use your element in a fight, should you ever need to."

"You will be required to choose an element, the one that you feel the strongest connection with, and we will treat that as your primary element. You will attend those classes at their scheduled times, with the other students of that element. We will then set you up with tutors, other students and perhaps some staff, to meet with you once a week and teach you what you have missed in that week's wielding class." A knock on the door interrupts his speech, and he pauses for a moment before instructing them to come in.

General Brand let himself in, the smell of freshly chopped wood and whiskey filling my nostrils as he moved through the doorway, closing it softly behind him. He was wearing black boots, cargo pants, and a fitted white shirt, the pure artistry of his muscles on full display as they strained against the seams. Inhaling deeply, I breathed him in before catching myself. Flushing, heat blooming across my cheeks, I turned my attention back to Professor Darmon, hoping neither of them caught my moment of pure admiration.

What was it about this man? Most of the time he was cold, any personality he had buried deeply beneath his role as Army General and the thick wall he'd built around himself. And yet, the way my insides warmed as his chocolate brown eyes looked me up and down was almost criminal.

Clamping my thighs together, I straightened my spine, determined to ignore the effect he unknowingly had on my body. Focus. I needed to focus. This meeting was important. My future in Danann was being outlined, and hopefully I'd be given some answers I'd been desperately trying to find.

"Perfect timing, Colin. I was just about to tell Riley how you've offered to train her in elemental combat." He turned back to me, grinning like he'd just offered the best solution in the world. To be fair, it was an excellent solution. It just also made butterflies dance violently in my stomach. The thought of being alone with the General had ideas flooding my mind that definitely weren't appropriate.

"Once a week, when your classmates are in their elemental combat lessons, General Brand will meet with you one on one." Professor Darmon continued, seemingly not noticing the internal turmoil I was subjecting myself to. "His element is fire, and he will also give you general lessons on that element. Wielding the elements for combat is all about control and creativity, though, and he will be able to talk you through some examples with your other elements. We will reassess at regular intervals and make changes if it's not working, however I think it will turn out nicely."

"I work with soldiers of every element every day. I have some tricks up my sleeve. Have you chosen your primary element?" General Brand added, throwing a wink in my direction. My jaw dropped, and I hurried to close it again, his flirtatious display catching me off guard. Was he warming to me? Maybe there had been a reason for his cold front so far.

Both men were looking at me, as though waiting for a response. "Yes. Great. I think I'd like to choose Earth as my primary element." I quickly choked out, pushing my wayward thoughts from my head and trying to refocus on the conversation.

"Great. That's settled then," Professor Darmon said, clapping his hands together. "I will confirm the students that will tutor you in other elemental basics later in the week. Now, let's move on to more serious matters. Your heritage, Riley. You were raised human?" He asked, though I knew he already knew the answer.

"Yes, I was raised in the orphanage in our village. The directress always said she found James and I wandering around, wet, cold, and starving just days after the Last War ended. We had no memories, nothing to identify where we were from. She took us in and raised us amongst the other orphans.' I shrugged, not having anything further to add. It was the story I'd been told from the moment I was old enough to ask questions myself.

Growing up, I'd never really felt different from the other children. I'd always been a bit of a loner, though, and as soon as I was old enough, I volunteered to leave school and assist Mr Cole, our head gardener. The directress claimed I had quite the green thumb and, to my surprise, hadn't uttered a word of complaint. Looking back, my talent in the gardens may have been a clue that I was somewhat different from my peers.

"You would have been two, maybe three, correct? James was older, though, by a couple of years. It is understandable that you would have no memory, or even simply no way to communicate any information that you had. I find it hard to believe, however, that James could not provide any information." Anger blazed to life in my chest and I felt both their eyes on me as my fists clenched by my sides. I was on my feet before I realized I had moved, quick to defend my brother. How dare they make that kind of accusation?

"Are you implying my brother is a liar? That—at the innocent age of five years old—he kept some bogus secret from the people who took us in and cared for us?" I could feel my skin heating as the intensity of my rage grew. How dare they question James? He was all I had. What reason would he have had to lie about where we came from? He'd been just a child, for god's sake.

The well of power in my chest bubbled faster and faster until it spilled over the edges of its containment and balls of fire erupted in the palms of my hands.

A red haze fell across my vision, the quickening beat of my heart deafening in my ears. I was losing control; I knew it; they knew it. Frozen in place, I watched as they both rose and backed away from me with their hands held out in front of them.

I had to do something, had to stop before I hurt someone. General Brand's mouth was moving as he tried to reach for me, but I couldn't hear him over the thundering of blood in my veins. Even as I backed away, the ball of flames in each palm grew larger and my back collided with the shelves behind me. I was trapped, fighting a battle of control deep within myself.

A sob tore from my throat as tears poured down my face and I realized I was crying. I kept my hands stretched out in front of me, trying to tame the flames, willing myself to bring them under control. I didn't want to hurt anyone, or burn down the school on my first day. The harder I tried to control the flames as they danced in my hands, the more erratic they became.

Someone sat down next to me, my eyes too fixated on the flames in my palms to look at who it was. Strong arms pulled me up from the floor and into their lap, cradling my body against their own. I couldn't look away from my flames, scared that if I did, the little control I was maintaining would collapse, and I'd set the room ablaze. Even with my attention elsewhere, I recognized him from touch and smell alone.

General Brand settled me between his legs, wrapping one arm around my waist, his fingers splayed against the bare skin of my abdomen. His other arm stretched out along mine, his fingers wrapping around my wrist. The scent of whiskey and pine surrounded me as he rested his chin on my shoulder and counted. "Breathe, Riley," he murmured, his hot breath caressing my ear, almost instantly distracting me from the panic that had been threatening to consume me and causing a different heat to bleed through my body. "In, 1, 2, 3, 4.... Out, 1, 2, 3, 4... That's it."

He kept counting as I focused on breathing in and out as he instructed. My heart slowly but surely returned to a normal rhythm, the deafening pounding in my ears reduced to a low thrum, and my vision cleared as the room came back into focus. The flames in my palms flickered and shrank in size. Letting go of my waist, he gathered both my hands in his, slowly forcing me to close them, extinguishing the flames altogether.

I closed my eyes, still counting my breaths, and tried to hold on to the sense of calm General Brand had helped me find. My emotions were scattered, and I could make little sense of how I was feeling. So much about my life had changed in such a short amount of time. I'd really need to work on controlling myself, especially if this was what happened when my emotions got the better of me. I could have really hurt someone.

I choked back a sob, leaning into General Brand's embrace, my back pressing flush against his firm chest as he remained wrapped around me. Focusing on the steady rise and fall of his chest allowed me to match his breathing with my own. I wasn't ready to move just yet, wanting to stay huddled up in his little pocket of warmth and safety.

It seemed General Brand wasn't as cold and emotionless as he tried to portray. Little by little, he was letting me in and showing me the softness that waited just beneath his tough man act. He was both gentle and kind; it hadn't escaped my notice that for all his hard ass fronting; he had now helped me twice. Once by physically healing me, and just now by emotionally supporting me through a panic attack of sorts.

I didn't want to leave the cocoon of safety I had found in his arms, but as Professor Darmon relaxed and moved back to take his seat at his desk once more, I forced myself to pull away. General Brand's hands lingered for a moment before releasing me and quickly pushing to his feet. Stretching out a hand to help me up, his eyes caught mine, something bright and hesitant shining there.

"Thank you." I whispered, emotions warring in my chest. "I'm sorry, I didn't mean to lose control, the anger just … took over." I lowered my eyes and took a step backwards, followed by another, before returning to my chair. I kept my gaze downcast, a little embarrassed by my outburst.

"It's not unusual for our emotions to rule us for some time after our elemental powers are awoken. I should have kept that in mind and perhaps broached the topic of your brother more sensitively, for that I apologize." Leaning forward on his elbows, he rested his chin on his hands, looking directly at me. "Whilst it is clearly a sensitive topic, it is one we need to discuss. I think we need to clear the air so that we can move forward on the same page. Are you okay to continue, Riley?"

I nodded, keeping my eyes downcast, hyper-focusing on a wooden knot in the front of his desk. General Brand's stare was burning into me as he assessed me and made his own decision whether I was fit to continue. He must have declared me so, as I felt the weight of his stare lift from me and I hazarded a peek to see him turning toward the Professor.

"Are we correct to assume that you applied for ascension in a bid to find James?" General Brand asked, his voice cold and cutting once more, jarring me out of my pity party. For the love of all that was holy; he drove me crazy with his constant fluctuating between hot and cold in the blink of an eye. Maybe I was reading too much into his behavior. Maybe the fae were just a particularly moody bunch, and his mood swings had nothing to do with me. They had just said our emotions ruled us for some time, though Stefan and Bee seemed pretty normal.

They'd figured me out; there wasn't much reason to hide the truth any longer. I belonged here more completely than if

I had ascended in the usual manner. "Yes, I did. Something has happened to him, and not a single person I tried to contact about it has offered me any help. He would not disappear on me, and I know he'd be searching for me if our roles were reversed." It was up to me to find him; I couldn't rely on anyone else.

Professor Darmon sighed, rolling his shoulders as he stood and made his way to the window. "Ascension is the way we try to bring our communities together, a way for us to feel more at peace with the divide between us, to build and foster relationships, even trust between our species." He was staring off into the distance as he spoke, hands clasped tightly behind his back, as though it pained him to admit what he was about to say. "It was a decent plan, in theory, but in reality, it seems prolonged exposure to our magic is detrimental to humans. Many of those that have ascended have become ill, physically, or psychologically. There are a few still here that are fine, but many have run, trying to return home and not quite making the journey; though a couple certainly have. Many of their ailments disappear when they leave our company."

He turned back to face us, his face grave. "Some of the more advanced illnesses remain. Once we realized what was happening, we began making changes, trying to come to a solution that allowed everyone to remain happy and healthy. Hence your ascension. If a human possessed magic of their own, perhaps they would not be driven to madness in our presence."

"We weren't sure if it would work, if there were any humans that possessed any form of magic, and regardless, it came too late. A faction headed by some of those made ill by living among us formed together to become what you would know as..."

"The Resistance." I said, more to myself than anything. So many puzzle pieces were coming together, answering questions I hadn't even realized I'd needed to ask.

"Correct. They believe we are here to claim your lands as our own, and not to save it as we promised. That we are failing in our mission on purpose," General Brand stated, frustration clear in his tone. "It has gotten to the point where, if an ascendant goes missing, they have likely joined the resistance. James' disappearance was treated as such."

My mind was swimming with this new information. The question of whether James might have left the fae city to join the resistance had crossed my mind multiple times. It wasn't impossible and I guess I understood why they may have assumed so. I couldn't quite bring myself to believe that he had. He had never expressed any unhappiness towards the fae, no inclination that he may turn against them. Hell, he'd always been the more positive of both of us, believing they were doing their best, where I'd always questioned whether they were doing anything at all.

Realizing I'd been silent for a while as I mulled over what this information could mean, I looked up to find both men staring at me, waiting for my response. "I understand why you'd treat his disappearance in that way," I said tentatively. "Respectfully, I know my brother. If he had joined them, he would have told me, or at least let me know that he wouldn't be in contact for a while.

I just cannot believe he would leave me without a goodbye." A sob caught in my throat, my heart aching as I allowed myself to voice those thoughts aloud.

"That may be, but it seems the resistance knows of you, Riley. The attack in the Dead Forest was well planned. They were after you and they were almost successful. It would be prudent to remain alert and consider the possibility you may not know your brother as well as you thought." His words hung heavy in the air, the seriousness of my current situation finally settling in on me.

I was fae, or something similar, with unheard of power that I couldn't yet seem to control. My brother was missing, maybe having joined the enemy faction, the same faction that wanted me so badly they would take me by force if they could, having already killed one of our men.

I certainly couldn't say my life was dull.

CHAPTER ELEVEN

Riley

The rest of the meeting passed quickly. Both men really had no idea why I possessed the power that I did. They weren't even sure whether I may be from Faerie or Earth or some other place they called the void. Eventually, deciding nothing would be discovered today, they dismissed me, advising me that my schedule would be delivered to my room this afternoon.

Wandering unhurriedly down the hallway, I headed back towards the dining hall where I was due to meet Bee for brunch. The luxury of being able to have brunch wasn't lost on me, it was not something we'd been able to do very often back in Sommers. Our meals were set at the orphanage, we ate what we were served when it was served.

Whilst my meeting with Professor Darmon had answered some of the questions I had, I still felt strongly that the fae could do more to help and improve the conditions those living in Sommers and other human communities faced. Figuring out who to speak to about the conditions back home might be difficult. Stefan and Bee had been really open with me so far, but this topic felt sensitive and I wasn't sure I wanted to put that kind of pressure on my new friendships.

Fiddling with my locket as I walked, lost in my thoughts, I arrived quickly at the dining hall. I spotted Bee and hurried over to join her at her table. She'd already grabbed an assortment of food from the buffet, and I plopped myself down in the chair next to her, burying my head in my hands with a groan. Lifting her head, she looked up from the heavy book she'd brought down with her eyes wide.

"What in all of Faerie is wrong with you?" She asked, surprised by my dramatic entrance.

"I lost control again," I moaned, not bothering to lift my hands from my face.

"And? It's to be expected, Riley. You're so new to your power, it's going to take time." She reached over, placing a hand on my shoulder and patting reassuringly.

"I nearly set the whole place on fire, Bee!" I exclaimed, wondering if I could just sink right into the floor and have it swallow me and the embarrassment I was carrying with me whole. "And it's not just that... General Brand helped me regain control. He held me, he was calm and gentle... and I liked it." I was trying really hard to keep the whine from my voice, but I knew I sounded ridiculous. I was embarrassed that he'd had to do that, and even more embarrassed that I wanted him to do it again. "I don't even know how old he is!"

Bee stared at me for a moment, her mouth falling open before she burst into an uncontrollable fit of giggles. I leveled her with a glare while she fought to control herself. It took a few minutes, but eventually she stopped, hands clutching her sides as she fought for breath.

"I'm sorry," she hiccupped, barely stemming her laughter. "He's twenty-five. I just can't picture it, that solid brick wall of a fae being gentle—are you sure it was him?"

"I'm sure. Ugh, I just keep making a bigger and bigger fool of myself. I can't make any sense of him either, he is so lukewarm!" Bee was still trying to contain her giggles, and I couldn't help but laugh with her. It felt good too, to let the stress of this morning's events go.

"Where's Stefan?" I asked when we'd settled enough to talk, filling my plate with some scrambled eggs and toast. I'd thought he was joining us for brunch. It may have only been a few days, but I'd grown to really enjoy his company. I'd only spoken to him briefly this morning after he disappeared with General Brand last night, and already I missed him.

Yeesh. These fae men had my head spinning.

"He had to deal with something at headquarters. He'll try to meet us later."

"Headquarters?" I'd heard it mentioned in passing, but I hadn't yet explored Danann and wasn't really sure what was inside the city walls apart from the Academy grounds and the stables across the way.

"It's what we call the Army base," she explained, taking a long sip of coffee. "I'll take you for a tour of the city on the weekend if you like?"

"Yes, please!" I needed to learn my way around, and quickly. Knowing where things were, and where to find certain people, seemed like the logical first step in finding out where James was. I was also going to need to learn more about what he'd been doing while he was here. Given how suspicious both General Brand and Professor Darmon were about James, it appeared I might have to resort to a little investigative work. The beginnings of a plan were forming in the back of my mind as I finished my meal.

"We'll head out first thing Saturday then and spend the day exploring!" Her excitement was clear, her brain mentally planning out our adventure and my introduction to the city. "Are you ready to head to the library? I really want to see if we can come up with any theories about what you are and where you might come from." She said, standing up from the table and slinging a bag over her shoulder.

"Sure," I stood too, piling our dishes onto a tray before following her through the dining hall. Apparently, the wait staff would clean it up. I was feeling well and truly spoiled in my time here. The children at the orphanage popped to mind, still living on their meager rations, and guilt settled heavily in my stomach.

Bee led us through the heavy double doors, out into the large open hall overlooking the ocean. The waves were a little stronger today, crashing harder against the sand than they had been yesterday evening. Something tugged in my chest, my water element responding to the volatile waves, wanting to join them. My magic surged then, pushing up against my barriers and I had to take a moment to stop and focus on keeping it contained.

I hadn't realized it was there before. It was buried so deeply in denial and a lack of self-awareness. Now that I'd discovered it, acknowledged its existence, I wasn't sure how I'd denied it for so long. This power was an innate part of me, and I knew, instinctively, that once I learned about it and embraced it, I would be able to wield control and do things beyond anything I had ever imagined. It was just going to take time.

Time I did not have.

Bee led me past the stairs that we came down from the dorms to another set of heavy double doors; these with a sign reading library. Before opening the door, she turned to me, a grin spreading across her pixie-like features. "This is my favorite place in the academy, the city, really. I love it here." With that, she pushed open the door and shoved me in ahead of her.

The inside of the library was nothing short of magical. The walls were floor to ceiling shelves in the same mahogany wood as the boards beneath my feet. A study area filled the space between the entrance and the large, arching windows lining the back wall. The view out of those windows was of the lake and gardens blooming with life. Cream rugs were scattered across the floor, a variety of tables, chairs, and couches to choose from. A large fireplace sat dead center in the wall to my left, filling the room with a flickering orange light that added to the ambience of the space.

To my right was what seemed to be a maze of shelving, leading back further than I could make out. There was so much knowledge in this space; I had thought that Professor Darmon's office had a lot of books, but it was barely a scratch on the surface. I spun slowly on my heels, taking it all in. "Where did they all come from?" I breathed, mostly to myself, as I wondered how the fae had found all these treasures.

"There was Fae whose sole task was ensuring that this knowledge traveled safely with us across the void. My father was one of them. It was not an easy journey, and this knowledge cost more than a few lives to protect," Bee said, her eyes darkening at the memory.

I didn't want to push her into reliving memories that might be hard for her, but curiosity got the better of me. "What is the void?" I asked. "I'd never heard of it before today, but it's been mentioned twice in a few short hours."

"Of course, you wouldn't have heard of it. It's something we try very hard to keep secret from the humans, we can't allow the fear and panic that knowledge might cause. Come, let's sit. I'll tell you what I know."

Frowning at her admission of secrecy, I followed her to a pair of armchairs in front of the fireplace. I probably should have suspected there would be things the fae kept from the human community; it hadn't crossed my mind before now and she'd caught me off guard by admitting it.

"I don't know much, only what I've overheard dad talk about. I've made a few assumptions too, so some of this is purely working theory. There's a full class dedicated to the void in our second year, and that's generally when we are privy to the information." She looked at me, studying me intently, searching for something. She must have found what she was looking for in my eyes because she continued on.

"Both Faerie and Earth are part of a multiverse. Both lands exist at the same time and space, but they are wholly separate from one another. However, disasters can be felt on both sides. The damage done to Earth is also damaging Faerie. If Earth dies, Faerie does too." I nodded along. I knew this much. It's what we were taught in our early schooling. The fae came here to save Earth, to save their own lands. The suffering that occurs here causes shockwaves of effect throughout Faerie.

"The only way to cross between the realms is through the void. It is wildly dangerous. There are things that reside there that don't even exist in your wildest nightmares. Mists that corrupt your soul, creatures that feed on fear, some that feed on magic. Only one return crossing had ever been made successfully." She paused for a moment, looking out the windows and across the Academy grounds. I waited with bated breath, hooked on her every word.

"Our God of Darkness, Kala, had crossed a few years before to see what was happening on your lands. He was the only one to ever make it through and back and was confident he could do it again, all while creating a safe path for us to cross in the future. So, he led our army, and many of their families, into the void, through the horrors within. I don't remember a lot of the crossing; I wasn't supposed to be there and had hidden amongst the books. I just recall an overwhelming sense of fear, and the almost constant sounds of those around us screaming as we were attacked. There were so many deaths. Too many," she shuddered with the memory, wrapping her arms around herself.

"I'm so sorry you experienced that, Bee. And at such a young age. That must have been terrifying." I reached out, placing my hand on her shoulder in comfort and reassurance. Placing her hand over my own, she smiled softly back at me. A sad smile, full of regrets and burdens no one her age should carry.

"Thank you. It was my fault, though." She didn't elaborate on that odd statement, and I didn't push. She was already telling me so much that perhaps she shouldn't. I filed it away for another day.

"We eventually escaped the attack and made the journey through, though our numbers were greatly depleted. Kala was weakened in body and mind. Some of the elders say he'd lost his mind in the end, that something had corrupted him on the crossing. He tried to keep a safe passage open; and instead ripped a one-way doorway into the tapestry between Earth and the void. Creatures of the void can cross to Earth, but they cannot return. We have been unable to access the void at all to even attempt crossing back."

"What happened to Kala?" I asked. Earth had many religions before the Last War; it was one of the reasons we fought amongst ourselves. The concept of gods was not exactly new to me. I'd never believed in any, though, so the idea of them living and walking among the fae was a little unsettling.

"No one knows for sure. He hasn't been seen since he ripped open the doorway. There's some who think he died with the magic, some of whom think he was sucked into the void, and others who think he disappeared once he realized the mistake he made." Interesting. I'd probably want to lie low if I let these monsters of the void loose on earth. This seemed like information we should know. How had it been kept from us? I'd never so much as heard a rumor about these creatures.

"Why is this kept from the humans? Shouldn't they be told so that they can protect themselves? Your leaders only visit us once a year. They shouldn't be left to fend for themselves against creatures they don't even know exist." I was on my feet then, not even realizing I'd stood. That red haze was making its way across my vision again. God, I hated feeling so volatile. The well of anger inside me just kept fucking growing. I wasn't angry at Bee in particular, more so at the general disregard the fae had for the human community. I couldn't fathom an explanation, especially not in this state. There was so much I didn't know, though, and I knew I should give them a chance to explain.

Now wasn't the time to lose it. None of this was Bee's fault. I thought back to this morning and the way General Brand had had me count my breaths to find my calm again. Practicing it now, I sat back down in the chair. Closing my eyes, I counted to myself and thought about his arms wrapped around me. That was probably a better distraction than counting. I focused on the way his arms had felt wrapped around me, the way his body had caged mine inside his own. I studied his face in my mind, finding calm in the deep pit of his chocolate brown eyes.

I opened my eyes to find Bee smiling at me. "That was so well done. You'll have full control in no time!" She leant forward in her chair and took my hand, placing it in her own. A fierce expression crossed her features, one in stark contrast to the placid fae I'd known so far. "I know that you feel strongly that we don't do enough to help the human community. I know that's how it seems from the outside. There are many of us that feel the same way. I promise, we are doing what we can, and working on doing more."

There was a fire flaring in her eyes. At that moment, I knew I could take her at her word. I wouldn't stop fighting for the human community, but I did have to trust that there were some Fae working on changing the way things were, and that there were reasons for the way things had been done so far.

Suddenly, a strong wind wrapped around my torso and I was yanked from the chair I'd been sitting in, immediately losing grip on Bee's hand. My ponytail fell loose, my hair whipping around me as the wind thrashes around my body, lifting me up, up, up into the air, and dragging me across the room at high speed. A scream tore through my throat, but as quickly as it began, the lashing wind ceased and I was plunging downward, falling directly into a pair of strong, familiar arms waiting to catch me.

Our eyes locked as I looked up at Stefan's handsome face, the silver in his eyes feeling as though it could see right into the depths of my soul. I'm sure he could read every thought I'd ever had just by focusing those eyes on mine. He smiled at me, amusement tugging at the side of his mouth, and for a moment, I was transfixed and completely vulnerable.

My heart was thundering wildly in my chest, not just from the shock of whatever this asshole just did, but from the closeness of him. His smell, rosewood and cinnamon, enveloped me, and I nuzzled into his chest, wanting to be closer to him. As close as I could get. My hands roamed over his chest of their own accord, down his sides, grazing back up his arms, feeling the large biceps underneath them.

Mine.

Stefan chuckled darkly, the sound of it so unexpected, so unfamiliar, that it tore me out of whatever spell I'd just been ensnared in. Stefan was grinning down at me. No sign of the joking, carefree man I've known so far. His smile didn't reach his eyes as shadows clouded over them, taking away the jovial sparkle that usually lit them up. This version of Stefan was all predator and for a moment, it was all I could do not to shriek in fear.

My body tensed as my self-preservation instinct finally kicked in and I pulled my hands away from his biceps, grimacing inwardly, unable to believe I did that.

Not the time, Riley. Get away from the monster, then you can berate yourself all you like.

Even my internal monologue wasn't going to cut me any slack.

Trying to maintain some dignity, I pushed hard against his chest and demanded he put me down. He obliged, placing me swiftly on my feet. Taking a few steps back, I worked to create some distance between myself and whatever this creature was standing before me.

I hardly recognized him. "What are you?" I blurted, unable to hold my tongue as I took another step backwards, closer to Bee. He didn't make any move to follow me. The tightness in my chest eased as I realized he wasn't following me, that he was allowing me to retreat. A move that didn't marry with the terrifying aura rolling off of his body in waves.

The bitter taste of fear burnt my throat as I forced myself to swallow. The man standing before me was somehow more than a man, more than a fae. There was something so otherworldly about him, something that screamed 'run away', but at the same time drew me to him. My thoughts scattered as I became caught in his gaze again. I stopped backing away, instead reaching forward, my fingers stroking the sharp lines of his jaw. He really was beautiful.

"Turn it off, Stefan." Bee warned, her voice closer than I expected. "Before you lose control and hurt her." I dropped my hand from his cheek, clenching it into a fist at my side, and turned to find her right next to me, glaring up at Stefan. Her hands ball into fists at her sides, vines slowly winding up her arms and trailing down to the wooden floorboards.

She looked ready to attack him, her back ramrod straight, feet spread apart in a fighter's stance. This petite little pixie, with sweet bells for a laugh, looked ready to go head-to-head with this monstrous version of Stefan.

What the fuck is happening?

"Now, Stefan." She growled, moving her hands up in front of her face, palms facing towards him, while at the same time moving her body between us.

He blinked. Once. Twice. The darkness clouding his eyes began to recede as his shoulders relaxed and the tension slowly seeped out of his body. Bee relaxed too, lowering her hands, though she didn't move from her protective position in front of me.

No one spoke for a long time. All of us caught in some weird, tension filled standoff. Just as I was about to ask what had just happened, Stefan spun on his heel and, in just a few long strides, left the library without so much as a word.

"Are you okay?" Bee asked as she turned around to face me.

"I don't understand what just happened." And I don't. The Stefan that was just here was not my Stefan. He had been someone else completely. Something else, maybe.

I shook my head, trying to clear my thoughts. I needed to sit down. Making my way back to the chairs Bee and I had been in before that shit show happened, I plopped down, closing my eyes and taking a few deep breaths.

My fingers fiddled with my locket as I tried, and failed, to make sense of all the new information and experiences that had happened over the last few days. I was starting to feel the weight of it, and I really needed some time to relax and process everything properly.

"Let's leave the research for another day. We can grab some subs, borrow a canoe and float on the lake for the afternoon? I think you need time to work through everything that happened before classes start tomorrow." This girl was seriously a mind reader—a saint and a mind reader.

I sighed heavily, wanting more than anything to take her up on her offer. I nodded quickly, deciding that there was no more I could do to find James until I found some kind of lead, and that I was more than deserving of an afternoon off.

My ascension had been anything but easy so far, and if that kept up, this might be my last chance to truly relax.

Self-care was never a bad thing.

⇝⇝⇝ ⇜⇜⇜

True to her word, Bee made sure the afternoon was nothing but relaxing. Lying in the small boat we'd managed to commandeer, the sun on my face, the warm breeze circling around us and the gentle lull of the lake were nothing short of heaven.

I felt at peace for the first time since I'd sprinted from the greenhouse back home. Bee had felt that Stefan should be given a chance to explain his behavior to me. She wasn't entirely comfortable in sharing what she felt was personal information about Stefan's past.

Fair enough, I could understand not wanting to divulge someone else's secrets. As much as I was dying to know what that scene in the library had been all about, I'd made the decision that Stefan could come to me. He didn't just need to explain himself; he had some groveling to do. Who just whips someone out of their seat and into the air like that? Not cool, Stefan.

We'd returned to our room in the early evening after spending some time strolling through the gardens. I'd been able to feel the well of power purring in my chest like a happy kitten, having replenished my reserves from all the exposure to the elements I'd indulged in.

Waiting on my desk when we'd gotten in had been a pile of student resources; notebooks, pens, and most exciting of all–a fae tablet. Bee had helped me set it up. I had no experience with this kind of technology. It was exclusive to the fae of Danann. The tablet itself was a sleek silver rectangular shape with the ability to fold in half to fit easily into your pocket or bag. It seemed straightforward, with some apps for note taking, research and messaging.

Bee had downloaded my timetable and added both her and Stefan's number–as well as General Brand's. She laughed heartily at me when I protested, a knowing look making her green eyes sparkle with glee.

It was Bee's first day of classes tomorrow too, and though she'd always been fae and had learnt some tricks from her father, she was eager to learn and hone her skills. We were in all the same classes, including elemental, as I'd chosen earth as my primary element. I'd always been drawn to the land. I never felt more at peace than in the garden or greenhouses, caring for our plants and crops. It made the most sense to me.

	Mon	Tue	Wed	Thur	Fri
AM	Faerie Races Introduction	Faerie & Earth The Crossing	Weapons Training	Foundational Magic Introduction	Earth Wielding
PM		Physical Combat		Elemental Combat Tutor - Colin Brand	
EVE	Fire Wielding Tutor - Colin Brand		Air Wielding Tutor - Stefan Saxe		Water Wielding Tutor - Lincoln Kai

My timetable had included information about my elemental tutor lessons. General Brand would be tutoring me in fire wielding on Monday. That was on top of the combat lessons he'd be giving me Thursday afternoons. I wondered if the forced proximity would help me crack open his outer shell, see some more of the kind fae inside. I couldn't help myself. The glimpses I'd seen made me want more. I wanted more of him, although I knew I shouldn't.

That night, I dreamt of brown eyes that morphed to silver and back again. Of shadows and darkness and a space filled with nothing. And of faceless monsters who doubled in size when they smelt my fear.

CHAPTER TWELVE

Stefan

The heavy double doors slammed shut behind me as I fled from the library, from her, from the accusation in those gorgeous hazel eyes. It took every ounce of restraint I had to control my pace and stop myself from bolting down the academy halls.

A few fae glanced my way as I plowed through the dining hall, the storm in my silver eyes enough to stop any from approaching me, and to send some slinking away into the shadows. They all knew not to come near me when I was in this state. She didn't know, couldn't have known. But they did. So, they all kept their distance. Not that I'd given her a choice anyway, ripping her through the air that way. Gods.

I was out the doors and striding quickly through the gardens before I'd even decided where I was going. It was almost instinct now. I'd find Colin, and he'd spar with me, helping me reduce the blinding fiery rage spreading through my veins until I could regain control.

But fuck. He was surely still at Headquarters and there wasn't a chance in hell I was going back there today. Not after the meeting I'd just come from. I had no desire to step foot through the barrack doors again today.

The debate had been endless. The elders wanted nothing to do with Riley. They didn't want her here and had come to Headquarters to protest her presence. She was an unknown, a threat, and in their eyes, she shouldn't have been allowed entry to Danann.

I don't know what they expected to achieve. The King had approved her entry to Danann and attendance at the academy. She was already here. There was no turning her out now. Especially not now it seemed like the Resistance wanted something from her.

Their protests had been the match that ignited the bonfire of emotion swirling in my gut. It had been a while since I'd lost control like this. I was always so careful to stay happy, light, and keep my feelings in check. They'd come after her though, and that had tugged on some deep instinct within me that screamed for me to protect her.

The first moment I'd seen her, I'd felt it. Not just her power signature, though that was intoxicating in its own right. No, I hadn't just felt her raw power, I'd also felt a pull, a connection to her. A golden thread that came from deep within my soul and tied me to her. I'd immediately wanted to know her, to protect her, to lose myself in her. I'd vomited out some lame line about being the best of friends and friend zoned myself by accident. I hadn't wanted to scare her with the intensity of the feelings she'd stirred inside of me.

That's exactly what I ended up doing, though. I'd attacked her, whipping her into the air and into my arms like she was some kind of puppet, and I was her master. Fuck. Why had I done that?

The desire to have her close had overwhelmed me. After the Elders had demanded she be thrown out, I'd needed to make sure she was alright. That no one had hurt her in the time I'd spent away from her. Sheesh, I'd only just seen her this morning. I was a lovesick fool at this point.

I hadn't been thinking straight. The feral part of me, the part I don't understand and that seems to exist almost separately from the main part of me, had taken over. I didn't understand what it was, why I had this... thing inside me I had to fight for control. No one else dealt with this. No one knew why I had to.

I'd scared her. I'd seen it in her eyes. She feared me at that moment. And I couldn't blame her. I feared myself sometimes. It was as though most of me was locked away, trapped in an inescapable cell, when the monster took hold. There were so many times I'd been trapped, clinging to the bars of my cell, shaking, and rattling them with all my strength, trying to get free and regain control.

My tablet dinged, pulling me from my dark thoughts, and I
pulled it out of my pocket to find a message from Bee waiting
for me.

Bee

> Lincoln will meet you at the training
> fields. Riley and I are having a girls after-
> noon. You'll need to explain yourself to
> her... and apologize. Take tonight, find
> your center, let her have some space. I
> hope your okay.

Guilt settled heavily in my stomach as I read her message.
Bee cared so much about those closest to her. It looked like
Riley had made that list. I was grateful she'd have someone else
looking out for her; I clearly couldn't be counted on to protect
her all the time.

Bee was telling me to stay away for the rest of today. Riley had
been through a lot in the short time since she'd left Sommers,
and I hated that I had added to some of the turmoil she was
experiencing.

Sighing heavily, I made my way through the academy grounds
to meet Lincoln. He was already waiting for me at the training
fields when I arrived. He must have responded to Bee's SOS
instantly.

The training fields were exactly what they sounded like. A
large grassy field we used for physical combat training. Metal fencing surrounded it, with some wooden benches lined
around it for viewing. Lincoln was waiting for me in the far
corner. I lengthened my stride, reaching him quickly.

"You attacked the girl, brother? Keep this up and the elders will assign you leader of their cause," He chuckled darkly. "Father would have your head."

"At least I'd be on his radar." I quipped, half heartedly. Prince Lincoln was the son of King Ronan, the fae Water King who had been given the responsibility of ruling the fae on Earth. I was his ward, and had been for as long as I remembered. Not that he acknowledged my existence most of the time, only deigning to when it was convenient to him.

The King and Queen of the water elementals had taken me in during their election to the throne. It had been a strategic move, a way to stand up against the other candidates vying for his position, gaining him votes from those more prone to humanitarianism. Once the election was complete, he forgot about me. I was raised alongside Lincoln by his governess.

Lincoln didn't have it much better. If his father lacked paternal affection, it was nothing compared to his mother. The queen was a vapid creature who enjoyed the benefits of her position to the fullest. The only attention he received from either of them was to ensure he was living up to the expectations placed upon him as the Water Heir.

"I'm not sure that's a good thing." He replied, cocking his head to the side, his feet planted in a wide stance. He was ready, waiting for me to make the first move, letting me attack first.

I rolled my shoulders, straightening my spine and cracking my neck. "Are you sure you're up for this today, Linc? I wouldn't want to make a mess of your pretty face right before school starts."

"Oh good, there's the Stefan I was hoping to find, the cocky, arrogant ass who thinks he's top shit and he'll always..." I lunged for him before he could finish his thought, kicking my leg out in a half circle and knocking his feet out from under him.

He hit the ground hard. Grinning wolfishly, he jumped back up instantaneously, raising his fists in front of his face in an offensive stance.

"You might have gotten in the first hit, but I won't be taking it easy on you."

"I wouldn't want you to. Give me your best, brother."

We began then, no more words passing between us as he helped me banish my personal demon, pushing it back into the cage it was breaking free of. We sparred until our lungs were burning for air, sweat pouring down our backs from the exhaustion. Lincoln took strike after strike, giving it back to me as good as he got, until the fire in my stomach dies out and the rage dissipated from my limbs.

We collapsed, laying side by side in the grass, watching as the sun sank behind the clouds, casting hues of orange, pink and purple through the darkening sky.

The salty smell of the ocean carried through the field on the breeze, and I breathed deeply, letting it soothe me and relax the tension from my mind.

The monster inside me had quietened and was again lying dormant, waiting for the next time my emotions got the better of me, when he could seize the opportunity to take control again.

The only thing I felt then was regret. I might have pushed Riley away and ruined any chance with her before I even told her what she was doing to me and how I felt about her.

CHAPTER THIRTEEN

Riley

"Good morning, Sunshine" Bee called as she threw open the curtains, letting the warm spring sun blind me as it fell across my pillow.

"Ugh, no. Less of the pep before coffee." I groaned, rolling and pulling the covers over my head. My eyes were gritty, my body exhausted from the lack of restful sleep. I'd been plagued by nightmare after nightmare last night, the worst of which was Stefan's handsome face morphing into some kind of monster with a jaw that widened beyond imagination, its mouth filled with row upon row of sharp jagged teeth.

A shudder rolled through me at the thought. I really hoped no creature like that existed. My hope was likely misplaced. The creatures from the void that Bee had spoken of were surely worse than any image I could conjure.

"We'll get coffee," she chuckled in reply. "You have to get up first, though." She yanked the cover back, and pulled me up from the bed, with a strength so surprising I was in too much shock to resist. Once I was steady on my feet, she let go and pushed me toward the bathroom. "Get dressed and we'll go get you some pep."

"I'm not sure I like you in the mornings," I grumbled as I entered the bathroom. "You're super bossy." Closing the door to the sound of her laughing, a small smile crept across my face. Oh shit, she was going to turn me into a morning person.

I showered quickly, dressing in the uniform provided for me. The navy and ruby tartan skirt fell a few inches above my knees, and paired with a crisp white shirt and ruby blazer, I felt fresh and well presented. Ready for my first day at Danann Academy.

I wasn't the only new student today. Bee had told me that Ascension had occurred just before the start of a new year, meaning all the fae in my class were new to the Academy, starting their version of what humans in the past had called college. Another luxury the fae had. We were too focused on survival to bother with more than basic education. Lining my eyes with liner, I went a little darker than normal, trying to hide the anxiety I was feeling about today—and hide the bags under my eyes.

When I was as put together as I was going to get, I joined Bee back in the bedroom. She nodded her approval and handed me my bag. It was a simple over the shoulder black bag, just big enough to hold my tablet and notebooks.

"Thank you," I said. "Let's go get that coffee before our morning class." I led the way out of our dorm and down to the dining hall. My stomach fluttered with nerves as we approached. I hadn't seen Stefan since the incident in the library yesterday, and I wasn't sure how to react when I did. I was both angry at him and longing for his company again.

Three days. That was all it had taken for me to fall for a guy I barely even knew. Three days.

I didn't need to know him. My heart already did.

How much could I really trust my heart, though? She seemed to want to claim the grumpy General Brand, too.

Little hussy.

Pushing those thoughts aside and filing them in a black box in my mind titled 'sexy fae men for consideration', I entered the dining hall with Bee and made a beeline for the coffee. I took a sip and moaned as the smooth creamy taste lingered on my taste buds, waking me up. The fae did coffee so much better than humans.

Grabbing some fruit and toast, I sat down with Bee and pulled out my timetable to look over my schedule for the day.

"I have Faerie Races this morning, nothing this afternoon, and fire tutoring with General Brand this evening." I said, examining the paper. "In fact, most of my afternoons are free. Why is that?"

"Most of us are assigned a part-time job somewhere in Danann, to contribute to the community and keep things running smoothly." She replied, shrugging as if it were no big deal.

"Your load is a little heavier than ours, with all your extra tutoring, so I guess you haven't been assigned one."

"Oh," I wasn't sure how I felt about that. On the one hand, not having any responsibility other than my studies left me more time to find clues that might lead me to James, but on the other hand, I would have liked to learn more about the fae community. I needed to find my place eventually. Future Riley problem.

We made our way to Faerie Races, taking a couple of seats towards the front of the room. Bee had been waiting her whole life to study here, and I was more than curious about the different Fae races. I hoped learning about them may give me some clue where I belonged; some idea of where I came from. We would not risk missing anything by sitting in the back.

The classroom itself was small, with only enough room for about a dozen students. The whole academy was smaller than I'd imagined, and I guessed that was because of the inability for more fae to cross from Faerie. I wondered briefly whether the fae in Danann were actively repopulating and whether the academy would eventually become irrelevant.

Right on time and interrupting that morbid thought, our professor entered the room. He was short and plump, his large round glasses sliding halfway down his long pointy nose. With his sweater vest, pressed slacks, and salt and pepper hair, he looked every bit the uptight scholar.

"I am Professor Ivan Burns," He began, pushing his glasses back up his nose with one long finger. "No, I am not a fire elemental; I possess the element of water. Yes, I know my name is ironic." A couple of fae behind us snickered, and I couldn't quite suppress the grin that caused the corners of my mouth to twitch upwards. Tucking my chin, I hid my face behind my hands—offending Professor Burns would do me no good, especially not on my first day in class.

Clearing his throat, Professor Burns made his way to the chalkboard at the front of the classroom, beginning his lesson. "There are four main types of fae. Four key groups that—more often than not—live separate from one another. Many of you have been on Earth for as long as you can remember and I do not expect you to have memories of these factions. However, I expect your families will have spoken about them." Curiosity got the better of me and I leant forward in my seat. Were the fae here not the only type that existed?

"Can anyone tell me about the ruling faction? Those of the highest power?" he asked, his eyes scanning the room. Bee's hand went straight in the air. That didn't surprise me one bit. She was self-aware, incredibly intelligent, and had an eagerness to learn that inspired me.

To my surprise, Professor Burns skipped over Bee, choosing instead a student seated at the back of the class.

"Ahh, Prince Lincoln. Could you tell me please, the ruling species of Faerie?"

Prince? I hadn't realized the King and Queen had a son. To be fair, I knew nothing about the King and Queen, beyond what General Brand had told me about them ruling the fae that had made the journey to Earth. I was eager to learn more about the hierarchy of Faerie, and the hierarchy they held here on Earth. This seemed like just the class to do it. Bee could fill in the gaps—if they weren't covered in class today.

I turned in my seat, wanting to see this Prince with my own eyes.

My breath caught in my throat as I took in the beautiful creature seated before me. His honey blonde hair was longer than any other male fae I'd seen, falling just past his shoulders in loose waves. A braid ran across the front of his head, almost like a crown. The lightness of his hair contrasted with his dark almond skin, making it seem even brighter in the rays of sun falling through the window and across his table.

He was tall and lean, possessing the body of an athlete. His full lips were set in a small smile, the shadow of a beard framing his angular jaw. There was a confidence about him, a powerful aura that captured me, drawing me in. I couldn't tear my eyes away from him.

His eyes flickered to mine, and I was stunned by the deep navy color of them, so dark it was like they held the secrets of the night sky and could see into the very depths of me. My heart beat a furious pace in my chest as he cocked his head to the side, looking me up and down, drinking me in, curiosity sparking in those gorgeous eyes and causing his brow to furrow. It was a marvel the entire class couldn't hear it.

"Ahem," Professor Burns cleared his throat abruptly, and I startled, tearing my eyes away from Prince Lincoln and staring down at my notebook instead. "An answer today would be most appreciated if you're done with whatever this is." He said, his tone full of disapproval as he waved a hand between myself and Lincoln.

There were snickers from throughout the room as I sank into my seat. My cheeks flamed with embarrassment. Our little moment had definitely not gone unnoticed. If there was ever a time for the floor to swallow someone whole, it would be right now. Please. I needed something to save me from this mortifying experience.

"The ruling faction of Faerie are the Gods and Goddesses, sir. They rule because they possess immortality, and because they are more powerful than you or I can ever hope to be," Lincoln said cooly, seemingly unfazed by our moment, or by Professor's Burns' clear contempt.

"Correct. Can anyone tell me anything about our Gods and Goddesses?" He pointed to Bee, who had raised her hand again.

"They each hold power over a fundamental component of our lands, elements, and worlds. For example, Goddess Faye controls the flame, and is also known as the dragon keeper. She maintains the fire lands, controls the dragons, and blesses the fire elementals."

"Correct, Miss Pollard." He turned then, making his way toward the board at the front of the class and writing the words: Faye - Goddess of the Flame and Keeper of the Dragon.

He continued around the classroom, choosing students at random until we had listed all the Gods and Goddesses of Faerie.

I took notes eagerly. There was so much I needed to work out, so many potential clues to uncover, that nothing was irrelevant in the grand scheme of things.

By the end of class, the board read the following, and my notes were much the same:

Faye—Goddess of the Flame and Keeper of Dragons

Kala—God of Darkness and Keeper of Lost Souls

Maya—Goddess of the Air and Keeper of the Wind

Avani—Goddess of Growth and Mother to All

Beyonte—God of Light and Keeper of the Sun

Jona—God of the Seas and Keeper of the Stars

Armani—Goddess of Heart and Love

"I expect a full report on a God or Goddess of your choice by the start of class next week. We will continue discussing the remaining factions of Faerie then." He moved around behind his desk, turning to face us once more. "A reminder that you are all to report to your assigned community jobs immediately after lunch. Class dismissed."

I stood along with the rest of the class, quickly packing away my things, ready to follow Bee out of the room. We'd barely made it into the hallway when a hand grasped my wrist from behind, stopping me in my tracks and spinning me around to face them.

He spoke before I could even react, his voice deep and soothing. "Can I have a word?" I looked up to find myself staring at Prince Lincoln. It took everything I had not to fall endlessly into his depthless navy eyes. I only just kept my feet planted firmly on the floor. "It's Riley, isn't it?"

"Hey Lincoln," Bee said cheerily, having stopped when I did. I turned to face her, contorting my face into a plea for her to rescue me from yet another tempting man, but she simply said, "I'll meet you in the dining hall, Riley." Winking at me as she hurried off, she gave me no chance to object to being left alone with Prince Lincoln.

"Stefan has told me a lot about you." Lincoln said, dropping my wrist as I turned back to face him, plastering a smile on my face that I hoped was kind and welcoming and did not resemble the internal hurricane of emotion I was feeling. Bee and I would be having words about when NOT to ditch our friends.

"Oh? All good things, I hope." My voice was stronger and clearer than I'd expected, with the way butterflies swarmed in my stomach.

"Well... mostly good things." He winked at me, my heart skipping a beat at his easy banter. "He said that on your very first night in Danann, you attempted to burn him alive."

I groaned, remembering how close Stefan was when my power awoke. "I didn't..."

He cut me off with a laugh that I felt all the way down to my core. "I'm teasing. I know you did no such thing."

"I could have hurt him, and others. I'm surprised those close to me all escaped unscathed." I admitted. I'd felt guilty since it had happened, despite everyone telling me it wasn't something

I could have prevented, even if I'd known what was about to happen to me.

"You didn't, though. You'll find us fae are resilient and able to protect themselves in various ways. They all likely blasted shields of various elements the moment they felt your power stir." He smiled at me reassuringly, the beauty and kindness in that smile causing my chest to tighten. What was happening here? These feelings were like what I felt with Stefan. "I'm sure you'll learn control soon enough, particularly with General Brand giving you private lessons. Walk with me," He said, gesturing down the hallway. We fell into step beside one another as we made our way to the dining hall.

"I'm sure his tutoring will be fantastic. I'll make leaps and bounds just so long as I learn quickly how to translate his grunting and growling into actual instructions." I muttered quietly, sarcasm coating my words and somehow easing the remaining threads of tension between us.

He roared a laugh as we walked down the empty corridor, void of any other students now, most of them having already made their way to lunch or their job placements.

"You've certainly got his number. I promise he's not as bad as he seems. He has a lot of... baggage. He takes time to warm up to newcomers."

Silence fell between us as I considered it. I had seen glimpses of a softer side of General Brand, one that wasn't as stone cold as he often tried to portray. Maybe Lincoln was right, maybe he'd warm to me. That thought alone made me happier than it should have. I settled into Lincoln's company, not as uneasy as I had been to start with.

"What did you want a word about?" I asked, remembering his words, curiosity suddenly burning through me.

"There's a start of term dance Sunday night," he said, stopping in front of the dining hall and turning to face me again. Taking both my hands in his, he took a steadying breath. "Would you come with me?"

I couldn't speak for a moment. Scratch that, I couldn't even breathe. Of all the things—that was the last thing I expected him to ask me.

"There's something here, Riley. I felt it the moment our eyes locked together. By the Goddess Armani, I'd like to explore it." His eyes were pleading with mine, tingles spreading up my arms from where our hands were intertwined. He had felt it, too. I hadn't imagined the pull I felt to him. Only it wasn't just him, was it?

"Yes, I'll go with you." I heard myself saying.

"Fantastic." His navy eyes sparkled, as though all the stars in the galaxy just brightened at my words. "I look forward to it. Pick you up at 8." He leant down, quickly pressing a soft kiss to my cheek before hurrying away with a wave, leaving me standing there stunned.

What. Just. Happened.

I entered the dining hall in a daze and found Bee at our usual table. She had grabbed us both bowls of pasta and a huge garden salad to share. The rich smell of bolognese hit me, and my stomach growled loudly as I flopped into the chair next to her.

"Is there a dance Sunday that you just so happened to forget to tell me about?" I asked accusingly, as I shoveled pasta into my mouth. I moaned at the freshness of the tomato and herbs, any anger I held dissipating as I savored the flavor.

Bee laughed, the musical sound calming me even more. How did she do that?

"Who are you going with?" she asked, taking her own bite of pasta.

"What do you mean, who? Lincoln just asked me. Remember, you just threw me to the wolves and left me for dead!" I wasn't angry with her, not really. Somehow, I knew she'd never leave me if I were truly in danger.

She shrugged, a playful smile dancing on her lips. "You have plenty of suitors. I was curious to see who would approach you first. My money was actually on Stefan." Her tone was matter of fact, as if she'd been totally convinced.

"Stefan and I are just friends. Maybe not even friends. He hasn't spoken to me since the library incident." I pouted, my bottom lip jutting out, and even I was surprised at how sad I sounded—how sad that thought made me feel. I was angry at Stefan, but I still wanted him around. Wanted to feel him near.

"He will. He just needs time. He'll explain himself soon. And if he doesn't, I'll give him a kick up the ass." She giggled as she spoke the word 'ass', which made me laugh too. We spent the rest of lunch in high spirits talking about the dance until Bee had to leave and make her way to job placement. She had been tasked with helping maintain various gardens around Danann. It seemed to be a mammoth task and once that was vital to maintaining the power reserves of the Earth elementals. Without them, Danann would be as barren as the rest of the earth.

Deciding to start on our assignment before I met with General Brand this evening for fire tutoring, I headed toward the library.

Butterflies start up again in my stomach at the thought of General Brand.

Damn, these men have really done a number on me.

CHAPTER FOURTEEN

Riley

A ding sounded from my tablet, drawing my attention away from the heavy leather-bound book I'd been perusing. After Bee left for her work placement, I'd made my way to the library to start research for the assignment Professor Burns had set.

I'd chosen to focus on Goddess Avani. I was intrigued by her title *'Goddess of Growth and Mother of All.'* What kind of connection might she have to Earth and its current state of decay?

I pulled my tablet out of my bag to check my notifications. To my surprise, the message that had come through was from 'Colin Brand'. Not once had I referred to the General as Colin. It was strange to think of him that way. I didn't hate it, it was just... different.

Colin

I'm free now if you want to start early.

Our tutoring session was scheduled for this evening at 7pm. It was only half-past three in the afternoon. If we met now, I might catch Bee for dinner and study with her later.

Riley

Sure. Still meeting at HQ?

Colin

Meet me at the stables in 10 minutes.

10 minutes! Shit! I wasn't sure if I could even make it across the academy grounds in that amount of time! Quickly throwing my things back in my bookbag, I slung it over my shoulder, grabbing the heavy tome I'd been reading and carting it to the librarian's desk. It was an effort to wait patiently as she checked it out for me.

When she was done, I stuffed the book into my bag and rushed out of the heavy double doors, through the dining hall, and out into the entryway. Pulling my tablet out again, I quickly shot off a message to let General Brand know I was on my way.

Making my way across the grounds and past the lake, I noticed there were surprisingly few students around this afternoon, just a couple of both water and earth elementals lingering in the gardens, using their magic to encourage the plants and wildflowers planted there to bloom and thrive, despite the lack of nurturing the land itself provided.

When I reached the path leading into the Academy's mini forest, I stopped short. Right where my powers were awakened. It was the first time I'd been here since, and the blackened scorch marks spreading out from the path shocked me. The fissures leading out from the center where I had collapsed were deep and erratic, shaped like lightning bolts as they extended into the trees. A few of the trees had blackened trunks and bare branches, the leaves either having been burned away by my fire or blown away on my wind.

I'd assumed that other fae would have repaired the damage I'd left behind. A wave of guilt washed over me, settling in the pit of my stomach. This wasn't anyone else's responsibility, it was mine. I caused this damage; I was responsible for fixing it.

My elemental powers were new to me. I hadn't tried to work with Earth yet. Where was I supposed to start? I pulled my bag over my shoulder and placed it on the ground, off to the side of the path.

Stepping over the fissures and blackened path, I knelt in the untouched center of damage, placing both hands to the earth and willing my magic to my palms, not sure if that was how it was supposed to work. The only magic I'd used so far had been accidental, provoked by either fear or rage.

A slight tingle started in my fingers, but it slipped away before I could harness it. I closed my eyes, focusing on pulling my earth element out from my core, from the well in my chest to my hands pressed firmly against the forest floor.

Nothing happened.

My stubbornness took root, and I kept trying, straining to pull it from myself. I had to fix this. I couldn't leave the land this way. She suffered so much already.

Still, nothing happened. Even the tingle in my fingers faded away. Tears welled in my eyes as I opened them and stared at my hands in frustration. *Why can't I make this work?*

My tablet dinged again, and I assumed it was General Brand, calling me out for being late. I pushed myself to my feet, dusting my hands off on my skirt as I stared at the ground for a long moment, silently promising to come back and fix the damage I had caused once I figured out how.

Grabbing my bag, I slung it back over my shoulder and started a slow jog through the small forest, out the gates and across to the stables.

General Brand was waiting for me outside, two horses saddled and ready behind him, their reins tied to the fence. As I drew closer, I realized one of them was Annie. I couldn't help the elated grin as it spread across my face at the sight of her. She'd been on my mind, some invisible thread between us making me want to know she was fine. Bypassing General Brand, I made a beeline for her, scratching her behind the ear and stroking my hand down her nose.

General Brand made his way over to us, the smile on his face disarming, causing my breath to catch in my throat. The effect made him look younger, lighter than he had before.

"I thought you might like to see her again. You seemed quite taken with her on the journey here." He was wearing a white button-down shirt and dark navy jeans today. He looked even better in this than in his Army uniform—not that I'd ever complain about his uniform. He looked hot in that too. There really was something about a man in uniform that did things to a girl.

"Thank you. I've been meaning to come see her. I just haven't made it outside the gates of the Academy until now." I said, looking up at him, my gaze catching on his full lips and the shadow along his jaw. Noticing him watching me, I averted my gaze quickly, looking back to the mare in front of me. "Why did you want to meet here, General? Aren't you supposed to be teaching me how to wield fire?"

He didn't answer me right away, and I glanced back up at him to find he was still grinning at me. It was a little unnerving, such a far cry from his usual serious, stoic demeanor.

"Please, call me Colin. I'm not here in a professional capacity, more as a favor to a friend." My brow rose in question. "Professor Darmon. He's.... done a lot for my sister and I." That made sense, I thought, nodding my agreement. It was Professor Darmon who had determined I required extra tutoring.

"I have some patrols to complete outside of Danann, along the edge of the dead forest, and I need to check in with our B station. I thought you could accompany me and, on the way back, we could use the fields outside Danann to unleash your fire element at full capacity without risk of damage. Really see what we're working with."

I looked at Annie, and the other horse, all saddled up, and gulped as the realization hit me. He expected me to *ride* her! I'd never ridden a horse, never even met one before I ascended. My heart started to beat wildly in my chest. How did you even climb into a saddle, for goodness's sake?

I continued to stare at him, completely dumbfounded that he just assumed I could ride. Anger bubbled in my stomach, his assumption a sharp reminder of the inequality between the way the fae and humans lived.

"Your entitlement is showing, *Colin*." I said, emphasizing the use of his name.

He raised an eyebrow at my snarky tone. Ignoring him, I continued, letting my frustration boil as I gave him a piece of my mind.

"Why would you assume I can accompany you? What gave you the impression that I know how to *ride a freaking horse*?" My voice rose, shaking as my temper rose, injustice fueling the anger coursing through my veins. Heat flooded my palms, and I stilled.

I was never this volatile back home. I don't think I'd ever had an angry outburst, or spoken to anyone rudely, or lost control of myself. Everyone kept telling me it was normal to lose control of my elements when I was feeling emotional. But my temperament seemed to be changing too. I was never an overly emotional person until I stepped foot inside Danann. Now every little thing got a rise out of me.

Deep breaths, Riley.

Colin chuckled as I actively focused on my breathing, feeling the heat slowly recede from my hands. His eyes twinkled with amusement as he reached past me, untying Annie's reins and leading her away from the fence. He clipped a long rope to her halter as he walked, turning and facing me again.

"Lead rope," He said, gesturing to Annie. "Come here, I'll help you up. All you have to do is sit; Annie will do the rest. Trust her." Funnily enough, I did trust her. Danann was new to me, Annie was new to me, these men were all new to me. But somehow I was tied to all of them. There were invisible threads connecting me to them, and I didn't know what that meant for me, for my future. It was unsettling, but not something I'd be able to figure out right away. This journey would take me where it would. For now, I'd have to hold on for the ride.

Colin was still smiling at me, and despite myself, I was entranced. I walked toward him, without having consciously decided I was going to do this. He moved aside, untying her reins and allowing me room to move right up to Annie. From the wall, he grabbed a mounting block, sliding it in front of me.

"Here," he said, handing me a helmet. "Put that on, then reach for the horn. Yes, there at the front of the saddle." He moved behind me, placing a hand on the small of my back, his fingers skimming the waistband of my skirt as he lifted me, his touch burning where it traced along my bare skin, waves of heat radiating through my body at the contact.

"Put your left foot in the stirrup, palm on the seat and push yourself up, swinging your leg over." I did as he said, the movement feeling more natural than I had expected. "That's it. Well done." Gods, if he kept smiling at me like that, I might just spontaneously combust.

I straightened my skirt, trying to cover some of my bare thighs as he turned and strode toward his own horse. If I'd had any inclination this is what we'd be doing, I would have changed. Before I knew it, he was mounted and had clipped Annie's lead to his saddle. With a click of his tongue, Annie lurched forward, and I tightened my hold on the horn, grappling for her reigns too as we moved toward the intimidating gates of Danann.

Colin waved at the guards as we approached. They recognized him instantly, and the gates opened, allowing us to leave. Annie moved up, trotting next to Colin and his mare of her own accord, her lead rope slack.

It dawned on me as the gates opened and Colin led us through them that I was willingly leaving the safety of the walls surrounding Danann. I hadn't even questioned it. This man, the General of the fae, Mr Hot and Cold, made me feel so safe that I'd jumped on a horse for the first time and let him lead me outside the gates of Danann, despite the fact that we were attacked last time we were outside.

"Is it safe to be out here? Will The Resistance attack again?" I asked Colin, as we crossed the barren fields toward the tree line. Could you call it a tree line if it was just a bunch of dead trunks and stumps?

He was quiet for a minute. A contemplative silence where I could almost see his thoughts as he considered my question. A gentle breeze rolled over us, masking the silence and leaving a slight briny tang to the air. I inhaled deeply, a fleeting sense of peace falling over me.

"I wouldn't knowingly put you in danger, Riley. You are too important. I know that you might not believe it, but you belong here, with us. I hope you will accept that in time." He answered softly, his low tone reassuring in a way that sent shivers down my spine. His words caused my heart to leap in my chest so violently it could almost have broken free entirely.

"I'm important? In what way?" I asked. To him? Or to the fae?

"Your power is immense. I think you might be what we've been missing. That you might hold the key to help us return home, to our own lands, to Faerie."

My stomach clenched, and I winced, disappointment spiking through me. So, not important to him. Why did that bother me so much? I squared my shoulders and straightened my spine. It didn't matter. I didn't need to be important to him. My worth was not defined by any man. *So why do I feel so disappointed?*

"What about Earth? Are you abandoning it? Leaving the humans here to fend for themselves?"

He pulled to a stop, staring at me hard, his mouth set in a hard line.

"Of course not," He said furiously. "We need more help, Riley. We need our reinforcements, our seers. We've been floundering blindly for fifteen years without them. It wasn't supposed to be this way."

I fell silent at his admission. This is the most anyone has ever said to me about the way the fae handled the state of the Earth, and I don't think he even realized it. Despite some snarkiness, no one had offered me much of an explanation for their failings before now. They had promised to heal our lands, but nothing had been done.

It's not a lot of information; it doesn't explain much. But it's enough to imply that they came here with a plan; some idea of how they might be able to help. Then they unfortunately found themselves without the resources they expected to have. Knowing this would ease so much of the tension back home in Sommers.

Some of the resentment I held towards the fae melted from inside me. I'd held these ideas and notions about them for so gods damned long. Some of those beliefs were wrong.

That thought sparked hope in my chest, in the hole left by the resentment I was learning to let go of. Just a small flicker, but it was something. Maybe things wouldn't be this way forever. Maybe there was some version of a future where the Earth healed and humans could take back their lands, or at the very least live among the fae, instead of beneath them, in what I was coming to realize has been a holding pattern.

"What was the plan, then? From a human point of view, it feels like the fae arrived on Earth with grand plans to save us all, took control and have done nothing since." I snuck a sideways glance at him, hoping to gauge his reaction to my questions. His expression remained stoic, though I thought I could detect a slight frown cross his forehead. It's gone before I could take a second look and he let out a long, heavy sigh.

"I guess it would seem that way to you." His voice was low again, quiet, the smile he'd greeted me with at the stables gone. I looked away, biting my lip as guilt washed over me. My questioning had taken away his smiling, carefree mood. I needed to know, though.

"Our first step was to take control. We felt that the more control and access to the lands we had, the easier it might be to discover the underlying issue, the cause behind the earth's deterioration. If the humans stopped attacking each other, if we prevented further damage, maybe the earth would have a chance to begin healing itself."

"To heal naturally, without interference?" I asked, my voice rising in surprise. "You were going to give it that chance?"

"Of course, that was the ideal solution. We came here not knowing how your world would be affected by our magic. We knew it didn't exist here, that humans had no control over the elements like we do, that different creatures existed here than at home." He looked over at me, his eyes holding mine. "We aren't the bad guys; we didn't come here with ill intent. We wanted to save your world, in order to save our own."

His voice was quiet, firm, and sincere. I sucked in a breath and tore my eyes away from his penetrating stare, looking ahead as I let his words sink in. Silence fell between us for a few minutes as we continued along and I considered all that I'd learnt.

I was quickly distracted from my thoughts at the sight of what appeared to be a small outpost ahead. A chain fence circled a small encampment. A tall stone tower sat at the back of the camp, a guard visible at the top. Behind the fence there were a couple of tents like those used at the ascension ceremony, a small fire flickering at the center of them, a couple of logs circling it, with men seated upon them.

This wasn't a long-term set-up, more of a temporary base. This must be the B station.

Glancing back, I realized we'd traveled quite far. Danann wasn't even visible anymore.

"This outpost sits between Danann and the location of the tear from the void. Have you learnt anything about the void, and the tear yet?" He asked as we approached the gate. The guard on duty recognized Colin immediately, opening the gate and nodding to him as we moved inside.

"Nothing in class. Bee told me a little about the crossing through the void and the tear. That it's a one-way door from the void to here, allowing some creatures through?"

"That's right. This base allows us to have soldiers nearer to the tear, to deal with anything that makes its way through to Earth, before it can become a threat to Danann, or Sommers." He led us toward one of the larger tents, stopping the horses. I watched closely as he dismounted, the muscles in his forearms tensing, sending a flush of warmth through me as he swung his leg over and lowered himself to the ground.

"Here, let me help you down."

He was by my side in an instant, his hands on me again as he helped me climb off of Annie. He placed me on my feet and I grabbed his arms to steady myself. He paused, his thumbs brushing against my bare skin, where my shirt had come untucked from my skirt. The scent of pine and whiskey fell over me, his scent, and I looked up from under my lashes, my gaze falling to his mouth. Licking my lips, I imagined what it might be like to taste him, to kiss him, to press my mouth against his. Would he taste as good as he smelt?

There was an almost palpable connection between us, and for a moment it was as though we were frozen in place, neither of us wanting to pull away, both of us hesitant to take that next step and cross the line between us. He was the fae general, my tutor. Was it wrong to feel this way about him?

"Ah, General, I heard you'd arrived!" A man's voice jerked us from each other, my hands dropping from his arms at the same time he dropped his from my hips. I smoothed my hands down my front, tucking my shirt back in. When I looked up, I saw an older gentleman shaking Colin's hand in greeting.

Tall, with fair hair and a friendly, familiar looking face, his eyes were kind as they swung between the two of us. He had a stack of books tucked under his arm, a bag overflowing with more books and random papers slung over the opposite shoulder.

"Reardon, how are you? I didn't know you were out here today." Colin said, shaking the man's hand and clapping him on the shoulder. "This is Riley, our newest ascendant."

His eyes lock on mine, a warm smile spreading across his freckled face.

"Ah, Riley, I've heard so much about you." I reached out my hand to shake his, but was surprised when he tugged me in for a hug. "I hope you're settling in well."

He pulled away, looking back at Colin.

"I was just here checking on Patch Two; it's not going as well as I had hoped." He frowned a little, then continued. "I'm heading back to Danann for the evening. Best be on my way. I don't want to be late for dinner with my daughter." He saluted, then spun on his heel, waving goodbye.

Bewildered, I turned to Colin.

"Who was that?" I asked, a little baffled by his easy familiarity with me.

Colin laughed, walking the horses into the large tent. It was set up as a makeshift stable of sorts. He led them to an empty stall towards the back. "That was Bee's father, Reardon. He's a bit of a character, but he has a kind heart."

"I'd be surprised if he didn't. Bee has the kindest heart of anyone I've ever met." I said, stroking Annie's nose as Colin removed her lead and harness.

He nodded in agreement. "She's always been available for Callie and I. She'd do anything for those close to her." We exited the stall, closing a small gate behind us. Annie whinnied softly as we turned to walk away and I smiled as a stable hand made their way over to her.

"Callie?" I asked. I don't think I've met her or heard anyone mention her name before. Oh fuck. Does Colin have a girl-friend? Am I fawning over a taken man? I subtly tried to put a little more distance between us as we made our way out of the tent.

"Callie is my little sister." I let out an audible sigh of relief, and he glanced at me, raising a brow. The smile was back on his face. And fuck me, but I melted a little. He'd always looked young, too young for his role as an Army General. But the way he was smiling at me made him look even younger, lighter, more carefree.

"She's just turned sixteen. Bee is two years older, your age, but she's always been a friend to Callie, and as they've grown, she's become a role model for her too," He stepped closer to me, closing the gap between us I placed there only moments ago, and taking my hand in his. I didn't want him to lose his smile again, so I didn't protest as he led me toward the tower. Plus, it felt kind of nice. "I've got to check in with Colonel Stubbe, then we can head back to the fields outside Danann and see if your power is all it's cracked up to be." He winked at me then causing my breath to catch in my throat. Still holding my hand, he led me inside the guard tower.

I hadn't been with the fae long. Had found no clues to lead me to my brother, and was no closer to finding out the truth about myself. But yet... I'd somehow gotten off track, feeling attraction towards three different men, for different reasons. I had the feeling that if I wasn't careful, I might just lose my heart to them.

CHAPTER FIFTEEN

Riley

Colin led me to the top of the guard tower, his hand holding mine as we climbed the stairs. The ascent was shorter than I expected, and it wasn't long until we reached the lookout and came face-to-face with Colonel Stubbe—a small man, not much taller than myself.

As soon as he spotted Colin, his posture stiffened. Standing up, he immediately saluted his commanding officer. His eyes were small and much too close together. They seemed to look right past Colin, to a spot behind his head. It was like Colonel Stubbe couldn't bring himself to look the General in the eye. He dropped his arm, his gaze still focused on that spot on the wall. His behavior didn't sit right with me. Something was off about him.

"General," Stubbe barked. "We weren't expecting you today. What brings you here?" His voice was rough and nasally, and a shudder rolled down my spine as I likened the sound to nails on a chalkboard. I glanced at Colin, raising an eyebrow as if to say, 'What is with this guy?' I'd never paid much attention to what kind of person is suited for a leadership role; I was probably the least qualified person to make any judgments. But something about Colonel Stubbe had me on high alert, my hackles raised, and my guard solidly in place.

"You failed to submit your activity report yesterday," Colin stated, authority radiating through his tone and coating the surrounding air. "It would be remiss of me not to check in and ensure everyone here is safe and accounted for, and see what the delay might be."

The effect his speech had on me was unexpected. My core clenched, desire for him flooding through me stronger than before. Gods, I was in trouble. Colin was older than me, around seven years older if Bee was to be trusted, but he was still young for someone in his position. I'd be lying if I said I hadn't questioned how he had secured the position of Army General at his age. But... holy smokes. He hadn't raised his voice, but the authority and command in his tone had me ready to 'Yes, Sir' the shit out of him.

Down, girl.

My gaze dropped to where our hands were still connected, his thumb gently stroking up and down the side of mine—setting my skin on fire as my need for him grew within me. It took a great deal of effort to force myself to focus on Colonel Stubbe again, needing to distract myself from the desire running through my blood, before I lost control and did something silly like wrap myself around this mammoth of a man in front of an audience.

Colonel Stubbe appeared nervous, his hands clasped together as he swallowed hard.

"My apologies, General." He hadn't once looked Colin in the eye. I wondered briefly what Colin had done to cause this kind of fear and subservience from his members, or whether this was all about the sniveling man in front of him. "We were adding some last-minute activity from the tear prior to sending the report in. It occurred just as we were about to send Romero to you last night. Why don't you head down to the mess? Johnson will have dinner ready for the night guards. Have some faerie wine, and I'll finalize the report and deliver it to you shortly."

Colin stared at him for a moment, as though he was assessing how true the man's words were. I could almost hear his brain ticking over as he considered Stubbe's explanation and decided whether it was worthy of trust. It was surprising to me that he would need to make that assessment. I'd have thought that every person under his umbrella would be someone who had earned his trust before their promotion.

After a moment, he nodded. "I appreciate that. However," he looked pointedly at Stubbe. "A message takes only a moment. Send one next time." With that, he turned in a clear dismissal and led me back down the stairs of the tower. I glanced back at

Colonel Stubbe as he saluted, catching what might have been a roll of his eyes as we exited, but he was out of sight too quickly to be sure.

I definitely didn't like that man.

The mess hall turned out to be a small tent set up by the fire we spotted as we approached. There were a few men outside, seated on the logs as the fire crackled beside them, chatting while they ate an early dinner. These must be the men about to start their night shift.

"Are you hungry?" Colin asked, nodding a greeting to the men as we passed by. He still hadn't let go of my hand. Not that I was complaining. It was hard being in a new place and not knowing many people. Colin was attractive, and holding his hand brought me a level of comfort so far only matched by Stefan and Bee.

My chest tightened at the thought of Stefan. We hadn't spoken since the incident in the library. I'd been hoping he'd reach out to me, my anger with him holding me back from initiating contact until he apologized for hurling me across the room like a rag doll. That same anger is currently being smothered by how much I miss him. I decided to confront him the next time I saw him and turned my attention back to the present moment.

"Are you kidding?" I said, closing my eyes and inhaling deeply. There was a strong aromatic smell in the air. Onion, garlic, and many other spices. "Who wouldn't be hungry when the food smells that good?"

"Wait 'til you taste it, pure heaven." An unfamiliar voice cut in and I opened my eyes to find myself face to face with a gorgeous young woman in chef whites.

She held out a hand to me, a friendly smile crossing her freckle splattered face. Her bright red hair was styled back in a tight bun, her blue eyes bright like the sky outside. "I'm Johnson, Amy Johnson." Her gaze followed my arm to where my hand was still intertwined with Colin's, surprise crossing her features. I quickly dropped his hand and shook hers, offering my own friendly smile in return.

"Lovely to meet you. I'm Riley." Amy instantly reminded me of Sarie, causing a pang of homesickness to hit me right in the stomach. How was Sarie? I wondered. How was everyone at the orphanage? Had they been able to keep my tomatoes alive?

"Riley, as in the not quite human, not quite fae Riley I've been hearing about?" Her statement and tone were teasing, the smile on her face still friendly, but her words stung. It felt like I was constantly being reminded that I was not who I thought I was. That my entire life had been a lie.

Tears welled in my eyes, and I looked down, blinking fast, as though that might push them back down. I didn't want or need to cry in front of a stranger, in a tent full of fae guards. What a display of weakness that would be.

"Hey," she breathed. "I'm sorry, I've clearly hit a nerve. Go. Sit. I'll bring out the best of the best. Nothing like some good grub and faerie wine to pick up the mood." She winked at me and moved towards the makeshift counter at the back of the tent while simultaneously waving us towards a couple of dining tables set up to the side.

Colin moved toward it, pulling out a seat, and gesturing for me to sit down. Once I'd done so, he pushed in my chair and took the seat across from me. He fidgeted a little, like he might be nervous. It was cute, if not a little strange, and I recalled what Bee said my first night about him being completely unavailable. Was I developing actual feelings for the surly, surprising man in front of me? Was that a mistake?

"I thought this would be a quick check in. I didn't expect to be waiting here at all. I apologize. We'll leave and get a start on your tutoring as soon as Colonel Stubbe brings me his report. I hope you don't mind." He smiled at Amy as she dropped off two small silver goblets and a bottle of what I can only assume is the Faerie wine, before hurrying back to her kitchen.

"I don't mind at all. Learning how things are set up, and gaining some insight into how things work in your community, is actually really interesting. The more of your history and goals I learn, the less... angry and judgmental I feel toward your kind—the fae." I offered, as he uncorked the bottle and poured the wine.

I wasn't expecting the swirl of pink and orange shimmering liquid that came out of the dark bottle. Somehow, the colors remained separate, although they looked as though they should merge as they poured.

Colin grinned at me as he poured his own glass. "It tastes even better than it looks." He said with a wink. "Like oranges and strawberry jam." He held his glass up in a clear invitation to cheers. Lifting my own, I toasted, clinking his goblet and grinning back at him. I was grateful he didn't comment or dwell on the change in my mood. My emotions had been all over the place, but for right now, enjoying a glass of Faerie wine with him feels like exactly the right thing to do—even if I might regret it later.

With that thought, I tipped my goblet up and downed the contents. He was right; it tasted just like oranges and strawberry jam. It flowed down my throat smoothly, a nice fiery warmth settling in my belly. I placed the goblet back down on the table and looked up to find Colin gaping at me, his eyes wide with surprise.

"I probably should have warned you," he began, clearing his throat. "Faerie wine is potent. One glass is more than enough to have a fae bigger than yourself tripping over their own feet." His face is conflicted as though he can't decide whether me downing the whole goblet in one go is funny, or something to be worried about.

I giggled at his confused expression, and his face broke into that lovely grin again. He shined so brightly when he smiled, his chocolate brown eyes becoming lighter, more amber in coloring, and his powerful jaw seeming more defined. My eyes tracked down that jaw, down to his muscly chest that was showcased by his tight shirt. If I had any artistic talent, I'd paint him. He looked so damn fine.

"You're pretty." I said just as Amy arrived back at the table with two large bowls of curry and rice. She raised an eyebrow at Colin, then looked back at me with a huge, toothy smile. She was enjoying this.

"He is, isn't he, love," she said, winking at me conspiratorially, placing one bowl in front of me and the other in front of Colin. "Best you get some of this into you, so you can make the most of his prettiness and not wake up with a banging headache tomorrow." She points at him and then back at me. "Make sure she eats; all of it."

She left again, and I looked down at the food in front of me. The smells I'd caught earlier were even stronger, wafting up from the steaming bowl in front of me, and my stomach let out a loud growl in anticipation. Another giggle escaped me as I shushed it and picked up my fork to dig in. Amy needn't have worried about having Colin make sure I ate it all—I was not one to pass up a free meal, especially not one that smelt this bloody good.

"Why are you so grumpy most of the time, grumpy man?' I asked, hiccupping between mouthfuls of curry. The Faerie wine had broken down any filter that might have held me back in the past. I wasn't even sorry; I liked the chunk of muscle sitting in front of me, and I wanted to know more about him.

He considered my question for a moment, a slight crease forming between his brows. Placing his fork down on the table, he took a small sip of wine and then answered with an honesty that took me by surprise, sobering me just a bit.

"I don't think I'm grumpy, not really. My job requires a certain amount of professionalism and separation from others. I have to ensure I earn the respect of the men that report to me, the respect of the community, and maintain the respect of King Ronan and the elders." He wiped his mouth with a napkin and my eyes were suddenly drawn to his lip as he looked at me for a response.

The room swayed a little as I tried to focus and ask him another burning question. He was being surprisingly open, and I felt as though I was peeling back his layers little by little, and getting to know the man behind the walls.

"Focusing so much on the respect of others sounds kind of lonely. What about friends? What do you do for fun?" I asked. I wasn't sure how much of that he'd be able to understand. My words slurred around a mouthful of food. God, the curry was good. I looked up and spotted Amy stirring a pot in the kitchen area. I gesture to my bowl and give her a thumbs up. She laughed lightly and went back to stirring as I turned my attention back to Colin.

He chuckled softly. "I have plenty of friends, Riley. I keep my circle tight, but I'm not lonely. Callie, for one, keeps me on my toes." Despite my addled state, it didn't escape my notice that he ignored the last part of my question.

"Do you spend a lot of time with Callie?"

"Every spare moment I have."

"It's amazing you're so close to her. James and I were really close." My throat stuck and tears threatened to flow. The faerie wine had loosened my hold on my emotions even further. "God, I miss him. I feel like I'm wasting time. I wish I knew what happened to him, where he is, what I can do to find him. I don't even know where to start." I buried my face in my hands, the feeling of despair sobering me—though that probably had a lot to do with the amount of food I consumed as well.

Colin wasn't the only one letting his walls down tonight.

I could still feel the warmth of the wine spreading through my limbs, and although I was on the verge of tears and incredibly frustrated by the lack of information I had regarding my brother's disappearance, I also felt energized, ready to move my body, to use my magic, and work towards controlling it.

I pushed to my feet, done with my meal. Energy buzzed through my veins, building quickly to a point where I could no longer fight it, no longer able to sit still.

"I need to move," I told Colin, bouncing on the balls of my feet. "I need to run, or dance... or something. Can we go?"

He chuckled, his baritone laugh causing little zaps of electricity to light up all over my skin. He stood, reaching to take my hand again just as an alarm blared around us.

CHAPTER SIXTEEN

Riley

The room exploded into a whirlwind of activity. Guards that had been quietly eating their dinner were on their feet in the blink of an eye, some drawing weapons to hand, others bringing their element to their fingertips, all while rushing out of the mess hall.

Colin looked at me, his eyes dark and wide, eyebrows drawn together in worry. He glanced toward Amy and back again, then grabbed my arm as the alarm continued to blare throughout the compound. My heart was beating against my rib cage as he pulled me over to where Amy and another girl—I'm assuming one from her kitchen—were huddled behind the counter.

"What is—" I said before I was cut off by the sound of guards shouting, interlaced with a distant growl, deep and guttural, that sent my pulse racing even faster and a chill wracking down my spine.

"Something has broken through from the void. Stay with Amy," Colin demanded in a whisper, pushing me down next to her, his face blank and devoid of emotion once more. He was back to stone cold General Brand. He turned to face Amy, a muscle clenching in his jaw as he said, "Get to the tower, into the bunker. Keep. Her. Safe." Amy nodded fiercely, but Colin was already sprinting out of the tent.

I opened my mouth, ready to ask what the fuck was going on, when Amy held her finger up, shushing me. She shook her head in a clear sign it was not the time to talk. I nodded my understanding as she gestured at us to stay down and follow her. I stayed close to her back; the other girl—Lori, if her name tag was correct—pressed up against me from the rear as we crawled along the counter, aiming for the back of the tent.

Amy peeked outside, lifting the wall of the tent slightly to create a gap. The path must have been clear as she motioned for us to follow her and wiggled underneath the canvas. With no time to hesitate, I scrambled under the lip as soon as her feet had disappeared. What was happening, I wasn't exactly sure, but I was not lagging behind to find out. Especially not after that bone chilling growl. It had been enough to sober me completely.

We emerged on a muddy walkway between tents, pausing for a moment to help Lori wiggle out to join us. I could see the guard tower a short way in the distance, a few rows of tents away from us. Shouting reached us on the wind and I looked in the direction it was coming from. Multiple elements were flying through the air, lighting up the sky as the sun began to set, all aimed at some unknown target that seemed to be just outside the gates.

A gravelly roar tore through the surrounding space again, setting the hairs on my arm on end. Metal screeched as it was crushed against itself, and the guards shouted more fervently. Whatever set off the alarms was quickly getting closer, maybe even breaking down the fence. Sweat beaded on my brow as I turned my attention to Amy, eager to get to the guard tower and bunker as quickly as possible.

She took off at a fast pace, moving on two feet, hunched as low to the ground as she could manage. Lori and I imitated her, following closely as she led us between the next row of tents as quickly as possible.

We zig zagged between a couple of tents, the noise behind us growing louder as more of the guards reached the front of the compound and whatever was attacking us broke its way through the gates. A fire was growing larger and larger in the distance, smoke thickening the air, the orange of the flame quickly becoming the only source of light as darkness fell swiftly. Shadows danced around us, over the walls of each tent we passed. Terror was building in my chest, making it hard to breathe as my heart knocked out a crescendo against my ribs.

Amy dipped into a gap between two tents, moving to the end of the row. She stopped suddenly, dropping low to the ground and holding up a hand, signaling for us to do the same. I fell to the floor immediately, crawling up next to her, my eyes darting around in the darkness. The guard tower was just across the way, highlighted by two torches on either side of the door. The door itself is wide open, the area in front of us deserted, nothing and no one standing between us and the safety the tower promises.

My legs itched to stand up and bolt across the path, to find the bunker, to get away from whatever creature has made its way on to our lands. But Amy hadn't moved, still lying flat to the ground, her right ear pressed firmly against the earth beneath our feet, almost like she's listening for something.

Oh, shit.

She was listening for something.

My heartbeat thumped in my ears, drowning out the mayhem of the battle behind us as I realized that the roaring creature behind us wasn't the only threat we were facing. Something else was stalking us.

All I could hear was the steady whoosh, whoosh, whoosh of blood flowing through my body. Calm down, Riley. I took a deep breath, trying to do just that and listen for the thing that had caught Amy's attention.

Turning my ear to the ground beneath us, I tried to focus on any abnormal noise radiating from beneath the earth. At first, I couldn't hear a thing. I strained, closing my eyes and listening as hard as I could. A scurrying, scratching noise caught my attention, but I couldn't figure out what would make it. Something burrowing through the dirt?

Just as that thought crossed my mind, Amy hissed. "Get ready."

She lurched to her feet and out of the gap between tents, into the space directly in front of the tower. "Elements out. Cover each other. They're surrounding us!" she shouted, and I watched in awe as she splayed her hands in front of her, mini tornadoes of swirling air visible in her palms. I was on my feet in a millisecond, Lori right next to me as we sprinted to join Amy. Banding together, backs pressed against one another in a triangle, we tried to cover every direction.

Lori raised her hands, and I followed suit, willing an element—any element—to come to my aid. I had no experience, no control. The best I could do was hope I didn't hurt anyone in my bid to protect us. I widened my stance, steadying myself and preparing to fight. Closing my eyes, I waited, trying to focus on my earth element, imploring it to come forth. Thick, woody vines wrapped themselves around my palms and I opened my eyes, examining them in awe.

There was no time to celebrate my victory before the earth rumbled beneath our feet, and a small scaly creature ripped through the dirt, flinging itself up into the air in front of Amy. It bounced once, twice, with a surprisingly loud thud before it landed on the ground, and charged forward.

I only had a second to examine it before Amy hurled a ball of air in its direction. It was almost lizard like, with a long, solid body covered in dark murky green scales. Its head seemed misplaced on its torso, more like that of a large angry cat, with a black mane separating the head from body. It growled menacingly, mouth opening wide, exposing a long snout like jaw, with multiple rows of razor-sharp teeth. Two giant, saber-like canine teeth protruded from the top front row, a rancid green drool dripping from them. Despite its smaller stature, there was no doubt that this nightmarish creature could tear me apart in the blink of an eye.

Amy's attack collided with the creature with a cracking boom, much louder than I expected, ringing through the air. It was thrown back with force, landing hard and unmoving on the ground a few feet from us. More and more of the creatures had ripped their way through the dirt, circling us, until we were surrounded by them. Swallowing hard, I ran my eyes over them. We were severely outnumbered, and I wondered briefly if this might be the end.

One by one, they threw themselves at us and I had no more time to consider what the hell we were facing and whether we'd walk out of here alive.

I was thrown into the fray. There was no more time to think about how I didn't have a clue what I was doing. No time to think at all. Only time to react. A creature rushed at me and I pushed my right palm toward it, willing the vines circling my wrist to strike. Shocked, I watched as they surged forward and wrapped themselves around their first victim. Instinctively, I closed my fist and tugged; the vine tightening around the creature's torso and yanking him closer to me.

From the corner of my eye, I saw another rushing me from my left and I held the first creature in the air, unsure of what to do next. It thrashed and growled, but couldn't break free of my vines. Facing my left palm in the second creature's direction, I willed a ball of fire to my fingertips.

My magic answered my call, spewing forth from the well inside my chest. The vines that had been wrapping around my wrist vanished, replaced by an orb of scorching flames. I tossed it forward, a guttering roar confirming I had hit my target as I lobbed more orbs at the nightmarish creatures surrounding us.

In my periphery, I could see Amy forcing the creatures back with punishing gusts of wind. Lori was shooting jets of water at as many as she could, fast and furious. It wasn't enough, though; they were gaining on us, tightening their circle. There wasn't any way for us to escape them, not when they had us trapped like this.

"Start moving toward the tower," Amy shouted. "Try to get close enough to make a break for it." It was the best plan we had. The only plan we had. Lori and I nodded our agreement and started inching toward the open tower door, still using our elements to push back as many of our attackers as we could.

"Ready?" I shouted when we were a few feet from the door. "On the count of three, let's all aim together, clear a path through them."

Amy immediately began counting down, raising her voice above the cacophony of shouts and roars around us. When she reached three, I whipped my vines through the air and tossed the creature still tangled in them toward the door. It skidded along the dirt, knocking back some of the other creatures in our way. As they scrambled to gain their feet and advance again, Amy hit them with a blast of wind, followed swiftly by a wave of water from Lori. I brought balls of flame to my palms as we sprinted, Lori in front of me and Amy bringing up the rear. Tossing flames at any creatures trying to close the gap, I made it through the door, spinning on my heel to cover Amy, expecting her to be right behind me.

But she wasn't. Instead, she was on the ground, scrambling to get up. Her face was full of panic as she tried to regain her feet and faltered, her ankle giving way, body slamming to the ground again. Leaving the safety of the tower without a single thought, I tossed more balls of scorching hot flame from my palms as I tried to reach her before anything else could. The sounds of battle were growing louder, and in the distance, I could spot some of the guards. Not close enough.

I watched in horror as one of the creatures leapt from behind Amy, too fast for me to blast in time, and clamped its jaw down around her calf.

She screamed as it sunk its teeth deep into her flesh and I sent another ball of flames at the creature, silently praying that it loosened its grip on her. Blood pooled on the ground around Amy as the venom of the beast made its way into her system and she quickly lost consciousness.

Lori hit the creature with a blast of water from behind me. The quick succession of blows knocked it off of Amy just as

I reached her. I knelt down, slipping in the blood that was spreading further around her still form. More and more guards were joining us, but they faded into the background as I focused my attention on Amy.

There was so much blood, her skin so pale... her body so still. No.

No!

She wasn't dead, she couldn't be. I refused to allow it.

"No, no, no. Please, Amy, hold on." I murmured as I took her pulse and examined her leg, trying to figure out what to do. There were so many puncture wounds, rows and rows of them, all still oozing blood. The flesh around each one had turned a sickly shade of green—as though they were infected or poisoned.

We'd had very basic first aid training back home—we had to. There were so many of us, so many children, that someone was almost always hurt. I didn't know much, but it was enough that I knew my first step should be to halt the bleeding by putting pressure on the wound. I tore my shirt off, leaving me in just a crop. I didn't care, way too focused on Amy to even feel the chill of the night air. I folded it over a few times and pressed it down on her leg. I leant my body over hers, praying that I was applying enough pressure, that what I was doing would be enough.

"Please," I whispered, a tear breaking free and sliding down my cheek, dripping onto my hands. I couldn't watch her die. She reminded me so much of Sarie. Of my best friend back home. "Please stay with me. Don't let go." I was not a fighter. I never had been! I'd always been more at home among the plants and seedlings in the orphanage's greenhouse. Plants weren't confrontational. They thrived when cared for and given the right nourishment. They didn't fight me.

I wasn't made for this. I couldn't keep watching people die—first the guard on the journey here and now Amy. It was too much.

My tears fell heavier as I kept an unrelenting pressure on her leg. They blurred my vision until I could barely see my hands in front of me. I couldn't stop them. There were more and more people crowding around us, fighting against the remaining creatures, but I couldn't see them. All I could see was Amy. Her still, lifeless body lying in the pool of crimson blood. Blood that was coating my legs as I knelt before her.

"Please," I begged one last time, lowering my head onto my hands as I willed life back into Amy's lifeless form. Exhaustion seeped through my body, taking hold of every piece of me. My eyes closed, and I couldn't seem to find the energy to open them again. I was sinking, consciousness fading from my grasp.

As I was falling under, a bright light built behind my heavy eyelids. It built brighter and brighter, from red to orange, before reaching a burning white crescendo.

Just as consciousness completely failed me and the bright light faded to black, I heard someone shouting my name; the voice was distorted but familiar. Then there was nothing.

CHAPTER SEVENTEEN

Riley

Sitting up with a start, I peeled open my gritty eyes and looked around, unsettled by my surroundings. The last thing I remembered was kneeling in the dirt beside Amy as her life faded from her body, guards and void creatures battling around us. It took me a moment to realize I was safe. That the sounds of battle were gone, replaced by the hushed tones of whispered voices in the night.

An orange glow flickered against the dark green canvas wall next to me, coming from the many candles clustered on tables within the space. The scent of fresh rain after a storm drifted in the open flaps on the other side of the room. Things were calm now, no more frantic yelling, creatures with sharp teeth snapping at us, or fae element attacks flying through the air.

Beneath me was a stiff stretcher bed, a crisp white sheet tucked over my legs. There were rows of beds just like mine filling the space, many filled with injured guards and a lot of other fae milling around the space, attending to the injured and speaking amongst themselves in hushed whispers.

This must be the medical tent.

Throwing the sheet off my legs, I swung them over the side of the stretcher as I looked, searching frantically for Amy. She had to be here. If she wasn't, if she didn't make it, I... I didn't know what I'd do. I couldn't stomach the thought of another life having been lost in front of me.

Suddenly, I spotted her flaming red hair, almost luminescent against the white sheets of the bed she was sitting in. Upright, an elderly fae woman was beside her, holding a glass of water and helping her to drink it.

Thank the gods, she was alive! Although I could see her, I needed to get to her, to make sure she truly was okay. It didn't sit right with me that she was injured while getting me to safety. Or that my efforts to protect all of us weren't enough.

I pushed to my feet and began moving toward her without even thinking about it. The edges of my vision darkened as the room swayed and my legs gave way beneath me. Strong hands gripped me under my arms, catching me before I could crash to the ground. I slumped against a warm, hard, familiar body as I regained my balance and my vision cleared. How long had it been since I passed out, I didn't know, but it had clearly been a while.

"Where do you think you're going?" If I hadn't already guessed who held me by the feel of him, I'd have recognized his growl anywhere, his touch too. I straightened, my body brushing against his as I turned to face him. Looking up, Colin's eyes locked with mine immediately. They were darker than they'd been this afternoon, almost black and dancing with shadows. His rage was undeniable. I could feel the anger emanating from him, searing across my skin as he assessed me.

I took a step back, his hands falling from my shoulders as I went. The fury flooding from every pore in his body confused me. It seemed to be directed at me. I wasn't sure what I could have done to deserve his wrath. It didn't matter, anyway. I just wanted to check on Amy. I'd deal with whatever this reaction was later, once I knew she was alright, that those monsters hadn't caused her any permanent damage.

She'd been trying to protect Lori and I, had been trying to ensure we made it to safety—and we had. But that shouldn't have been at her own expense.

I crossed my arms over my chest, tilting my chin and narrowing my eyes as I stared back at him. "I'm going to see Amy. Excuse me," I said, my frustration building. What was his problem? I spun on my heel, storming off without giving him a chance to respond. His heavy footsteps let me know he was right behind me as I marched away and I sighed heavily. Whatever was bothering him wasn't going away. Whatever. He could stew in it for now. Amy was my priority. Fuck the drama.

I reached her side as the elderly fae stood up to leave. She offered me a soft smile as she walked away, empty glass in hand. Plopping into her vacated seat, I turned my attention to Amy. She looked at me, an elated grin splitting across her face as she realized I was there.

"Riley! Come here," she yelled, her arms held out wide as she pulled me in for a hug. "Are you okay? By the gods, you were incredible! I've never seen such raw power! Where did it come from? How did you do it?" She barely took a breath as she spoke, holding me in front of her as she examined me for injuries. She was no longer deathly pale, a soft flush coloring her cheeks and her eyes sparkling with good health. She looked great, radiant, so far removed from how she was the last time I'd seen her.

I had no idea what she was talking about, or why she was so worried I might be hurt. "Me? Are you alright? Your leg—there was so much blood. I was worried you weren't... that you were... that you wouldn't..." I trailed off, tears stinging my eyes as I looked away from her.

She grabbed my hand with both of hers, the smile dropping and her face turning serious as she stared at me. "I'm fine, Riley. Completely healed. I wouldn't be if it weren't for you. Thank you."

"What are you talking about? I didn't do anything. I was trying to stop the bleeding, but there was so much—"

"Riley," Amy said, her voice firm. "You saved me. I don't know how you did, but you did. I remember the creature biting my leg, the pain of all those teeth puncturing my flesh, the burn of its poison as it seeped inside my skin and began to spread. Then nothing. It was dark, a darkness that was thick and cloying and terrifying. And then it was gone, light flooding everything, a brilliant white light that almost blinded me. I struggled to open my eyes against the brightness of it, but I did. And it was coming from you."

What was she saying? Had I healed her? I knew the fae had some healing powers. Colin had healed me on the journey from Sommers to Danann. But I did not know how they used them, how they differed from their elemental powers. Only that it was different. Stefan had mentioned that type of magic coming from the Origin.

"I... It wasn't me." I muttered, unable to believe I was capable of that kind of magic, that kind of power.

"It was," Colin barked. He'd followed me over and stationed himself right beside the chair. "It was you. I watched it all. I reached the fight just as you knelt at Amy's side. I saw the wound on her leg, the blood pooling around her. If I hadn't, I might not have believed they had injured her at all. You are a powerful creature, Riley. No other fae here has shown the ability to heal from the poison the void creatures possess. None. Ever." He said it so matter-of-factly, there was no space to argue with him. I had healed Amy. Me. Riley.

"But how? How can I have done something like that? I don't know how to heal someone. I wasn't trying to. I just wanted her to survive. I had no idea that's what I was doing." I couldn't really argue against the evidence. Amy was alive and well. Right here in front of me. I must have healed her, saved her life. There was no other explanation for it. I couldn't keep denying what they were telling me. I looked down at my hands gathered in my lap, turning them over as I examined them.

I was beginning to scare myself.

How was I so powerful?

What was I?

Where did I fit in?

I wished James was here to reassure me, to tell me everything would work out in the end. He always knew the right thing to say; he'd always been so kind and supportive. I needed my big brother.

I looked back up at Amy to find her staring at me, concern etched across her features.

"I'm glad you're okay, that I was able to help you." Switching my gaze to Colin, still standing stiffly beside me, shadows dancing across his face and his rage still palpable. I dropped my eyes, looking at my hands again. "I'd like to go back to the Academy. I'm tired."

"King Ronan has sent extra carriages and guards to transport those who fought today back for rest or further treatment. I'll escort you." He held out a hand to help me stand, and I took it, the contact sparking between us. I quickly dropped it once I was steady on my feet. I'm too tired to play this game tonight. Too tired to examine why he was so angry with me or why he'd taken a step back again.

"Don't be a stranger," Amy said, smiling at me gently. She was trying and failing to hide her concern. "Let me know when you venture into the city next. Maybe we can go for coffee."

"Sounds great," I said, smiling for the first time since I awoke. I offered her a small wave as I gathered my things from beside the bed I'd been in, and Colin led me out of the tent.

A small gasp escaped me as I took in the damage outside. Some of the tents in the small encampment were completely destroyed, others covered in scorch marks. The surrounding fence had been knocked down in places, the ground muddy, small tunnels where those monsters had dug through.

"Where is Lori?" I asked as Colin stomped through the base ahead of me. I almost had to jog to keep up with him. "I didn't see her in the tent?" She'd made it inside the guard tower with me during the fight, but I'd been so focused on Amy that I didn't know if she had followed me back out or stayed in safety. I hoped it was the latter.

"She's fine." Colin grunted, not even turning to look back at me. Anger flared inside of me, my hands clenched into fists at my side. His attitude was exhausting. He'd gone full blown General on me since I woke in the tent. Earlier today, he'd been so kind, so gentle. Like we were two regular people getting to know each other. I'd been starting to think that whatever was between us might actually work, that we might be able to pursue whatever it was that had been drawing us together. I wasn't going to stand by and take this treatment from him. I didn't have to. I had Bee and Stefan—if the asshole ever apologized.

And I already had a date for the dance this weekend. I didn't need Colin and his drama.

"I've got it from here. You can get back to your duties. I won't inconvenience you any further." I gritted through my teeth. Picking up my pace and storming right past him, I gave him a wide enough berth so that he couldn't get in my way. I headed directly for the gates at the front of the base, where I assumed the carriages would be waiting.

"Riley, wait." I heard him call, but I didn't stop. Exhaustion had seeped into my bones. I couldn't deal with this tonight. I just wanted to get back to the academy, take a long hot shower and forget this evening had ever even happened.

CHAPTER EIGHTEEN

Riley

Apart from some hushed whispering and not-so-subtle glances in my direction, the carriage ride back to Danann was uneventful. Most of the passengers were guards who had fought hard. Their exhaustion was written clearly on their faces, in the dark purple bags under their eyes. So, I let them whisper and steal glances my way, choosing to ignore them and instead stared blindly out at the scenery as we passed the dead forest and barren fields.

The carriage dropped me off just outside the academy grounds, having already let off a couple of guards at the stable. The rest would go into the center of Danann. The gates recognized me, opening as I approached and closing again as I made my way down the path into the academy grounds. It was a strange feeling to know they read my magical signature. Magic

I hadn't known I possessed until a few days ago. Magic that I didn't understand, but which felt wholly like a part of me that had always been there.

The frigid night air pressed against me, and I shivered, wrapping my arms around myself in an attempt to keep warm. I was wearing only a crop top and my skirt, having used my shirt in my attempt to save Amy, my bare skin offering no resistance to the chill of the night air.

Something shifted in the trees ahead, and I stopped, squinting through the darkness to see what it might be. My senses were on high alert after the attack tonight and my shoulders drew back, my whole-body stiffening with tension. The moon fell behind thick clouds, taking away what little light I'd had to see by. Shadows thickened and danced over the path ahead. A rustle and crack startled me and I willed fire to my palms to protect myself, amazed at the ease with which the balls of heat and light appeared there. A dull ache pounded in my chest and I wondered briefly if my magic reserve might need replenishing.

"Woah, woah, woah little dove, it's just me," said Stefan as he appeared ahead of me on the path, his hands held up in the air in a sign of surrender. He grinned at me, like he hadn't just snuck up and given me an unnecessary fright after everything else that had happened tonight. Cocky asshole.

I frowned at him, straightening from the fighting stance I'd fallen into and extinguishing my balls of flame. His silver eyes sparkled as they locked with mine, and he took a cautious step toward me.

"I heard about the attack," he said softly, his voice barely above a whisper as he closed the distance between us. "Are you alright?" His eyes were wary as he stopped, his body just a foot from mine. Raising a hand, he cupped my chin, tilting my face to his, examining me for any injury.

A sob tore its way from my chest as his words, his presence, broke down the walls I'd built around myself tonight. All my fear and anger burst forth in a tidal wave. Trembling, tears poured down my cheeks as I surrendered to it. Reaching for me, Stefan pulled me in hard against his body, wrapping his arms around me. His touch grounded me, keeping me in place physically while emotionally I shattered into a thousand pieces.

So much had happened in such a brief space of time. My world had been turned on its head and the toll of adjusting to my new reality was hitting me hard. Stefan held me while I fell apart, letting myself process the events of the last few days, and even some of my grief at losing my brother. I buried my face in his chest, the smell of rosewood and cinnamon wrapping around me like a second set of arms. An overwhelming sense of safety enveloped me, and in that moment, it didn't matter that he'd scared me the other day, or that he'd been an ass by staying away for so long. He was here now, right when I needed him the most. That was what mattered.

When my tears finally stopped, and I could breathe again, I sagged against him. The adrenaline and emotion of the night's events finally escaping my body, flowing away from me and out into the darkness of the night, leaving me limp and exhausted.

Without a word of protest, Stefan scooped me into his arms, cradling me against his chest, and started strolling towards the Academy.

He carried me in silence, brooding but comfortable and I rested my head on his shoulder, too tired to demand he put me down to let me walk; too weary to worry about what was passing through his mind. I realized then that I felt content in his arms. Safe. Warm. Cared for. Like I might just be someone's priority again.

I hadn't felt this way for a long while. Not since, well, since before James had ascended and left me alone at the orphanage. I wanted to hold on to it, grab it tight, and never let it go. I wanted to hold on to him, so I did. I lopped my arms around his neck, nuzzling into his neck and breathing deeply. Something in my chest settled, instinct telling me this was where I was meant to be.

He looked down at me, one brow raised in question, a soft smile dancing on his lips. I smiled back, closing my eyes and soaking in the moment.

He carried me all the way through the trees, through the gardens, and up the stairs to my dorm room. He didn't bother to put me down to open the door, instead shuffling a little to free one hand and crossing the threshold quickly, closing the door behind us. The room was dark, cold, and empty.

"Where's Bee?" I asked, as he gently placed me on the edge of my bed. He knelt down, placing a hand on my ankle and untying my shoelaces to remove my boots. I tried to lift my leg in protest, but he pulled it back down, shushing me.

"Let me look after you, little dove." He said, sighing heavily. "It's the least I can do." He looked up at me, pausing for a moment, waiting for confirmation, and I nodded. Reaching back down, he lifted my leg again, his fingers trailing down from my calf to ankle, sending shivers down my spine.

Stefan removed my second boot and placed my foot back down before rising and turning to the bathroom. He disappeared inside and I heard the water turn on, as though he was running a bath. He reappeared a few moments later, a cloud of steam billowing out of the bathroom behind him.

"Go rinse off that blood and mud in the shower, then soak in the bath—you look exhausted and much too pale for my liking. I'll go scavenge up some supper." He stated, leaving no room for argument. A bath sounded amazing, and he wasn't wrong. I was exhausted, right down to the very core of me. The well of power I could usually feel ebbing and flowing inside my chest was faint, almost empty. It was an uncomfortable feeling and one I did not wish to grow familiar with. I understood then why the fae surrounded themselves in their elements as much as possible.

He turned to leave, reaching for the door handle. The thought of being alone sent wave after wave of anxiety through me, causing my hands to tremble. What if something found me here? Could those creatures get inside the walls of Danann? I took a steadying breath as he started to close the door behind him.

"Stefan," I said, my voice dry and gravelly, shaking a little. "Please hurry, I—I don't want to be alone tonight," I admitted, my eyes cast downwards as I twisted my fingers in my lap. I wanted to be strong. I wanted never to need anyone else. But the reality was that I was scared and exhausted, all my strength gone for the night.

He stared at me, hesitating in the doorway. "I'll be back long before you're out of the tub, I promise. I'll stay as long as you need me to."

"Thank you." I whispered, and it was his turn to nod, his expression solemn as he closed the door behind him.

I mustered up the strength to stand, then stripped off my clothes before heading into the bathroom. The claw-foot tub was nearly full, a layer of bubbles on the top and tendrils of steam dancing in the space above the water. I turned off the tap and rinsed myself quickly in the shower, removing the majority of dirt, grime, and blood—Amy's blood—from my body. I shuddered at the memory. Things could have ended so much worse tonight. Those creatures, whatever they were, could have killed her. If I hadn't been there, if my magic hadn't taken over and healed her, I hated to think about what could have happened, what state she'd be in now.

I stepped into the bathtub, sinking into the warm scented water. A heady floral scent washed over me—orange blossom, my favorite. I allowed my body to relax; the water working soothing my aching muscles. I was grateful for my newfound power. That I could heal and protect those around me. But I hoped I didn't have to face too many more nights like tonight.

I was so far out of my comfort zone it wasn't even funny.

I soaked in the softly scented tub until the water cooled. I climbed out, too tired to dress, instead drying off quickly and shrugging into a soft cotton bathrobe.

True to his word, Stefan had already returned. He was sitting at my desk, a platter of sandwiches in front of him. He must have lit some candles scattered around the room, as well as a small fireplace in the corner beyond Bee's bed that I hadn't noticed before. The air was warm; the orange flickering light calming my frayed nerves.

His eyes darted to me the second he heard me enter the room. The silver in them sparkled, glittering in the dimly lit room as his gaze roamed up and down my body. His tongue darted out, licking his lips as his stare became almost predatory. My cheeks flamed at the intensity of that stare, heat flooding through me and desire pooling in my lower stomach.

"Sit. Eat." He growled, motioning to my bed and standing to hand me the platter of food. I took a sandwich, my stomach growling. It felt like forever since I last ate, though I know it had only been a few hours since I'd had dinner with Colin. I'd burned through so much energy; my body needed the fuel.

Stefan cleared his throat, sitting down next to me on the bed, twisting his hands together before rubbing his palms down the front of his pants. He was nervous. Curiosity surged through me. I didn't know what he could make him feel that way, but I was dying to find out.

"I owe you an apology and an explanation. If you want me to leave after I've said my bit, I will. I won't like it, but I'll understand if you don't want to be around me any longer."

"Stefan, I won't—"

"Please, little dove. Don't make any promises. Let me explain, and then decide if you still want to be my -" He paused for a moment, looking down at his lap. "My friend."

"Alright," I said, gently placing my hand on top of his in a gesture of support. "I'll hear you out. Go on."

"So," he began, taking a deep breath to steady himself. "I'm not sure how much of this you know, but I am going to start from the top. I am a ward of King Ronan and Queen Ciara, the fae Water Elemental King and Queen. They took me in when I was just an infant, during their bid for the throne. My background is unknown. No one has ever identified my mother or father, or where I come from, other than I was left on the doorstep of the orphanage one stormy night. Cliche isn't it?" He glanced at me quickly, too quickly, a sad sort of smile on his face. I squeezed his hand in reply, worried that if I said anything, muttered even a single word that I'd throw him off and he wouldn't be able to continue.

"I don't remember anything from before the crossing. I don't even remember the crossing itself, though Lincoln and Bee both have memories of it. My first memories are of Earth, of the wall being built around Danann, of the gardens flourishing. Those memories are scattered among periods of darkness. Periods of time that I have no physical memory of, just a feeling of absolute terror, of being trapped and fighting to get out, to get away from whatever had captured me within my mind." His voice broke a little, the fear he described tangible and affecting him even now. My heart ached for the little boy who had experienced such a thing.

"What was happening to you?" I asked, taking his other hand in mine and gripping them tightly. I wasn't sure I really wanted to know the answer, but Stefan continued.

"We don't truly know. I'm not sure we ever will. There are theories, but without access to Faerie, to our historians, healers, and gods, we just don't know. As I've grown older, stronger, I've gained control over the monster inside of me. I no longer have blackout periods, though I still have periods where his rage affects me, where I'm not myself."

Realization hit me then and my chest felt like it was caving in. He looked up from his lap and faced me, desperation shining in those bright silver eyes and tearing my heart apart. A single tear slid down my cheek as I tried to imagine how that must feel, to have an unwanted visitor in your mind, not knowing what it is and always worrying it might take control.

"That's what happened in the library, Riley. I was furious at the Elders. I let my control slip and that put you at risk. I'm so sorry, little dove. The last thing I want is to hurt you or scare you or risk you. I want to hold you, protect you, care for you. I have from the first moment I saw you in the candidate's tent. I wanted you then. Fuck, if I don't want you more now. Can you forgive me?" He pleaded, his eyes begging me, burning even brighter.

He wanted me. Me.

Though I knew it wasn't his intention, that he really was trying to explain himself and apologize, that Stefan wanted me was the key message sticking in my mind.

I let go of his hands, and they dropped to his sides. Sliding across the bed, I closed the small distance between us, grasping his shoulders as I climbed on top of him, into his lap, my knees either side of his waist.

I took his chin, tilting his face so that his eyes meet mine from my new vantage point above him. His hands gripped my thighs, his fingers brushing against my skin and sending a fresh wave of desire through me.

"Thank you," I whispered, my mouth mere inches from his as I leaned in. "For trusting me enough to confide in me, for explaining yourself. You have nothing to apologize for." I paused, taking a breath as my heart pounded in my chest and electricity crackled between us. "Of course, I forgive you." He licked his lips, drawing my gaze to his mouth. I wanted nothing more than to kiss him at that moment.

So, I did.

I leant forward, wrapping my arms around his neck, gently brushing my lips against his. He responded almost instantly, groaning as he tugged me closer, one hand moving up my body and gripping my hair, pressing harder as he fused his mouth to mine. He nipped my lower lip, causing my lips to part, opening for him. He pushes his tongue inside, stroking my own, teasing me.

I gasped, my breasts tightening as I met his strokes with my own rocking against the hard length of him. My nipples pebbled against the soft cotton of my robe as our kiss continued, wetness flooding between my legs. The realization that my robe was the piece of fabric covering my nudity caused butterflies to dance in my stomach and need to throb at the apex of my thighs.

This connection had existed between us from the moment we met. I felt it then, and I felt it even more strongly now. There was some kind of invisible thread tying me to Stefan, and I didn't want to fight it.

Giving myself to him entirely, I dropped my head back as his mouth trailed light kisses along my jaw and down my neck to the collar of my robe. He stood suddenly, twisting us, and dropping me onto the mattress beneath him. He clambered onto the bed, kneeling between my thighs, his eyes searching mine and watching as my hands reached for the tie around my waist. I untied it, pulling the robe open and baring myself to him as he sucked in a sharp breath.

"You are a stunning creature, Riley Emmett." He murmured, continuing to kiss down my collarbone. "Are you sure?" He asked, pulling his head back a little, waiting for my confirmation.

I nod. "Yes. I'm sure. Please, Stefan." I begged, squirming beneath him as the need for him filled every part of me. He pushed off the bed and stood at the edge, something akin to deference shining in his silver eyes. He pulled his shirt over his head to reveal a toned olive chest and abs for days. Sitting up, I tugged the robe off of my arms, throwing it to the floor as I watched him unbutton his jeans, pulling them off, followed by his boxer shorts.

His erection sprang free, the impressive length of him causing my mouth to dry as arousal beaded at the tip. I quickly slid off the bed, to my knees on the floor beside him, craving a taste of him.

He twisted toward me, his mouth falling open in surprise as I wrapped one hand around the base of his shaft, licking the tip gently, the saltiness of his pre-cum causing more heat to flood through me.

Stefan moaned loudly, dropping his head back and tangling his fingers in my hair as I licked along the length of him before taking his head into my mouth. I moved, pumping my hand in time with my mouth alternating between sucking and licking him.

I was so turned on, so feverish with desire, that I couldn't ignore the throb between my thighs any longer. I reached my free hand between my legs to my core and began circling my clit in slow, lazy circles. Ripples of pleasure rolled through my body and I moaned around his shaft, taking him deep.

"Fuck," Stefan growled, watching as I pleasured myself and him simultaneously. "Let me look after you, little dove." He pulled his hands free of my hair as I released my mouth with a pop. He lifted me gently, placing me back down on the bed with a soft thump. I scrambled away from the edge as he grinned wolfishly at me, as though he planned to devour me. No complaints here.

He climbed over me, his mouth falling to my breast and tugging a nipple into his mouth. I gasped as he rolled his tongue over the sensitive numb. He pinched my other nipple between his fingers before swapping to ensure each received enough attention. I arched my back, my body screaming for more, the need for release overpowering me.

He moved downward, trailing kisses down my stomach, which sent shivers down my spine. He reached a hand between my legs, running a finger between my folds, feeling my drenched center. Moaning loudly, I flexed my hips, craving more of his touch.

He groaned at the wetness he found there, before gently pushing one, then two fingers inside my aching core. He lowered his head, his tongue stroking a long line up the center of me before focusing on my clit, his fingers inside me curling in a lazy come hither motion.

My back arched again as he lapped at me, pumping his fingers in and out of me in a slow, heady rhythm, circling them and hitting my g-spot just right. Tension coiled in my core, building to a crescendo.

"Stefan," I moaned, as my climax neared. "By the gods." My orgasm washed over me as it reached its peak, and I found my release. Wave upon wave of pleasure rolled through my body, my toes curling and skin tingling at the intensity of it.. Stefan slowed, lifting his head and grinning at me as my entire body relaxed. Even after my bath, I'd been holding onto so much tension tonight. It was a relief to feel it leave my muscles and release with my climax.

"I'm not done with you yet, little dove." He purred as he crawled back up over my body, kissing me deeply, passionately, the taste of me on his lips only fueling the flames of my lust all over again. His hands roamed my body before gripping my hips and making their way to my breasts, where he began teasing my nipples.

I'm ready and aching for him all over again. The need to feel him inside of me almost driving me out of my mind.

"Do you have protection?" I asked, breathlessly, as a trickle of sense broke through my hazy lust-filled mind. I was just discovering myself and my place in the fae world. I didn't know what I was or where I had come from—neither did Stefan, it seemed. Now was not the time to take risks.

"I'm not sure what you mean by protection. Fae are immune to human diseases, if that's what you're getting at. No fae have been conceived here on Earth, and intention is required when we reproduce," he stated, an eyebrow raised in question. If any of the men back home had tried a line like that on me, I'd have been running for the hills, but I couldn't deny the truth radiating from Stefan. Intuition told me he spoke true.

"Great. I want you Stefan, please. I need you inside of me." I purred, watching as heat flared in his eyes.

"Your wish is my command," he said, some of his usual snark sneaking back into his tone, making me giggle as he leant down to kiss me again. He lined himself up with my entry and pressed forward, gliding slowly inside, filling me to the hilt. He stilled for a moment while I adjusted to the size of him. Ecstasy filled every fiber of my being as he moved inside of me.

I wrapped my legs around his waist as he pumped in and out, his movements becoming faster, more frantic as he chased his release, my own beginning to build again. He lowered his head, forehead resting against mine as I cried out, my climax reaching its peak again. Lights flared across my vision with the force of it, my body vibrating as waves after waves of pleasure rolled through me. With a few more thrusts, Stefan moaned my name as he found his own release before collapsing on top of me.

We laid still for a moment, panting as we caught our breath. Stefan rolled to the side, pulling me into him with my back against his chest, spooning me as he wiggled us under the covers. An orange glow flickered on the walls as the fire guttered, the room still warm and soothing.

Contentment like I'd never felt before settled in my chest. I was safe, warm, and cared for. Stefan came with baggage twin to my own and that made me feel more understood than I ever had before. Somewhere deep down, I knew I'd found my person—or at least one of them. I nuzzled into his arm, letting his scent envelope me as I drifted off, finally calm after a night full of twists and turns.

"Rest now, little dove." Stefan whispered, placing a kiss on my hair as sleep beckoned to me, swiftly pulling me under.

CHAPTER NINETEEN

Riley

Soft morning light poured through the open window, gently stirring me from my slumber. I rolled over, groaning as my muscles protested the movement. My entire body was aching and tender. Most of the hurt came from the fight at B station, though some of it most definitely came from my time with Stefan last night.

Smiling, I propped myself up on one elbow, taking a moment to really look at the beautiful fae still lying in the bed beside me. His eyes were closed, the lines and angles of his face relaxed in sleep. His pink hair was mussed, far from the perfectly styled mohawk he usually sported, and bright against the pale white of my sheets. Sheets that were draped only across the bottom half of him, revealing his chiseled chest and defined abs.

Memories of what we did last night, of his mouth on my skin and his hands roaming every inch of my body, flood through me. A fresh wave of desire makes my core molten, beginning to ache with need. I'd been involved with men before; but I'd never wanted them the way I wanted Stefan. They had been a means to an end. I took what I needed and none of them complained when I didn't ask for anything more.

It was different with Stefan. I wanted more. I wanted to be around him day and night. I wanted to get to know him and to see if we could build something together. I felt drawn to him in a way I couldn't quite explain, like there was an invisible band tying us together, tugging us ever closer. I'd felt it grow stronger and stronger in the short time we'd known each other, and I had to wonder how deep my feelings could grow if we were given the time to explore them.

The smile on my face firmly set in place. I gently pulled the sheet off my body and slid my legs over the edge of the bed as quietly as possible. It was still early. I didn't need to wake Stefan yet, and I definitely needed some time to sort out my own thoughts and feelings.

Standing, I circled the bed, my bare feet padding gently across the cool wooden floor. The fire had burnt out while we slept last night; the warmth overtaken by a cooler air in the early hours of the morning. I gathered my robe from where I'd tossed it on the floor last night as I made my way to my bathroom.

Making a beeline for my closet and tossing my robe in the basket, I grabbed a fresh uniform from its hanger. I dressed quickly before moving to the vanity and inspecting myself in the mirror. After everything last night had entailed, from the attack to Stefan's revelation and our intimacy, I was almost surprised to see the same familiar face looking back at me.

I felt different. Discovering my magic, healing Amy, being with Stefan. Those things had all made me feel so far removed from the Riley that had walked into Danann last week. It was a positive change, mostly. But my eyes were still the same hazel they'd always been, my complexion still a light olive, my nose still slightly upturned in what I'd always imagined being a cute pixie look.

I sighed to myself as I braided my hair. The changes had been on the inside, down to the very core of my being. It made sense that there wasn't any sign of it on the outside. At least James would recognize me, if I ever found him.

Guilt flooded through me at the thought, leaving me unsteady and shaking. I sat on the edge of the bath to stabilize myself. Since I'd arrived here, I'd done nothing to find him. Nothing at all. Instead of looking for some clue where he might be and what happened to him, I'd spent last night having dinner with the fae General and then having sex with Stefan.

Tears welled in my eyes, and I blinked against the burn, causing them to spill over the lids and flow down my cheeks. I let them come, let them pour as I stifled my sobs.

Gods, I needed this release. Needed to let it out so I could refocus. Despite having a cry last night, I found there was more. I couldn't continue this way. If I did, I'd end up resenting everyone around me, including myself. I didn't want that. I wanted to find my brother and make a new life for ourselves. If I possess the elements, maybe he does too. Maybe we could work it out together.

The bathroom door opened suddenly, and Stefan appeared in the frame. He was still shirtless, but had taken the time to pull his pants back on. I wiped at my face, trying to hide the evidence of the pity party I'd been having for myself. I shouldn't have bothered. He could see right through me.

All it took was one glance at me and he was striding across the room, lifting me from where I was sitting on the tub and pulling me into his arms and down into his lap, right there on the bathroom floor.

"Shush, little dove. What's wrong?" He asked, his gentle voice soothing as he stroked my hair, one arm still wrapped tightly around me.

"I'm sorry," I sobbed, unable to stop the tears now I'd let them flow. "I'm a mess." His hand left my hair as he drew gentle circles on my back.

"We're all a little messed up." He said, a flicker of humor in his tone. "Join the club."

I barked a laugh, sniffling and wiping at my cheeks again as I glanced up at him. A small smile tugged at the corner of his lips; though his silver eyes were still heavy with concern.

"Tell me what's bothering you, Riley." He kissed the top of my head, his fingers still tracing patterns along my spine.

"I.. I miss James." I said, letting out a heavy breath and dropping my eyes. "He was all I had for so long, the only family I've ever known. He is the whole reason I'm here. And I've been letting him down. I'm all he had, too. And I'm letting him down. I haven't got a clue where he is. I don't even know where to start. He's gone, and he's been gone so long. What if he's dead, Stefan? What if something terrible happened to him and I've taken too long to find him? What if–"

"Hey, hey, hey. Take a deep breath, little dove. You aren't letting anyone down." He stopped tracing circles on my spine, instead placing two fingers under my chin and lifting my face back up so our eyes meet. "Riley, babe, look at how much you've already done trying to find James. You're here. You're living among the fae that, until recently, you resented with ferocity. You've traveled far from the only home you've ever known, survived both an attack by the resistance and an attack of Void creatures, all while coming to grips with your newfound elemental power."

Well, when you put it like that.

His words hit something deep inside of me, easing the guilt and stopping it from smothering me.

He was right.

I had worked hard to be here; I'd worked hard since I'd arrived in Danann.

As I sat there, cradled in Stefan's arms, feeling a little more at home in this new strange place, I vowed to keep working hard until I found my brother.

>>>>>   <<<<<

Stefan stayed a while longer, hovering over me, trying to make sure I was alright. I ushered him out with a promise to meet him for lunch and head over to physical combat together this afternoon. I needed some space to prepare myself for the day ahead, and he needed a shower and a fresh change of uniform before his morning classes.

I was so used to doing things on my own that it was going to take some time for me to be comfortable around so many people all the time. Back home I'd had James and Sarie, and then just Sarie after James left. But we both worked so much we really hadn't had much time to spend together.

I was missing Sarie too. Her fun, bubbly, no bullshit personality had always made my day brighter. I'd write to her this week. Hopefully, she'd write me back.

In an attempt to reduce the evidence of my tears this morning, I splashed my face with cool water while I contemplated what to do next.

I'd continue to attend my classes and learn as much as I could about this world I was now a part of. The more I learnt, the closer I would come to finding out where I fit in.

I just needed a break. Needed to find somewhere to start my search for James, find something to help me continue my search in the right direction.

I needed to find his apartment. Maybe have a look through his belongings and see if anything jumped out at me; if there were any clues to be found. That would be my goal now. Find where he lived. He'd said he lived in the heart of Danann. If I could find out his address, I could visit when Bee took me there this weekend.

Happy with my plan and feeling more at peace with myself now that I had a path to follow, I turned off the tap and grabbed a fluffy towel to dry my face.

That was better. My eyes were only a little red now, and I could cover that with some kohl.

I went to work on a thick smoky eye. People were starting to view me as some kind of powerful being. I didn't feel powerful; I felt like I was scrambling, making mistake after mistake that somehow helped me. Fake it till you make it, right?

When I was done lining my eyes, I headed out of the bathroom, grabbing my bag and pulling my tablet out from inside.

I frowned at the number of unread messages there.

Shit. I hadn't checked my messages since I'd left to meet Colin yesterday afternoon. There were a couple of messages from Bee and Stefan from last night, two from Amy and one from Colin from this morning.

I ignored the messages from Stefan and the others for now, choosing instead to check Bee's. She had such a gentle soul; she was probably worried sick.

Bee

> I heard what happened tonight—are you okay?

> Riley?

> Call me when you get this! Colin said you aren't hurt and are on your way back. I'm at my dad's and asked Stefan to meet you.

> Girlllll! I'm mad. You better meet me at breakfast.

Riley

> Shit, sorry Bee. I didn't check my messages. I'm not used to this technology. I'll be in the dining hall in 5 minutes

I quickly checked the rest of my messages. Stefan had been letting me know he'd be meeting me—he hadn't snuck up on me after all—and Amy had thanked me again and asked what I was doing on Saturday. I shot her a quick reply, letting her know I was likely coming into town with Bee and asking if she would be free for that coffee.

I ignored Colin's message, not even bothering to read it. I'd thought we'd been making progress before the attack last night. He'd been sweet and attentive and had seemed to come out of his shell a little. Then he'd clamped right back up and become an arrogant jerk again. Nothing he could say would tamper my anger with him today.

I liked him, felt drawn to him in the same way I felt drawn to Stefan. Like a moth to a flame. But I wasn't here for the drama. He either liked me or he didn't. He needed to work his shit out. I didn't plan to be burned.

I threw my bag over my shoulder and hurried out of our room and down the hall, offering a tight smile to a few fae lingering around as I made my way past them.

I made it to the dining hall before Bee, grabbing two cups of coffee and a jam scone to nibble on before taking a seat at our usual table. I pulled my tablet out again and checked my message from Colin.

Colin

I'm sorry.

I reread those two words over and over as my heart constricted in my chest.

An apology was the last thing I'd been expecting from him. I wasn't sure how to reply. Bee saved me the trouble, arriving at our table and plopping into the seat next to me with a huff.

I closed my tablet, shoving it back into my bag as I turned to face her. She crossed her arms over her chest, and I could almost see the steam billowing from her ears. It would almost be funny if she didn't look so serious. I swallowed the laughter bubbling in my throat and forced my features into a morose expression.

"You better have a good explanation, Riley. I've been up half the night worried sick. What could have possibly kept you so busy that you couldn't take one goddamn minute to message me back?" She said sharply, her chest heaving.

I threw my hands in the air, surrendering to her fury. "I'm sorry, I was with Stefan," I confessed, a blush staining my cheeks. I pushed the second cup of coffee toward her, trying to smooth the tension. "I forgot to check my messages."

She stared at me; her mouth pressed into a thin line. "You were with Stefan? All night?" She asked, raising an eyebrow, some of the anger in her eyes dimming as she let her shoulders drop just slightly.

"Ummm," I muttered, unsure of how best to tell her. She'd caught on to the tension between Colin and I—had even put her money on Stefan being the first to get close to me. They were such close friends, though, they'd grown up together. I wasn't sure how she'd feel knowing I'd slept with him, without having resolved anything with Colin—and still set to attend the dance with Lincoln.

"By the gods, I knew it!" She exclaimed, any lingering anger vanishing as excitement flooded her. "You slept with Stefan!" A couple of students seated nearby turned to face us as her voice echoed across the room.

"Shhh, Bee. Not so loud." I said, shrinking into my chair.

"Oh, it's nothing to be embarrassed about." She said, waving her hand dismissively. "Fae are naturally promiscuous, jumping from one bed to another until we find our mate. No one is going to judge you for it."

"Mate?" I asked, raising a brow and taking a sip of my coffee now that I knew she wasn't about to knock it out of my hands in her anger. "Like soulmates?"

"Yeah, kind of," she said, shrugging like it wasn't a big deal.

"What does it feel like? When fae find their mate?" Could this explain the pull I felt toward Stefan and Colin? Lincoln too?

"I don't know," she said, a brow raising before her expression turned serious, the excitement she'd felt after hearing I'd been with Stefan, dissipating as she remembered where this conversation started. "I'll look into it. Are you alright?"

"Honestly? I'm not sure. I'm still trying to process the attack last night." Avoiding her gaze, I stared down at my coffee. "I keep wondering what's next, and feeling like I might never find what I came here for."

Bee's small hands grasped mine, holding it between the two, the action causing my gaze to move to her face.

"You haven't had an easy start here. It seems like everything is being thrown at you, one after the other. I think…" she gnawed on her bottom lip as she searched for the right words. "I think you're being tested. And I think so far you're passing these tests with flying colors. You are incredible, Riley. A powerful, kickass woman who might just show us all a thing or two. You'll get through this and be stronger for it. And you'll find James. I'm almost sure of it." The sincerity in her words warmed something inside me, giving me a renewed sense of hope and strength to face the day ahead.

"Thanks, Bee." I said, my voice barely above a whisper as I fought to contain the tears threatening to fall. She smiled at me softly and nodded, dropping my hands and standing quickly.

"Come on. Dad teaches our morning class. He'll never for-give me if we're late."

Chapter Twenty

Riley

According to my timetable, that morning's class was about Faerie, Earth, and the Crossing. I'd learnt a lot about why the fae segregated themselves from the human communities, but I still had many questions about what was and wasn't being done to help them. They were suffering, scrounging for the bare necessities, while the fae lived in relative comfort. Surely there was more they—we—could do to help.

Learning that Bee's father was the Professor had made me even more excited to get to class this morning. I'd only met him briefly, but he seemed like the kind of teacher who'd be willing to give me the answers I sought without judgment or vague responses.

We reached the classroom door just as Reardon was bustling out of it. He seemed flustered and stressed, almost walking right into us in his rush to leave. His hair was messy, standing up in odd directions, and his bag was overflowing with papers. All of it combined gave him a frantic look.

"Hey dad, where are you going? Isn't class about to start?" Bee asked, concern furrowing her brow.

"Oh girls, I'm glad I caught you." He said a little breathlessly. "I've canceled class today. I'm needed over at B Station. They've caught one of the creatures that attacked last night. It had been injured and hid inside the tower. They have it alive, too weak to fight against the vines used to move it. I'm heading over now to study it."

"Is that safe?" Bee asked her father, reaching out and swiping a hand over his head to flatten his hair in a gentle, affectionate gesture.

"I'll be fine, darling." He said reassuringly, the corner of his mouth quirking in the corner as he leant down to kiss her on the top of her head before turning to me with a small smile. I guess I'd have to wait to pepper him with questions. "Professor Darmon would like to see you, Riley. Can you head down to his office?"

"Oh, of course." I said, my stomach sinking as I wondered why he wanted to see me. Had something else happened? Was it about what I'd done last night?

"I'll come with you." Bee offered, glancing at me from the corner of her eye, somehow sensing my unease. "I'll call you later, dad."

Reardon waved as he bustled off down the hall, leaving Bee and I to make our way to the Professor Darmon's office.

"What do you think he wants with me?" I asked Bee, fiddling with my locket as we walked along.

"I'm not sure." She answered honestly, her face set in concern. "Maybe it's about the attack last night? No one has checked in with you yet, have they?"

"No, you're probably right." We arrived outside the office, and I raised my hand, knocking softly.

"Come in." Professor Darmon called.

Pushing open the door, Bee and I stepped inside. Professor Darmon was sitting behind his desk, pouring over some papers and looking every bit as frazzled as Reardon had. Everyone seemed rattled this morning. Not that I could blame them, I was too. Word of last night's attack must have reached the entire academy by now. I wasn't sure what repercussions the attack might hold for the people within Danann, but it was clearly unexpected news. Unease settled in my stomach at the thought.

I took a seat, Bee plopping down into the twin chair next to me. We sat in silence for a long minute, while the Professor finished reading the document laid out in front of him.

"Sorry, girls. Thanks for waiting." He said, straightening his papers and placing them to the side. "I was just finishing the report from General Brand about last night's attack at B Station. I understand you were present, Riley?" He asked, his steely gray eyes settling on me.

My fingers found my locket, fiddling with it again, tracing the intricate engraving on the front as butterflies danced in my stomach and I nodded. Why had the attack occurred at the exact time I was there? "Yes, I was. I was with Co—General Brand."

He nodded at me thoughtfully, standing from his chair and beginning to pace back and forth behind his desk. There was a nervous energy emanating off him, setting my own nerves on edge. As if they weren't frayed enough.

After a few minutes of awkward silence, Bee cut in. "Why did you summon Riley here, Professor?" She asked, tilting her head to the side as she watched him pace curiously.

He paused, clicking his tongue and turning to face us.

"I am breaking protocol by speaking to both of you, however I am concerned for your safety, Riley, and would be remiss not to make you aware of the potential threat." He took a heavy breath and sat back down in his chair.

I risked a glance at Bee, raising a brow in question. She shrugged, clearly not knowing any more than I did. Was this about the Resistance? Could they have something to do with a void creature attack?

"I don't believe, and neither does General Brand, that last night's attack was the random act of Void creatures acting alone." He looked between the two of us, his expression drawn and serious. "We know there's a threat against you, Riley. And that the Resistance knows of your existence and is interested in having you join their ranks. I would hope you do not consider that an option, but that is not what I called you here to discuss."

A shiver ran down my spine at the mention of the Resistance. They had attacked us and killed one of the fae guards transporting me to Danann. I had never, and would never, consider joining them. They were ruthless, soulless, their agenda unclear.

"The General and I believe there may be a group within our own community hoping to get rid of you, Riley. The Elders have been quite vocal about their desire for you to be sent back to Sommers. They didn't want you here to begin with, despite King Ronan giving his approval." He looked at me apologetically. "People tend to fear what they don't understand. It is often easier to ignore these things, will them away, than to take the time to understand them. We are facing many more challenges here on Earth than we ever expected, and there is a fear that you will grow to be one of them. My personal belief is that you will be our salvation. One way or another, I believe you will help us save these lands, these people, and help our own kind return home."

His steely gray eyes captured my own, and I quickly swallowed the lump that formed in my throat at his words. His expectations of me were great, and the fact there may be fae wanting me out of here... it was a lot to take in. The power in my chest thrummed, reassuring me it was there, that maybe I could protect myself. That was the problem, though, wasn't it?

"I..." I didn't know how to respond to his declaration, to the idea that there were fae angry enough about my presence that they might order an attack on me. Was that even possible? "Do you think someone targeted B station while I was there?"

I asked. "That they had enough control over the void creatures to do that?"

The Professor nodded as he stood again, clasping his hands behind his back and taking up the same path he'd been pacing earlier.

"Yes. That is exactly what I believe. I need you to be careful until we figure out what it is we are up against and how best to protect you from it. I would ask that you do not wander around alone, particularly outside the grounds of the Academy, and that you do not leave Danann at all—even with the General, it is too dangerous and you have very little training. You did brilliantly last night. You proved that you have a natural affinity for wielding your elements and more. Some of that is likely luck, and we do not want to risk that luck running out."

"I can do that," I replied, straightening in my chair as I tried to hide the tendrils of fear taking hold of me.

As much as I wanted to explore Danann, I didn't really need to leave the academy grounds. And I really hadn't been alone very much since I'd arrived here. It shouldn't be hard to make sure I was always with Bee or Stefan. I just hoped I didn't become a burden on any of them.

"I'll help, too." Bee said, twisting slightly in her chair to face me, her green eyes dancing with some untold emotion. "You are meant to be here, Riley. I feel it deep in my soul. We need you. Dad believes it too."

Warmth spread through me at her words. Perhaps there was a faction of the fae that didn't want me here, but those that did made me feel more at home than I ever had before.

⟫⟫⟫ ⟪⟪⟪

After meeting with Professor Darmon, Bee and I spent the morning in the library working on the assignment Professor Burns had set.

Wandering through the shelves, I tried to find the row dedicated to the gods and goddesses the librarian had directed me to. Turning at the end of the current row, I found myself in a small study area, tucked into the corner.

Hunched over the small table, piles of books surrounding him, sat Prince Lincoln. Ignoring the tug in my chest urging me toward him, I leant on the shelf beside me and watched him for a moment instead.

Engrossed in the book spread out before him, he hadn't noticed me enter his space. I watched as he turned the page, chewing on the end of his pen, before jotting down a few notes. The braided crown he'd had the day we'd met was gone, replaced by four individual braids pulling his hair away from his face and hanging down his back.

We'd barely had a full conversation, and yet the draw I felt toward him matched what I felt toward Stefan. It made no sense to me.

"Riley," he breathed, without lifting his head. "I thought I felt you coming. Come sit with me, Tyas."

"Tyas?" I asked, as I moved toward the empty chair beside him. The desk was littered with notes, crumpled paper and pens.

"It means 'my heart'. I think it suits you." He lifted his eyes from his book, blinking slowly and capturing mine as I sat beside him. Those words should terrify me, instead I found them intriguing. There was something between us. Maybe he knew what it was?

"Can you explain that to me? I'm not denying there is something here, but I don't understand the pull I feel toward you." Not any more than I understood the pull I felt toward Stefan or Colin.

His smile was slow and lazy, his eyes lingering on my lips for a moment before he spoke.

"We are a long way from home," he began. "So, my theory may be wrong. We don't know how being on this plane affects some of the things we took for granted back on our own lands. Did you know that fae have mates?"

I nodded. "Bee mentioned it, briefly."

"From what I've read," he gestures towards the pile of books before him. "If one takes the time to look, it's not difficult to find your mate. The pull is described as undeniable. You are drawn to your mate from the moment you lay eyes on them, like something unseen binds you to them. It's said that some fae have found their mate simply by following that pull in their chest before they've ever even met their other half."

Lincoln set down his pen, scooting his own chair closer and resting a hand on my knee. The tips of his fingers had ink smudged on them from the studying and notes he'd been taking. Notes about mates. He'd been looking into what that meant. "I think you might be my mate, Riley, and therefore my heart, my Tyas."

I sucked in a breath, shocked at the directness of his admission.

"You felt it too, didn't you?"

I nodded, unable to deny it. I had felt it. But... I hadn't only felt that pull toward Lincoln. Could the fae have more than one mate?

"Yes. But I've felt the same pull toward others." Was that okay to say? He was being direct with me. It felt as though I should be the same with him.

His midnight eyes sparkled as he nodded, turning back to the book in front of him and tapping the page with his finger. "This book says there is a chance we can have more than one mate, that it often occurs among the more powerful of our kind. That seems to fit, given the power you hold. I don't expect anything of you, Riley. I know your start here has been anything but smooth and easy. But I would like to explore this connection, get to know you."

"I'd like that, too." I said, rising from my chair, his hand sliding off of my knee as I went. The fight, discovering my healing powers, this admission. There was so much I needed to process. I would like to get to know Lincoln, but I needed to process first. "Can you point me to the gods and goddesses' shelves?" Judging by the surrounding piles of books, he knew his way around the library.

"Of course."

After perusing the shelves Lincoln had shown me to, I selected a brown leather-bound book, small enough to fit in my pocket, that I'd found tucked into the back corner behind some of the larger texts. Finding my way back to the lounge area, I curled up in an armchair in front of the fire, the same one Stefan had wrenched me out of and given me the fright of my life only a few short days ago, and had spent the last half an hour reading

It was untitled, with intricate golden patterns sewn into the corners. Each corner was different, the swirls and lines almost seeming alive with the way they glittered in the firelight thrown from the hearth. I traced my fingers over the delicate pattern before opening the book to find a tidy cursive script; the words reading more like a diary than an informative history book.

I flicked through the pages, stopping when I came across a hand painted picture of one of the goddesses. The detail was phenomenal. So much so that I could almost see the sun shining off of her long golden locks, her green eyes bright, shining with some untold emotion. I couldn't put my finger on it, but there was something familiar about her, the set of her mouth, the green of her eyes. Like I'd seen them somewhere before.

My brow furrowed as I tried to remember where. I'd spent my whole life in Sommers. I hadn't seen many fae outside of the Ascension ceremonies until recently. I'd certainly never met one of their Goddesses. They were back in Faerie, right?

A soft tap on my shoulder startled me, tearing me away from the page and causing me to twist around, sitting up straighter in my seat as I assessed the room for threats. I glanced up quickly, my posture relaxing as soon as I spotted Stefan standing before me, a wide grin lighting up his face and laughter dancing in his eyes. I was still on edge from the attack last night, and from my meeting with Professor Darmon this morning, but I grinned back at him, welcoming his happy, easy company.

"Ready for lunch?" He asked, holding out a hand. I took it, letting him pull me to my feet.

"I'm famished, actually." I stuffed the journal into my book bag along with the other books I'd checked out to complete my paper and glanced around for Bee. "I feel like I could eat a horse. Like there's an empty pit where my stomach..." Realization struck me then. "I'm not hungry, am I?"

Stefan smiled and hooked a finger under my chin, lifting my face to his. "No, you're not hungry. Your magic might still be replenishing. You must have used an incredible amount of power last night." He leant forward and pressed his lips gently to mine.

Pushing up on my toes, I wrapped my arms around his neck and pressed my body against his. He pushed a hand through my hair while running his tongue across my bottom lip, a request for me to open.

Moaning softly, I parted my lips and deepened the kiss. A desperate heat built in my core as our bodies pressed together and our tongues danced. I wanted to be closer, needed to feel him wrapped around me again.

"Oh my gods, get a room—wait, don't, we share a room." Bee's laugh tinkled through the library as she approached, her eyes glittering with amusement. "Let's go get lunch before you eat each other." She threw a wink at me before grabbing her bag and striding towards the exit.

"Bee!" I exclaimed as I pulled away from Stefan, reluctantly untangling myself from him. A pang of relief flitted through my chest, relief that it had been Bee to call us out, and not Lincoln. I'd been clear I was interested in others as well as him... but still.

She laughed again before pushing through the large doors and heading toward the dining hall. I pouted at Stefan.

"Best you save your energy for class, anyway. First years always take a beating in physical combat, for the first few months at least." I scowled at the grin on his face before following Bee.

I'd take any beating I had to, as long as it helped lead me to James.

CHAPTER TWENTY-ONE

Riley

I rubbed my neck, trying to stretch out the aching muscles as Bee and I made our way to the training fields. The morning was fresh, a cool chill in the air and a gentle mist hanging over the academy grounds. Stefan had not been kidding about first years taking a beating in physical combat yesterday. I'd been knocked on my ass more times than I could count, and now every muscle in my body ached.

"By the gods, I could barely lift my spoon this morning. How am I going to lift any of these weapons?" Bee moaned as she rubbed at her arms. I snorted a laugh as we joined the rest of the first years huddling together to one side of the combat field.

I spotted Lincoln on the other side of the group, talking to the same guys he'd been seated with during Faerie Races. He hadn't been in Physical Combat yesterday, and despite my blossoming relationship with Stefan, I'd wondered where he was, disappointed not to see him after our conversation yesterday.

I hadn't been able to explain the pull I felt to him and to Stefan and Colin, too, until yesterday. Not that I was sure we were mates. But it was like there was something deep inside me that recognized all of them and desperately wanted to be closer to them. Undeniable. Just like Lincoln had said.

I watched him as he chatted with his friends. He'd shaved since I last saw him, his beard more of a soft shadow across his powerful jaw. His honey blonde hair was braided across the top of his head like a crown again, before splitting into dual braids falling down his back, reminding me he was a prince. Not just here, but in Faerie.

He turned, catching me watching him and offering a warm smile in my direction, his navy eyes brightening before he made his way over to where Bee and I stood. Bee winked at me, offered Lincoln a wave and a smile, and moved away to chat with a few other classmates.

"Good morning, Riley." He said, taking my hand and planting a gentle kiss upon it, catching me completely off guard. Butterflies fluttered in my stomach as his eyes locked with mine, the depth of them capturing me the same way they did the last time we were this close. "How are you feeling? Father told me about the attack and how you saved Amy. I apologize for not knowing earlier, I was... too engrossed in my studies. It sounds like you performed a miracle."

"Oh, I wouldn't go that far," I murmured, embarrassment causing my cheeks to flush. "It was a fluke, really; I don't have very much control over my elements yet." I shrugged, hoping he'd catch the hint and let the subject drop.

Did everyone know about the attack and what I'd done? I wasn't sure how to feel about that. I didn't know how I did it… or if I could do it again. What if someone wanted me to replicate it? I wasn't sure I'd be able to.

He studied me for a minute, his eyes searching mine, looking for something I wasn't sure he'd be able to find. "I am intrigued by you, Riley," he said finally, his voice low and husky, the sound of it causing desire to course through me, my core tightening in response. *Down girl.*

"Good morning class. I am Florian Darkov; you can call me Flo." Lincoln dropped the hand he was still holding, but didn't let go, twisting and standing beside me to face our new Professor. Flo was a tall, willowy woman, with skin as pale as moonlight and jet-black hair set in a long braid down her back. She was dressed in a tight black leather outfit—fighting leathers, I realized—that only highlighted the paleness of her skin further.

She set down a large, heavy looking duffel bag before her, leaning down to unzip it before straightening and continuing. "This class introduces you to some of the basic weaponry used by our kind. Most of them are ordinary, some are enchanted, and others are blessed. Our elements can only do so much; our reserves only hold so much power. If you ever run empty amid battle, you will want a skill to fall back on. There is physical combat, and there are weapons."

She waved her hands in front of her, and one by one different weapons rose from the bag into the air, floating on the wind before dropping to the grass in a line before us all.

"Wow," I muttered under my breath, marveling at her control. I really needed more practice using the power within me. I could feel it stirring now, the well inside of me feeling replenished and full.

"Today we'll determine whether you have a natural affinity for a particular type of weapon, or a connection to one that is enchanted or blessed. We will not begin training with any of them. Today is all about *connection*. Hold them, weigh them in your hands, close your eyes and *feel* them. If we're lucky, maybe a few of you will find a bond. Ah, here is the rest. Begin, I'll come to speak with each of you shortly." She waved to two men carrying a large crate, directing them on where to place it down and immediately unpacking it.

I dropped Lincoln's hand and took a few steps forward, my eyes running over the long line of weapons lying before me. I felt him following me as I examined the pieces laid out before us.

There were daggers, swords, throwing knives—even brass knuckles. I'd never seen anything like this before. The bow and arrows the Resistance had attacked us with were the most violent weapon I'd been witness to.

"I know my way around a greenhouse. I'm comfortable with a pair of pruning scissors. But I've never even held anything like this," I murmured, more to myself than anything.

"That's what this class is for. Unfortunately, learning to fight and defend ourselves has become a necessity. Most of the class has no experience, just like you." I glanced at Lincoln as he spoke, spotting a darkness crossing his expression.

"What about you? Have you been taught to defend yourself as Prince, or do you have guards for that?" I quickly scanned the field, noticing no guards were in sight. If he had any, I had yet to see them following him at all. None in class and none in the library.

He chuckled darkly, "My father believes a good king shouldn't rely on guards for protection. I've been training to defend myself and my people my entire life. I particularly favor a trident. Come, I'll show you."

He held his hand out again, and I took it, craving the comfort his touch provided. I swallowed against the guilt I felt at that. I liked Stefan. I liked him a lot. But we hadn't defined things. It was way too soon for that. I resolved to tell Stefan I'd agreed to go to the dance this weekend with Lincoln and see how he felt. We're adults, right? We could have an adult conversation about this.

We walked along the line of weaponry, passing Bee, who was crouched in the grass, examining a pair of throwing knives with large rubies set in the silver hilt.

"These feel right," she said, grinning up at us as she weighed them in her hands.

"You'll look badass with those, Bee, small but mighty." I winked as Lincoln led me past her, continuing across the field to where Professor Flo had finished laying out the crate of larger weapons. "What did she mean when she said we'd be lucky if some of us bonded?" I asked, tipping my head toward Professor Flo.

"Some weapons are blessed. They hold their own power and have some level of sentience. If your power matches the weapons, if they connect, the weapon may choose to share their power with yours. It's said to be handy in battle, though I don't have any firsthand experience with that."

"Huh," We walked in silence for a moment while I pondered that. There was more variety to the magic fae had access to than I'd ever understood before. I wasn't sure I understood now, but I wanted to.

"Why do you like a trident?" I asked as we reached the weapons. "I mean, I thought they were just accessories for mermaids—and mermaids aren't real. I never considered that they'd be a useful weapon."

Lincoln laughed, the sound sending a wave of warmth through my body, gathering in my belly. Man, this guy was gorgeous. He flicked one of his golden braids over his shoulder as he turned to face me.

"Mermaids are real, Tyas. There are many of them back home in Faerie. They aren't what your human fairytales describe. Less human, more animal, and much more vicious. They definitely don't have tridents as accessories." Butterflies swarmed my stomach at his casual use of the nickname he'd given me.

"Huh. Well then, I guess dragons are real then? What about genies? Talking wardrobes? What isn't actually real?"

He snorted. "Talking wardrobes? That might be going a bit far. You won't find any animated furniture in Faerie. Djinns—if that's what you mean by genies—exist but are rare and keep to themselves. Dragons live mostly in the fire lands." I stared at him, the revelation that dragons exist—freaking dragons, man—causing my brain to short circuit.

He stepped closer to me, reaching forward and cupping my chin before whispering softly, "I forgot how much you have yet to learn about us, about your heritage. It's refreshing. I hope that one day you can see Faerie. That we can do the work we came here for and return home. I think you'll like it there." He rubbed his thumb over my bottom lip, and I found myself getting lost in his eyes.

I wanted to kiss him. To press my body against his and see how well we fit together. I swallowed hard, tearing my gaze away from his and turning to look at the group of tridents leaning against the crate. We were in a freaking class. I needed to pull myself together. Stop letting these Fae men make me feel things I wasn't sure I wanted to feel.

"Back to the tridents." I took a small step back from him, pretending not to notice the way his brow furrowed. My feelings for him scared me. They were too strong, too quickly. "If they aren't just pretty sticks to wave at enemies, what do they do?"

He snorted again, the tension in his body fading as he turned and picked one up, weighing it in his hands. "They make a decent club. They're sharp and can impale an enemy with one shift jab. But most importantly they act as conduits for our magic in both directions. They help refresh our reserves at a faster rate and can concentrate the power we push into it into a much stronger attack."

He passed the trident to me, and I took it with both hands. It was lighter than I expected, coated in a smooth layer of silver. Each of the forks had three small sapphires inserted into the metal. I tested it, swishing it through the air in front of me before holding it above my head and examining the gems more closely. The bright blue almost seems to be moving, swirling inside of itself. I could almost hear water softly lapping against a distant shore.

"This trident comes from the water lands in Faerie. It is imbued with the magic of the Kai family–Lincoln's family. It usually calls to those with a strong reserve of water magic. Can you hear its call, dear?" I looked away from the trident to find Professor Flo standing next to Lincoln.

"I can hear something," I said, turning back to examine the weapon again. "I don't think it's calling to me, though. It doesn't feel... right."

"Interesting. You possess all the elements, don't you? Would you say any of them are stronger than the others?" She asked, studying me closely.

I passed the trident back to Lincoln, who grasped it and spun it through his hands with ease, winking at me. "I'll go see how Bee is getting on with those throwing knives. Join us when you find your weapon."

I nodded at him and turned back to Flo. "If I had to pick one element, I guess I would say I'm strongest with earth. I've always had an affinity for growing things, crops, flowers, anything."

"Interesting," she said, more to herself than me. Turning away, she moves to the other end of the crate, leaning inside of it and rummaging around. "Let me see. Let me see." Her voice was muffled as she hung over the side of the crate, and I moved forward, concerned that she'd topple in completely.

She straightened suddenly, tendrils of her jet-black hair gently whipping around her face as a light breeze drifted across the combat field. I felt my magic stir, the wind wakening my air element. I hadn't had much of a chance to play with air, to test my control, only really having used it consciously at B station the other night.

I smothered the urge to let my wind free, saving it for my lesson with Stefan tomorrow. We could get to know each other then, I said to my power, to myself.

I turned my attention back to Professor Flo, to the weapon she held in her hand. It could only be described as a beautiful sword. Its hilt was a carved dragon's head with two emeralds where its eyes would be. It looked freshly polished, the metal shining brightly in the morning sun.

"Does it call to you, dear?" She asked, tilting her head to the side curiously, like she could sense the pull I was feeling and was intrigued by the fact.

It *was* calling to me. A tug in my chest pulled me toward the sword. Urging me to take it from Professor Florian and feel the weight of it in my own hands. The longing to hold it, to claim it as my own, grew stronger as my eyes darted to its beautiful carved hilt and back to the Professor.

"It does," I admitted quietly, wringing my hands together to keep myself from snatching it from her.

"Here, try it. Grasp it tightly." She handed it to me, offering the hilt and my eyes zeroed in on the green jewels, the sunlight catching them and making them glitter, the way the light danced on the gem inviting me in.

I reached for it, time seeming to slow, the sound of my classmates trying out their own weapons dulling. I could vaguely hear a commotion, someone shouting, but my focus stayed completely on the sword before me. I'd never felt a pull like this before. Such a powerful urge to claim this possession before me.

Strong hands gripped my shoulders at the same time mine closed around the dragon head hilt, a power like no other coursing through my body. Wave after wave of pure energy engulfed me as I gripped the sword, not daring to let go. The energy, the raw power, was some kind of test. One I did not intend to fail. Though I had no idea why.

"The weak will falter, only the strong can hold me." A voice, feminine but not entirely of this earth, hissed in my mind. "Which one are you?" I realized that the sword itself was testing me, ensuring I was worthy of it and the power it held. I couldn't respond, couldn't think past the desperate desire to master the sword held in my hands.

My own magic rose to greet it like they were old friends. The two energies pushed and pulled against one another as the threads of them wove together in my mind and soul.

Goosebumps rose on my skin as I stood frozen to the spot; my body simply a vessel for the joining of these two powers. I could hear someone calling my name, the sound muffled, like the speaker was underwater. It was a familiar voice, one that nearly pulled my attention away from the power roiling inside of me.

My body shook and I couldn't tell if those hands gripping me were trying to shake me out of the reverie I was trapped in or if it was internal, a reaction to what was occurring within my very soul.

"The latter, it seems. You are familiar, girl. Like we've met before. Are you the blessed one? I think you are."

My ears rang as the hissing voice faded away. The two energies inside me continued to knit themselves together as black clouded the edges of my vision. Just a little longer. I just had to hold on a little longer. I didn't know how I knew that, but it felt like the truth.

My power finished joining with that of the swords in one last burst of energy that flooded through me from the top of my head to the tips of my toes. The hands gripping my shoulders released suddenly, people around me shouting as my hearing and vision cleared.

I blinked once.

Twice.

My jaw dropped as I glanced around, the class suddenly falling quiet.

I was still standing in the combat field, but instead of an expanse of flat grass I had been standing on before, the entire field was covered in wildflowers as tall as my waist, and Lincoln...

Lincoln was unconscious on the ground, surrounded by the freshly grown flowers.

CHAPTER TWENTY-TWO

Riley

"Lincoln!" I shouted, running to where he was lying sprawled in the grass, Professor Florian already kneeling beside him. I fell to my knees on his other side and placed my hands on the hard muscles of his chest as I gripped his shirt and shook him a little.

"Lincoln, I'm so sorry. I didn't mean to hurt you." I sobbed.

I did this. My *magic* did this; and the magic in that sword. That god's damned sword that said it knew me. Which was not possible. I'd never held a weapon like it before.

I leant over him, placing my forehead against his as panic coursed through my veins, my heart beating hard in my chest. This was what I'd been afraid of. Hurting with my newfound power instead of helping. "Please wake up."

"He will." Professor Flo said gently. "He's just unconscious. He hit his head when he... fell." I glanced up at her to find she was watching me, caution shining in her eyes. "I think if you gather yourself and focus, this could be a learning opportunity for you. I hear you possess healing power beyond anything known to Fae. Use it."

"I don't know how to use it. What if I hurt him more? Look what I've just done!" My voice was shrill, unfamiliar, even to me.

"You won't hurt him. I believe if your intention is clear, you will do just fine." She lowered her voice to just above a whisper, just loud enough for me to hear. "You have great power, Riley. You must learn to harness it sooner rather than later. Before it consumes you. This—" she said, gesturing to the wildflowers surrounding us. "This was the sword. We'll talk more about that later. Calm your mind. Try to heal him."

I swallowed hard, nodding as anxiety pooled in the pit of my stomach. She wasn't wrong. I needed to bridle my power. To take back control. That knowledge calmed me, and I took a deep breath, holding it for a moment before breathing it out, just like Colin had taught me. I repeated it a few times until my hands stopped shaking and I felt a little steadier.

I pressed my hands flat on Lincoln's chest and closed my eyes. The well of power in my chest felt full and eager to be released. But I didn't know how to access it, how to shape it into a form that would undo what I'd done to Lincoln.

"I... Nothing is happening. What do I do?" My voice shook again as I fought to stay calm, knowing there'd be no chance I could do this if I didn't keep my emotions in check.

"Visualize it. Follow the magic's path from where it lives in you, down to your hands. Feel its warmth and set your intention."

I did as she said, keeping my eyes tightly closed as I concentrated, focusing on the well in my chest. Picturing my power as a white light—that's what Colin had said he saw when I healed Amy—I imagined it flowing freely through me, splitting in two in my chest and flowing down my arms, through to each of my fingertips.

Those same fingers began to tingle and heat, and I opened my eyes to find my hands encased in white light.

"That's it. Now push it in to him. Tell it to find where he's hurt and heal him." Professor Flo's voice was eager, excited.

Closing my eyes again, I imagined just that. I pictured my power sinking into his chest and sweeping through his body, looking for anything amiss. My arms shook with the strain, but there... There it was. He was hurt. It was only minor—perhaps a concussion. He wouldn't die and would wake soon anyway, but I focused my energy on healing it now. My power latched on to the part of him that was injured, surrounding it and knitting it back together.

I took a shuddering breath as I pulled my power back within myself, where I felt it settle in my chest. Keeping my eyes closed, I tried to calm my racing heart. Did it work? Did I do it?

"Give him a minute." I opened my eyes, glancing at Professor Flo, finding her studying me intently.

Lincoln stirred beneath my hands—still resting on his chest—and my eyes darted back to him just as his navy-blue eyes fluttered open, glassy at first before focusing on me.

Quicker than any man should be able to move, he sat up and pulled me into his lap, grasping my face in his hands.

"Are you okay?" He whispered, his face so close to mine that our breath mingled. The proximity of his body to mine sent a flush of warmth through me, even though we had an audience.

Professor Flo cleared her throat, and I felt her move away. "Shows over, class dismissed." She said, clapping her hands. The sound of students muttering among themselves became more distant as she ushered them away.

"I'm fine." I breathed, barely able to concentrate as I stared at his mouth, his plump lips calling to me. I wanted him to kiss me so badly it almost hurt. The relief I felt knowing he was okay, that I didn't hurt him too badly, made me want to hold on to him and not let go. In reality, I barely knew him, though my heart felt differently. I was always meant to find him. "I didn't mean to hurt you, the sword... I'm sorry."

"Shhh, I'm alright. You healed me. I felt it." he whispered, and I licked my lips, desire drying my mouth out as I tried to remember how to breathe. His blue eyes settled on my mouth, watching the movement, a hungry groan rumbling from his chest before he slammed his lips against mine.

He tasted like a warm spring day, and I lost all ability to think as I wrapped my arms around his neck, leaning into him and kissing him back.

Our tongues danced together, and I moaned softly, my nipples hardening with desire as his hands released my face, skimming down my shoulders and back.

"Come on, guys. I'm right here." Bee's voice startled me, and I pulled away from Lincoln, breaking our kiss.

"Sorry, Bee." Lincoln said in a tone that said he wasn't, not even a little bit.

I grinned at her sheepishly. "Sorry, Bee." I echoed, glancing around to see most of the class heading back to the Academy. Professor Florian was busy packing her weapons back into crates.

I couldn't help but stare at the wildflowers filling the field around us. I didn't know how, but I'd done that. The *sword* and I had. But how? I didn't understand how a weapon, an inanimate object could have affected me—controlled me how it did.

Now that I knew Lincoln was okay, I needed to know what the fuck just happened. Lincoln stood, offering me his hand, and I took it, letting him pull me to my feet before straightening my skirt and marching over to where Professor Flo was packing up the crate.

"You knew something was going to happen when I held that sword." A statement, not a question.

She turned slowly; her face wary as she glanced between me, Bee and Lincoln standing just behind me. "I suspected you'd bond with it, yes." She admitted, wiping her hands on her leather pants.

Some of my classmates had bonded with weapons throughout the class today. Bee had bonded with the throwing knives, but no one else had reacted the same way I had. No one else had caused a tidy, well-maintained field bloom with knee high wildflowers. I wasn't sure I wanted to know why, but I asked anyway.

"Why did my bonding cause this?" I gestured to the field. "No one else's did."

"The sword is blessed by the gods and goddesses. It has rejected all that have held it since our arrival on Earth, long before that too. It sucks the power from all those that try and leaves them drained as punishment for thinking they may be worthy."

She twisted back to the crate, pulling the lid across to close it again before pulling herself up to sit on the top of it.

"I don't think you're entirely Fae, Riley."

I snorted. "Tell me something I don't know. I think we can all agree I'm some kind of mystery freak."

"You aren't a freak. You are powerful and unknown, but not a freak. Faerie is a vast land; we cannot claim to know of all the power that lives there."

"You think Riley is from Faerie?" Lincoln asked, stepping forward to stand beside me.

Professor Flo frowned at him before shrugging and jumping down from the crate. "I don't know. But she certainly isn't from here. Not with power as potent as that. I won't pretend to have the answers you're looking for, Riley, but I would like to help you find them. I plan to do some research, to see if I can find anything that will point us in the right direction. Is that alright with you?"

I was a little taken aback by the fact that she was asking for my permission. "Uh, I guess. Thank you."

She clapped her hands together. "Fantastic. I will let you know what I find. Now that's settled, I better be getting ready for the next class. Off you go, dear. Have some lunch—outside—you used a lot of power, you'll need to replenish it."

She waved us away and the three of us began our trek across the field and back to the Academy building. Lincoln took my hand as we walked but remained silent, each of us mulling over the events of the morning. The weight in my chest, the worry over what I was and where I came from eased a little at his touch, at having him so near.

It didn't seem to matter what I did or how hard I tried, my power kept revealing more and more of itself. I couldn't help but wonder, and fear, what might be next.

CHAPTER TWENTY-THREE

Riley

I could feel the well inside me filling slowly as I lounged in the sun before the small lake in front of the academy building. Surprisingly, given the size of the field and the sheer number of wildflowers I'd grown, my power reserves weren't that low. I'd definitely felt more drained during my time here. Most of the power must have come from the sword.

Lincoln had to return to the royal mansion in the heart of Danann and Bee had her work duties to attend to, so I was on my own. A restless energy buzzed through me as I soaked up the warmth of the afternoon sun. With a few hours to go before I was due to meet Stefan for air tutoring, and no inclination to spend the afternoon inside, I needed something to do. Some way to distract myself from the constant worry I'd been subjecting myself to.

I pushed up from the ground and pulled the picnic mat Bee had grabbed from the dining hall. I stuffed it into my bag and walked towards the academy gates. I knew I shouldn't be wandering around alone—I'd promised Professor Darmon I wouldn't, and I'd reassured Bee I'd head up to our room to study until she returned—but I wanted to see Annie.

I'd felt a connection to the mare from the second I met her back home in Sommers. She'd been at B station during the attack by those Void creatures. I'd ridden her there and then left her after I stormed off and rode the carriage back to the academy. I needed to see her with my own eyes and make sure that she was alright.

I moved into the trees and followed the path through them to the gate, which swung open at my approach, sensing my magical signature. I hadn't believed it when we first arrived. I'd been positive there wasn't a trace of Fae in me. I'm something though. Something powerful. I've proven that beyond a shadow of a doubt.

Like it could sense me thinking about it, I felt my magic swell inside me, pushing against my control. I took a deep breath, fighting for the ability to push it back down as I exit the academy grounds and continue along the path through the large expanse of grass and flowers, to the stables across the way.

I was able to temper the surge of power. I could still feel it within me, roiling and unchecked, completely regenerated from my use of it this morning. *Later.* I thought to myself. I would be meeting with Stefan later to learn how to wield air. I could burn off some of this excess energy then.

A young man, maybe a few years older than myself, was leading a couple of mares around the training ring as I approached. I stopped to watch them for a moment, leaning against the round white fence. I'd spent my entire life so far without having met any of these creatures. They were majestic, strong, and proud. Elegant in the way they trotted circles around the stable hand.

The sun was beating down on me and I turned my face to it, letting the rays warm my skin as a gentle breeze brushed loose strands of hair across my face. I breathed in slowly, deeply. It was quiet here, peaceful. The academy grounds were nice—paradise compared to Sommers—but there were always plenty of Fae crowding around.

"Can I help you, miss?" My eyes snapped open to find the stable hand passing by me, leading the two mares to the gate between the ring and the stables.

He looked like he might be around the same age as James. His white collared shirt clung to his thick stocky muscle and tucked into a pair of tan cargo pants. His dark hair shaved short and close to his head.

"You here to see Annie?" He asked in a deep voice before I'd even opened my mouth to respond. "I'm about to bring her out. Wait here."

"What are you? Some kind of mind reader?" He laughed but didn't stop; didn't wait for an answer. He disappeared into the stables, and I shrugged. "Guess I'll wait here." I murmured to myself.

I leant against the fence again, eyes locked on the stables, waiting for the stable hand to bring Annie out. It was only a few minutes before he was moving through the doors with her lead rope in hand.

She whinnied when she saw me waiting and I grinned, pushing off of the fence and jogging over to her slowly. I rubbed the white strip on her nose softly when I reached her.

"Hi girl," something in my chest loosened, like it had been coiled tight with worry and could now relax. "Sorry I left you behind the other night. That grumpy general rubbed me the wrong way, and I had to get out of there."

She snorted, air puffing out of her nostrils and tickling the skin of my arm. It was an amused sound, and I marveled at her intelligence. There was something about this horse.

"Grumpy General," the stable hand chortled. "You've got that right."

He held out his hand to me and I took it, shaking it as I peered around Annie to look at him.

"How'd you know I was here for her?" I asked, letting his hand drop and stroking Annie again.

Maybe he was a mind reader. Gods, I mean dragons exist in Faerie. And apparently seers had been meant to cross before things went sideways for the Fae. They see the future, right? The idea that someone might be able to read minds didn't seem as farfetched as it once had.

"I saw you here with the General the other day and you seemed... attached to her. Affectionate." He frowned a little, as if considering something. "Anyway, I recognized you and since the General isn't hanging around today, I took a guess. Turns out it was spot on. I'm Garner."

"Riley." I said, offering him a smile. "I felt a connection with her the moment we met. I'm still trying to work out what it means."

What did it mean? Was it a part of my connection to the Earth element, or something else entirely? A hint about my heritage, maybe? I sighed.

Why was where I came from such a mystery? Somehow, I'd ended up in a human community with no clue I didn't belong there. Where does James fit in? Is he my brother? Where has he gone?

"Riley? Riley Emmett?" His voice cracked a little as he spoke, causing me to glance quickly at him in concern.

"Yes. Riley Emmett. Why? What's wrong?" His reaction made me nervous. Anxiety caused my stomach to twist as I wondered what I'd done to make him react this way to simply knowing my name.

"James was my friend. He told me about you. I didn't realize you were here. Why are you here?"

Pain barreled through my chest, the air cleaving from my lungs. He'd known James. James had spoken about me. I tried to remember how to breathe. Why couldn't I remember how to breathe?

Annie nuzzled me, whinnying softly. Her touch grounded me. I just needed to breathe. In. Out. In. Out.

I tried to pull myself together, trailing my fingers through Annie's soft mane to keep myself from falling apart. This man was a stranger, and I was falling apart in front of him. *Come on, Riley.*

"I'm sorry. It's just—" I sniffled and wiped away a wayward tear making its way down my cheek. "No one I've spoken to has known James. Gods, I miss him. How did you know him? Were you friends?"

"Yes. We were friends." His eyes were sad as he gathered Annie's lead rope again and began moving toward the training yard. "Come on. Let's walk and talk."

Annie nudged my hand as she followed Garner, and I nodded. I couldn't pass up an opportunity to talk to someone who knew James. Who'd seen him and known him more recently than I had. He'd never told me much about what he did here, or what the Fae were like and how they treated him. His letters had always asked about me, about the orphanage and the other kids we'd grown up with. The focus had never been on him.

It had never struck me as strange before. Until now, it had seemed like such a big brother thing to do. I don't know where he worked, or where he'd lived, or even who his friends were.

Fuck. I should have asked more questions, pressed him harder for information. At the time, I'd just been so happy to hear from him. If I'd known and taken more interest in the details…

Maybe then I'd have some clue as to where to start looking for him.

I couldn't even be sure Garner was telling the truth. Maybe they weren't friends. I had no way to verify the information. I trusted the Fae more now than I did when I first came here. I still believed they could do more to help the struggling humans and the dying lands, but I was starting to see clearer what they were up against.

Even so, I couldn't just blindly trust everyone I met.

I fell into step beside Garner as we passed through the gate and began to walk, following the fence that circled the large yard.

"How did you and James meet?" I asked, genuinely curious. Had they worked together? Met at a bar?

"We worked together. He helped here part time, and part time at a café down in the city center. The horses liked him, trusted him. So, I did too. We hit it off quickly." His brows furrowed as he continued. "He spent a lot of time championing for change, for more help for your human communities."

That sounded like James. He's always been passionate about the way the Fae had treated us and left us to our own devices. He was very vocal about wanting them to do more, to care more. It's where I'd gotten it from.

"He never wanted you to come here, Riley." Garner lowered his voice, almost whispering. Like he didn't want anyone to overhear us, despite the fact that there was no one else in earshot.

"He shouldn't have disappeared then. I wouldn't have had to come looking for him." The words came out sharper than I intended, the pain in them clear, even to my own ears. It was true, though. I would have stayed in Sommers, would never have applied to ascend if he hadn't disappeared. I'd been happy at the orphanage, tending to the gardens and the crops. I think I'd have been content to stay there if I'd known James was safe and well.

"He was always looking over his shoulder, worried about things he wouldn't voice to me. He seemed worried you'd be in danger here."

"Why would I be in danger here? Aside from the obvious magic making humans sick or crazy?" Not to mention the resistance, the void creatures, or the group of Fae the Dean seemed to think didn't want me here. James was spot-on actually; I wasn't safe at all.

He snorted. "You've got us pretty worked out, don't you?"

"The opposite, actually. I thought I had a clear picture of your kind—our kind—but you are nothing like I expected."

"What did you expect?" He asked, raising an eyebrow at me.

"Honestly? I'm not sure. I'm having trouble reconciling the anger I feel at the lack of help given to Sommers with the kindness and acceptance I've experienced here." I halt and Garner does too, Annie coming to a stop beside us. We'd almost made a full lap around the ring. "Life in Sommers is hard. It's fucking hard. We work our asses off and often don't have enough food. The air is stale, the scenery gray and dull and the crops struggle to grow. *We* struggle to grow." I blew out a breath, frustration building as I struggled to explain myself. "Everything is so god-damn nice here. It is literally like walking into another world. I used to be so angry that it was kept from us. So angry that nothing was being done to help us while the Fae lived it up. I understand better now that some of the help I wanted would have been detrimental to us, but I still feel like there's more that could be done to help."

He studied me for a moment, considering my words. "You might not belong to the human community anymore, but maybe you can be their advocate. If you're the new girl I've been hearing about, your power is incredible. You'll be able to use that to your advantage. I don't know what James was worried about, or why he wanted to keep you away. Maybe he knew something about your heritage. Whatever it was, I think it caught up to him. Maybe chasing him down will only lead you to get caught up in it too."

"I can't give up on him. I won't. I will find out what happened and where he is. I need to discover who I am and where I came from and whether James even is my brother. If you know anything, Garner, please help me."

"Alright," he said after a minute. He reached into his pocket and pulled out his tablet. "Put your details in. I'll message you his address. I miss James too, and I've been worried about what happened to him. His disappearance was written off as just another rebel joining the resistance, but that doesn't sit right with me."

I took the tablet and put my details in before handing it back to him.

"I think you're wanted," he said, nodding his head toward the gate where Stefan stood leaning against the rail. How did he find me? "Look after yourself, Riley."

"I will." I said, rubbing my hand along Annie's neck in good-bye. "And thank you, I haven't met anyone who knew James. It was nice to talk about him, no matter how briefly."

I turned and walked toward Stefan. I felt a little lighter, glad that someone else knew James well enough to know he wouldn't join the resistance. Garner had made a good point about advocating for the human communities. Maybe that was something I could do. I could push a little more, dig a little deeper into the whys and why nots.

I smiled to myself at the thought. I might not know where I came from. I might not totally belong here, but I could make a difference.

CHAPTER TWENTY-FOUR

Stefan

I watched as Riley said goodbye to both Garner and Annie and made her way over to me. She was glowing today, her skin as vibrant as the bright sun shining overhead.

I'd heard about what she'd done earlier with her earth element. Covering the combat field in wildflowers was no easy feat. That kind of magic took an incredible amount of energy. I'd expected her to look tired, drained, but she looked refreshed and lively.

She smiled to herself as she approached me, something she was thinking about making her feel more content than I'd seen since she'd been here.

I lunged for her, grabbing her around the waist and pulling her to me. She squealed, her laughter sounding like music to my ears as I tugged her in, pressing our bodies tightly together.

I pressed my lips to hers, groaning as I tasted her, the citrusy flavor of oranges lighting up my senses. She melted into me, wrapping her arms around my neck and deepening the kiss.

Fuck. I could not get enough of this girl. The draw I'd felt to her the moment I saw her in the candidate tents had not lessened. Not even a little. It was growing. I craved her. Wanted to spend every minute basking in her presence. The idea that it might be more than lust, that maybe this girl was destined to be mine, that maybe we were mates had crossed my mind a few times now.

I growled as she pulled away and she laughed, stepping back and pushing me gently on the chest, creating distance between us.

"Poor Garner doesn't need to witness this." She said, winking at me.

"I guess you're right," I muttered, pulling her under my arm and leading us back to the academy. "We have work to do, anyway. Did you forget our tutoring session?" When she hadn't shown, I'd let intuition guide me to her, somehow sensing where she'd be. Maybe it was a lucky guess, but it felt like more.

"Shit, I'm sorry!" She exclaimed. "I didn't forget. Not really. I just lost track of time." She chewed on her nail as we walked.

"What's on your mind, little dove?" I asked, wanting to know what had caused the little crease between her brows to appear.

"Garner knew James," she said without hesitation. Her trust in me blew me away. We'd only known each other a couple of days, but she was so open with me. She didn't treat me like the monster lurking under my skin could take over at any moment. She treated me like I was just Stefan. It was a feeling I wasn't overly familiar with. I knew most people were wary around me, waiting for the moment I switched. I could sense it.

It made me want her even more than I had before. This beautiful, gentle, powerful creature.

"He doesn't think James would have joined the rebels." She looked up at me then, the hope in her eyes burning brightly. "He's going to send me James' address. Maybe I can check it out. Maybe there's something there that will give me a clue where he went."

The hope in her voice caused my chest to tighten. "Officers have already searched his apartment, Riley. I'm not sure there's going to be anything there," I said softly, giving her a little squeeze as the academy gates swung open to admit us.

Her shoulders dropped a little, and I kicked myself internally, angry that I'd been the one to dampen the bright hope she'd just found.

"Maybe not. But it's worth a look. No one knew him the way I did, Stefan. Maybe I'll find something that wouldn't mean anything to anyone else..." Her voice trailed off, the soft sound of a sniffle reaching my ears and I stopped, twisting to face her and lifting her chin so I could see those beautiful eyes.

"Hey. We'll go there and I'll help you turn his place upside down, if that's what you want to do. I'll follow you anywhere you need to go to try to find him. I promise."

She blinked, surprise coating her features before she quickly looked away. "Stefan, I—"

Maybe I shouldn't have said anything and let her hold on to that hope until she got to wherever James had lived and found nothing.

"You don't have to say anything. You don't have to thank me. Let's find your brother and figure out your heritage. Maybe even save the planet."

"No. I—I need to tell you something." She chewed on her lip; her gaze averted.

"You can tell me anything, little dove."

"This," she said, her voice shaking just a little. She gestured between the two of us. "This is all new. I don't know where we're going. I'd like to find out, but I need to be honest with you."

My brow furrowed as she took a deep breath, steadying herself. I had no idea what might be bothering her this much. A small part of me was elated that she was comfortable enough to broach the topic—whatever it was—despite how nervous it seemed to make her.

She let out her breath and continued. "I agreed to go to the dance this weekend with Lincoln, and today in weapons training... I hurt him, and then I was so relieved that he was alright that when he kissed me, I didn't think. I felt a pull toward him, a pull he thinks means we were mates, and I kissed him back. I'm sorry. We haven't defined things. Hell, we've been together once, and I don't know what your expectations are. But I don't want to hurt you."

I blinked. What was she sorry for? I waited for her to keep going, to explain her apology further. We hadn't defined our relationship, and whilst I would hunt down anyone who hurt her, I wasn't possessive. Polyamory wasn't unusual among our kind. Most couples were monogamous, but there were enough who weren't that it wasn't a shock.

When she didn't continue, I asked, "What are you sorry for?"

"For kissing Lincoln?" Her brow was furrowed as she asked. The statement seemed more like a question, given my lack of reaction. Maybe she didn't know. I needed to reassure her. Show her I wasn't upset. I only wanted the best for her. I wanted her to be happy and loved, to find her brother and discover the secrets of her path. It didn't bother me if she needed more than just me to make her happy.

"No, Riley. You don't need to apologize. Fae aren't always monogamous. There are many that do not settle for just one partner, many that have more than one mate. And you're right, this is still early days. I like you, I *fucking* like you a lot and I want every piece of you that you'll give me. But I'm not against sharing, not if that's what you want. Lincoln is a pretty damn good choice too. He's my brother, my best friend. There isn't anyone better than him. I am not hurt, and I don't want you any less than I did a minute ago. We are fine. Alright?"

She stared at me for a long moment, absorbing my words, before she nodded. I took her arm as we walked through the grounds back to the combat field. She remained subdued. It might take some time to convince her I was okay with this situation.

I sighed. Maybe a change of topic would bring back the cheerful mood she'd been in as we left the stables.

"How are you feeling about using your air element today? Have you taken control of it yet?"

She shook her head. "No, the only time I've used it was when you threw that ball at me." She glared at me sideways, the smile on her pink lips letting me know she wasn't actually mad at me. "I've felt it, though. Twisting and building inside of me like a storm that needs to be released. I think it might be a relief to let it out today. I've been looking forward to it."

Her smile was genuine and I was glad to see that the light in her eyes was back.

"Holy shit." I stopped short as we reached the combat field. I'd been told what had happened today; had known what I'd see when we arrived. But actually seeing it? It was a different thing altogether. The entire field was a rainbow of wildflowers, the grass as high as our knees.

It was beautiful and wild.

"I have no idea how you did this today and still have power to spare." I cannot fathom the depth of her power.

She shrugged. "I don't know either. One day, we'll have answers. Today is not that day." She moved toward the center of the field, the beauty of the flowers surrounding her nothing compared to the ethereally beautiful woman standing among them. "Now, show me. Or tell me. What should I do?"

I couldn't deny her, not when she was so eager to learn.

"I think we should start with releasing it in controlled bursts." I moved toward her, wrapping my arms around her waist and pulling her flush against me, her ass rubbing against me in a way that almost had me groaning out loud. That was *not* what we were here for today. "I'll guide you."

I tucked my chin into the space between her neck and shoulder, inhaling the orange blossom scent of her.

"Close your eyes and find the power within you. That shouldn't be too hard. You already described how it feels."

She shivered against me, her body relaxing into mine as she let her head fall back against my chest and raised her face to the sun, letting it warm her.

"Are you ready?" She hummed softly, and I took that to mean she was ready, that she'd found it within her. "Alright, let it flow through you, down your arms, into your fingertips. Let a small amount gather there. And when you're ready, release it. I've got you."

She took a deep breath, steadying herself against me as she raised her arms, palms facing away from us. The air seemed to still and crackle with energy as she gathered the power within her, goosebumps rising on my arms in anticipation of its release.

"Just a small burst this time." I murmured in her ear.

She nodded, face still raised to the sun, her eyes closed and her brow furrowing as she concentrated.

Suddenly, she released it, the wind whipping through the wildflowers in front of us, flattening them as it burst from her with more force than I'd anticipated. I dug my heels into the earth beneath our feet to stop us from falling backward as she continued her release.

She raised her palms to the sky, and I could feel the force of her wind pushing us into the earth. I gritted my teeth against it, holding on to her as tightly as I could. This power, the strength of it, the well that must exist inside of her, was like nothing I'd ever felt before.

I should have expected this, been better prepared for it. She possessed all four elements after all, we had no idea what she was capable of. This might very well only be the beginning.

"Riley," I grunted, the pressure still pushing down on me. "Pull back, little dove."

Miraculously, she did, the pressure easing until she pulled the wind back into her completely, opening her eyes and spinning around in my arms.

"That felt incredible!" The smile on her face could have lit up the darkest room. The tension in my spine melted, and I grinned back at her in spite of myself, pulling her a little closer to me.

"I bet it did. It was pretty damn impressive. Do you feel depleted at all?" I quirked an eyebrow in question, genuinely curious about how she'd feel after using that much power.

She shook her head. "No. I feel rejuvenated, like I'm only just getting started and could go on for hours."

"Go on then," I pulled myself away reluctantly, taking a few steps back and offering her some space. "Try a small, short burst this time. Like you're in combat and want to knock your enemy backwards a bit."

"I can do that. I *did* do that with my fire at the outpost."

We practiced in the field for an hour longer, her skill and control growing with each minute that passed. By the end of our session, she was not only releasing small, sharp bursts of air, she was able to aim them and send them out in quick succession.

"What's next?" She asked, her voice breathless with a mix of elation and exertion. Her body was relaxed in my arms and I relished the feel of her against me.

"We'll need to stop soon; you don't want to burn yourself out." I was worried about the amount of energy she'd used this afternoon. Her power seemed endless, but I didn't know how close she was to the bottom of her well.

"I've got a bit left in me. Please, Stefan. This is the first time I've enjoyed my magic. I feel powerful and in control for once. Teach me something else." She *was* enjoying herself, that much was clear. She hadn't stopped smiling the whole time we'd been here. Joy was sparkling in her eyes. Who was I to deny her that feeling?

"Okay," I said, planting a kiss on the top of her head and pulling her down to the ground with me and into my lap. It took me a moment to work out what to show her next. It was a little advanced for an ordinary first year. But she was far from ordinary in every way.

"Try to wrap the air around us, kind of like a shield. It can be moving or still. Do whatever feels natural to you."

"Like a shield," she murmured in agreement. She fidgeted in my lap, getting comfortable before closing her eyes and focusing.

Slowly, dark twisting shadows started to flow steadily from her hands, wrapping themselves around us in a dome. My jaw dropped as I watched them surround us, twisting together in a way that seemed all together unnatural.

"Riley," I managed to whisper as they closed in around us, thickening and darkening, forming what looked like a solid black shield around us.

"Am I doing it?" she asked, her eyes still closed tightly. "It feels like I am, but I'm too scared to look." I couldn't say I blamed her, even if she didn't yet realize what she's released. It was growing darker inside the dome she'd created by the second, the shadows thickening, beginning to block out the light from the sun high above us.

"You need to look, Riley. You're doing... something, but it isn't an air shield. Open your eyes, little dove."

She did, a look of horror crossing her features and causing her eyes to widen as she took in the dome surrounding us, blocking us from the world outside. She dropped her hands quickly, and it vanished just as fast, the sunlight almost blinding in comparison as the outside world was exposed again.

I blinked against the bright light a few times, giving my eyes a moment to adjust. Riley was shaking in my lap, and I wrapped my arms around her, offering comfort.

"Hey," I said, cupping the back of her head and pulling her closer against my chest. "It's okay. You haven't hurt anyone. You've done nothing wrong."

"But what was that? It looked like shadows. I don't have shadows, do I? Is that even possible?"

"It seems like you do, so it must be possible." I murmured, my mind racing with thoughts of what this could mean. There was only one entity I knew of that had the ability to wield shadows. And he'd disappeared, hadn't been seen since we crossed through the void.

"Kala. Kala could wield shadows." I whispered, not wanting to startle her.

"Kala? As in the God of Darkness and Keeper of Souls, Kala?" She laughed, a little hysterically, clutching her locket tightly in her hand. "I've never met him, never knew of him until a few days ago." She pulled back from me, twisting in my lap, her face turned to mine and full of a desperate need for answers. "Why do I have them? What am I, Stefan?"

My heart broke at the anguish in her voice, the longing and desire to know where she belonged. This girl had been through so much. Not only had she lost her only family and was in a desperate search to find him, but she also had to face new questions about herself and her heritage at every turn.

"Maybe there's a connection there we don't know about," I mused. "I wish I knew the answers for you, Riley. I really do. I think we should keep this between us for now until we can talk to Professor Darmon, at least. This feels big. Like it might help you figure out what you are and where you truly belong."

She nodded and nestled her face into the space between my neck and shoulder. I held her tightly, praying to the gods and goddesses that we could work this out. That we could find the answers she so desperately needed.

CHAPTER TWENTY-FIVE

Riley

Colin had sent me a message earlier to meet him at the gates to the academy for our combat training session. I hadn't replied, still pissed at him for his attitude the other night. But I was going to meet him. I had to. I wasn't about to skip my scheduled classes. Exhausted and wrung out, I was unsure what to expect, but I was dragging myself there.

The other first years had all been headed to the training field, and it felt odd to be heading away from them. It felt like pointing a neon sign at myself that screamed, look at me, I'm different.

I let out a sigh as I wandered up the path that led me through the trees to the border of the academy. I took my time, enjoying the warm spring day and the way the sun broke through the lush thick canopy here and there. I'd quickly grown used to the greenery here, but I hadn't forgotten how barren the lands were back in Sommers.

There had to be something we could do to help. I understood that our magic could affect the humans adversely, but surely there was something to be done, supplies we could provide. Healthy seedlings, or nutrient rich soil. Maybe the healthy start would allow more crops to go without the risk of harming the community with magic.

Colin had told me the King and Queen were eager to meet me, yet I'd seen nothing of them. Maybe it was time to seek an audience and put my thoughts forward. Another thing to add to the list. It had become almost as important to me as finding James, now that I'd been here and could see the inequality first hand.

I was too tired to hurry, and I knew I was going to be late. Colin could wait. I didn't care much what he thought of it. This last week had been intense, and it wasn't even close to over yet.

Being able to fight and defend myself with my magic seemed like a vital skill to have. Especially after the attack at the outpost. I'd held those creatures off with the help of my group for a little while. But maybe if I'd known more, had more skill, maybe I'd have been able to help Amy sooner, stop her from being hurt altogether.

Amy and I had been messaging the last few days, and we'd agreed to meet for coffee at a bakery near the city center on Saturday. Its name—The Boardwalk Cafe—made me think it might be near the ocean. I was looking forward to taking a break.

I was so lost in my own thoughts that I didn't realize I'd reached the gates until the clearing of a throat pulled me back to the present.

I startled, my heart racing as I brought my hands up in front of me in a defensive position and immediately scanned the area.

"Oh, it's just you," I mumbled as I found Colin staring at me from beside the gates, his eyebrows raised. I let my hands drop, running one through my hair. I refused to be embarrassed by my reaction. I felt like I was always under attack in this place, whether it was internal—my magic going haywire—or external. It didn't matter. I was on edge, and I felt like I had every right to be.

"You're quick to react. I'll give you that." He grinned at me, his brown eyes sparkling with amusement, the afternoon sun making them appear almost liquid gold in color. "Can't say the same for your ability to communicate. You're here so you haven't lost your tablet. Ignoring me then?"

By the gods, he was something to look at. I clenched my thighs together, trying to smother the flames he set alight in me as his molten gaze raked over my body.

I'd changed out of my academy uniform and into a pair of matching teal blue leggings and crop top. This session was about elemental combat. I'd figured it was a good idea to be mobile and flexible. But I hadn't expected this kind of attention from him, not after the way we'd left things.

I ignored the way my body reacted to the intensity of his gaze. Ignored the flush building in my cheeks and the desire coursing through my blood as I rolled my eyes at him. I wasn't letting him off that easily. He'd been an asshole, and I was sick and tired of his hot and cold act.

"I'm not in the business of entertaining assholes, or forgiving them easily," I said haughtily. If he were expecting friendliness and hand holding today, he was sorely mistaken. "Let's get this over with." A huff of amusement left him as I reached where he stood on the path. "Where are we training today?" I wasn't supposed to go beyond the walls of Danann at all, even accompanied by the General.

"Headquarters. We'll use one of the training rooms there to give you a bit of privacy and protection for others if you lose control. Plus, no risk of void creatures attacking." He offered me a wink before leading the way through the gates.

I clenched my fists in frustration as I followed him out of the gates and down the path towards the city center. He was back to the charming version of Colin. The version I had so much fun with and felt so comfortable beside before things went sideways the other night.

I liked this side of him. Just as much as I liked Stefan and Lincoln. I stopped dead in my tracks. Really? I couldn't wrap my head around the fact that I felt this strongly about three different men. By the gods, they'd be the death of me.

"Alright, Riley?" Colin halted just ahead of me, frowning slightly, his eyes glowing with genuine concern.

"Fine. I'm fine." Waving him on, not sure what had gotten into me today, I kept walking. It was time to shake off thoughts of dating more than one man. There was no time for that. My focus needed to be on finding James.

I could see Garner walking a few horses around the training yard at the stables, but otherwise it was just Colin and I, the area quiet and empty of other Fae.

"Where is everyone?"

"Most are in the city center at this time of day. Not too many venture this close to the gates unless attending the academy, stables, or headquarters."

It didn't take us long to reach the army headquarters. It wasn't too far down the main path, past the stables. Colin led me inside, nodding to his men as we passed, but not stopping to introduce me to any. That was fine. I wasn't in the mood for niceties today, anyway. Plus, the last time he introduced me to a bunch of new people, the whole place ended up being attacked.

He opened a door halfway down the plain corridor and gestured for me to go ahead. I stepped down into what could only be described as a half inside, half outside space. It was walled, protecting the space from the weather, the large windows currently open and letting in the light of the afternoon sun and a gentle breeze to keep the space cool. The floor was unfinished, non-existent, soft and grassy like the fields outside.

I guess if you were sparring in here, it would be a more comfortable fall than a hard concrete floor.

Colin stepped in behind me, closing the door and making his way to the middle of the room. I followed behind him, anxiety causing me to drag my feet. I wasn't sure if I'd be able to control my magic enough today. I really just wanted to get this over with so I could head back to the academy, have some dinner, and take a nice, long bath.

"What do you want to start with, Riley? Any element in particular?"

I couldn't care less what element we started with. I was already mentally soaking in the hot, orange blossom scented water. I could almost feel my muscles relaxing as the heat worked its magic on the tension in my body.

"Earth to Riley. What's going on with you?"

"I'm tired," I said, shrugging my shoulders. "And I really don't think it matters. You said yourself that the concepts can apply to each element. I don't have much experience or control with any of them. Stefan taught me to throw balls of air yesterday. That is the extent of my experience."

"Right. Let's stick with air then." He stepped back a few paces, creating some space between us and planting his feet firmly in the grass. He grinned wickedly at me. If I hadn't been in such a foul mood, it might have been enough for me to forgive his mood swings. As it was, some of the resentment I felt toward him melted slightly. "Show me what you've got."

He was taunting me. The playfulness I'd experienced from him the other night out in full force. My anger and frustration rose again, my blood boiling in my veins. He needed to make up his gods damned mind. We're friends or we're not. He either likes me or he doesn't.

I planted my own feet, bracing myself against the force I could feel building inside me. My magic was awake, roiling inside of me, responding to what I was feeling. I knew I should try to rein it in. Harness it. Not let my emotion take control. But in that moment, I just didn't care. I'd had enough.

He'd said to show him what I had, and I really hoped he meant it. I was not about to pull any punches. The full extent of my power was screaming at me to be released, and Colin had just volunteered to be my punching bag.

Without giving it another thought, I threw my hands out in front of me, flinging my air forward with so much force that I was pushed back, my feet ripping through the dirt and grass at my feet.

Colin was quick to react, his movements strong and fluid as he flung his own hands out in front of him, throwing a shield of fire in front of him. The flames rippled violently as my blast of air collided with it and he grinned—actually fucking grinned—as he himself was pushed back a few feet.

"Come on. You're not tired. You're angry. Full of pent-up rage and that's all you've got? You can do better. Again." His tone was light, teasing, as he dropped his shield and beckoned me forward.

I bit down on my retort and instead focused on bringing that power to my fingertips. Letting it gather and build, before pushing it out toward him again in what I imagined being a more concentrated ball of rock-hard air.

I didn't even blink and his shield was up again, the whole thing flickering and flexing toward him as my attack hit dead center.

The sound of Colin grunting with the effort to maintain his shield made me smirk, the taste of victory on my tongue. The desire to knock his shield out, to get one up on the grumpy, flirty general, took over and without thinking I leaned forward, throwing another arrow of air directly at him.

Colin gritted his teeth and clenched his jaw as he worked to maintain his shield. My eyes were drawn to his forearms, the muscles there flexing and bulging with the effort he spent trying to break my attack.

The flames flicker, warp, and flicker again before guttering out completely. His eyes widened in shock, and I lunged, throwing one last ball of air in his direction. Not as strong as the previous ones, I didn't want to seriously injure him. But strong enough that when it collided with him, he was knocked back on his ass.

I stalked forward, hands still raised in front of me. I might have been completely new to magic, but I knew enough not to drop my defenses so quickly.

"Was that good enough for you?" My voice was laced with false sweetness as I fluttered my lashes at him, still sitting half sprawled in the grass. "Was that better? Did you feel *it*, sir?"

Surprise and amusement flashed across his features, followed by raw, unbridled desire. The air in the room shifted as he pushed himself to his feet, brushing off the front of his uniform.

He stalked towards me, a predatory look shining in his eyes. I backed away as he closed the distance between us. My breaths came in quick shallow gasps as electricity burned between us and my whole body ignited under the weight of his stare.

"I shouldn't want you the way I do, shouldn't be planning what I'm about to do to you."

"And what are you planning to do to me, *sir*?"

The huskiness of my voice, the clear desire in it surprised me as my back hit the wall and I swallowed hard. Any anger, frustration I'd been holding onto fizzled into nothing as he reached me, leaning his arm against the wall above my head, his face only inches from mine.

"Fuck," he growled, the sound causing wetness to pool between my thighs. "Call me that again."

"You like it when I call you sir?" My voice was barely above a whisper. We shouldn't be crossing this line.

But his warm breath was on my mouth, and I couldn't think straight. I was drowning in need and desire. Need for him to kiss me, touch me, take the edge off, and make me forget all the gods damned shit I had going on.

Groaning, he shifted closer, his body pressing against mine as he whispered in my ear. "Fuck yes, I do, sweetheart. Now, do you want to tell me what's going on with you today, or do you want me to make you forget all about it?"

A soft moan escaped me as he brought his lips to the space between my neck and shoulder and nibbled softly. My pussy fluttered in anticipation. This is exactly what I needed. Time to allow myself to be free and wanton, and not weighed down by all the different things I had to worry about.

"Make me forget, please."

CHAPTER TWENTY-SIX

Colin

I should not be doing this. There were so many reasons urging me to step back, pull away from her, to stop this thing before it goes any further. My position as General, our ages, Callie, that Riley was such an unknown. Such a wildcard.

But fuck. This girl had gotten under my skin. I couldn't tear my attention away from her or dampen the desire she ignited in me. I hadn't been able to stop thinking about her since we met, and I brought her back to Danann.

I felt lighter when she was around, like the sun was shining brighter than it had before she came around. Almost as if the weight on my shoulders wasn't as heavy. I wanted to lose myself in her, get lost together and forget this world existed.

"Make me forget, please." She pleaded, her voice husky with desire.

I groaned at the words, at the invitation in them. I pulled my face away from the crook of her neck and pressed my body more firmly against hers as I examined her face, searching for confirmation that she truly wants this. Truly wants me.

She gasped as my erection dug into her belly and turned her face to mine, her eyes dropping to my mouth as she wet her bottom lip.

I claimed her mouth with my own, stifling her moan as our tongues danced with animalistic need. Fuck. I'd been such an asshole, so fucking hot and cold toward her. I needed to show her I was sorry. I couldn't think of a better way to apologize than with my mouth.

I broke our kiss and nibbled along her jaw, tugging at her earlobe and working my way down her collarbone. Her hands were on my back, under my shirt, roaming the hard muscles there.

I grasped her hips, sliding my hands around to cup her ass and lift her away from the wall. She wrapped her legs around my waist, her hot core pressing flush against my rock-hard erection. I could feel the heat of her core through both of our clothes and groaned as I kissed down her collarbone, reaching the supple flesh of her cleavage.

"I want to taste you," I growled against her skin. Stepping away from the wall, I spun and deposited her on the grass before me—a section undisturbed by our combat 'lesson'—and knelt between her thighs.

I ripped my shirt off before gesturing for her to put her arms up. She obeyed immediately, and I pulled her top over her head before laying her back on the ground, taking a minute to admire the view.

She was fucking perfection. Her light olive skin was unmarked, her breasts full and perky, small pink nipples were peaked from the fresh air. Or arousal. I didn't care which. I was going to *devour* them.

It had been a long time since I'd been with a woman, since any had caught my eye or made me feel even a hint of desire toward any of them.

"Colin," she gasped, her face flushed with arousal.

"Mmmm?" I murmured, my gaze fixed on her perfect breasts and the way they bounced slightly as she breathed in and out.

"Get on with it."

I barked a laugh at her demanding tone and obeyed immediately, leaning forward and sucking one of her perfect pink buds into my mouth. I palmed her other breast before running her other tip between my fingers as I bit her gently. The scent of orange blossom reached my nose as the taste of her lingered on my tongue.

My cock throbbed, straining against my jeans as her back arched off of the grassy floor beneath us.

"Oh, please, Colin." Riley moaned, panting as her excitement built around us, the air changing, becoming charged, electrified. Her hands were in my hair, and she pushed down slightly, her desire clear.

That demand, the clear indication of what she wanted—needed—from me, was all the encouragement I needed.

I dipped my fingers under the waistband of her leggings and yanked them down, tossing them to the side. Eager to give her what I could and make her forget whatever was bothering her.

I placed my hands on her knees, spreading her legs wide. As I did, she reached down, her fingers running through her folds, gathering some of the wetness pooling there, before bringing it back up and circling her clit. A moan escaped me as I watched her touch herself.

Fuck. If I wasn't falling for her before, I would be now. She was something else.

Grabbing her wrist, I pulled her hand away, replacing it with my own and tracing my fingers through her soaking wet pussy.

She lifted her head, her eyes dancing with amusement, a triumphant smile spreading across her beautiful face.

Winking at her, I buried my face between her thighs before running my tongue down the length of her, dipping into the heat of her core before coming back and circling her clit.

Fuck, she tasted as good as she smelt. Orange blossoms with a hint of coconut. If this was my last meal, I wouldn't be complaining. I would happily die here between her thighs.

I repeated the movement of my tongue, circling her clit once more before sinking a finger inside of her. She gasped at the instruction, her hips bucking as she sought more.

"Fuck, Riley, you're so fucking tight." Her pussy clenched around me in answer, and a growl escaped me. Perfect, so fucking perfect.

"More, Colin, more," she begged. Unable to resist her, I added a second finger, filling her as I pumped them in and out of her, my tongue still working her clit. "You're so fucking frustrating, Colin."

She ran her fingers through my hair, gripping it tightly as she tightened her thighs around my head. I couldn't say I minded the idea of death by suffocation in her beautiful pussy. What a way to go.

Sensing what she was about to do as her pelvis lifted from the ground beneath us, I withdrew my fingers and gripped her ass, letting her roll us until she was straddling my face.

She was angry with me, and this was her way of taking back some control. She could have it. I was at her mercy.

Reaching up, I grasped one of her breasts in my hand, the other remaining on her hip as she fucked my face. I rolled her nipple between my thumb and forefinger, at the same time I plunged my tongue inside her wet heat.

Her gasps and moans told me all I needed to know. She was close, right on the edge. It wouldn't take much for her to fall over it.

Sliding my hand down her hip, I cupped her perfect ass, squeezing tightly before trailing down between her legs and lightly circling her backdoor.

A keening sound spilled from her lips, and I grinned against her pussy, dragging my tongue from her entrance to her clit again, my fingers following behind, gathering some of the wetness there and dragging it backwards.

I lapped at her clit as I continued circling her backdoor, her moans growing louder and more frantic as I teased her. Gently, and making sure she was lubricated enough, I pushed a finger inside her ass. She arched, her pussy almost smothering with the movement.

She was shaking now, so close to shattering. I sucked on her clit. Hard. And just like that she came undone.

She screamed, her back arching pushing those perfect breasts into the air, her whole body tensing as she came. Her ass clamped on my fingers, and I released her clit, licking it gently before pressing a soft kiss to the swollen nub. I laid my head back on the grass, wanting to watch her ride the waves of pleasure, pleasure I'd given her. Or as much of it as I could see from between her sun kissed thighs. I'd never seen anything more beautiful.

Slowly, her body relaxed, releasing my finger and I pulled it out and easing her down onto the grass beside me, her body still trembling from the force of her release. Leaning over her, I placed my hands on either side of her head. There was no way I could resist pressing a kiss to her mouth.

Her hazel eyes fluttered open, her smile wide as she looked up at me, a post orgasm glow making her look almost ethereal.

"I needed that," she said, barking a laugh. "I'm sorry I was being a brat. It might not be your intention, Colin, but you've been... hot and cold with me." She doesn't break eye contact with me, needing to get this off her chest.

I pushed up, sitting back on my heels, my cock still hard and longing for more of her. This wasn't about me, though. It was about her. *Down, boy.*

"I know. I'm sorry. I don't have a good excuse. Except that the draw I feel toward you scares me and—"

Before I could finish my thought and explain myself, no matter how feeble my excuses were, a knock sounded at the unlocked door.

CHAPTER TWENTY-SEVEN

Riley

I was on my feet in an instant.

Throwing my hand toward the door, I willed an air shield into keeping it closed, praying I could buy us some time and stop whoever was about to enter the training room from catching me buck naked with General Brand.

Colin's eyes locked with mine as he pushed himself to his feet, the panic in them mirroring my own. My gaze flicked back to the door, mentally reinforcing the air shield as I felt a press against it.

Fuck. This was the worst kind of compromising position to be caught in!

I needed to get myself dressed, but if I moved, I might very well break the shield. A shiver ran down my spine, intuition telling me things wouldn't go well if those on the other side of that door knew the General and I had been intimate. He was my tutor and the head of the Fae army. I knew there was some unrest about my presence here. Would they consider him a traitor for this relationship—if you could even call it that—with me?

I flushed at the memory of what we'd done, at what I'd let him do to me. Bee had said the fae were naturally promiscuous, and it certainly seemed that the awakening of my magic had woken a sexual hunger in me I'd never experienced before. I was ravenous for these men. All three of them. Fuck.

Now was not the time to ponder my newfound promiscuity. Our visitors would grow suspicious if we didn't open the door soon.

I'd had my first foundational magic lessons yesterday, where we were told about some of the non-elemental magic that most Fae could wield. Including the trick Stefan had done in the candidate tent back in Sommers, where he changed my outfit. We'd only learnt the theory; it was all about your intention. The ability to vanish and re-conjure objects was innate. You just had to want it enough. Unfortunately, we hadn't had the time to put the theory into practice.

Just as I was trying to recall the steps, the silky, stretchy feel of my clothing wrapped around my body, and I breathed a sigh of relief. Colin had done it for me. His own shirt was back on too, and he was already moving toward the other side of the room.

"Thank you," I whispered, offering him a small smile of gratitude. "Who is it? Do I let them in?"

"It's Colonel Stubbe." He whispered back, a dark look flashing across his face. He didn't seem fond of Colonel Stubbe. Not that I could blame him. Something about that man gave me a bad feeling. It explained the prickling sensation on the back of my neck and the warning bells ringing in my mind. "The King is with him. Step back, brace your feet, try to look as though we've been sparring. Your hair is wild enough to seem like I've knocked you on your ass a few times."

I scowled as he threw me a wink, but did as he said.

"Just so we're clear, Riley. I am not ashamed of the way I've begun to feel about you, about what just happened, or about what might come next. I will shout it from the rooftops if you'd like me to. But you will probably make a better impression on King Ronan if he doesn't know."

I nod, surprised by his words. I'd half expected him to turn back into the cold General, the one with the stony face and constant frown. I liked this version better. This version made butterflies flutter in my stomach and the apex of my thighs throb.

We could continue to explore each other and those feelings later.

Now, it was time to meet the Fae Water King.

Another knock sounded at the door just as I pivoted my body so that I was facing away from it, moving my air shield in place in front of me. Colin, seeing what I'd done and acting without missing a beat, threw a few small balls of fire in my direction. I felt the burning heat of them as they slammed against my shield, one after the other.

I gritted my teeth, actually having to focus to maintain my shield and protect myself from his fire. The back of my neck prickled again, and I knew our guests had entered the room, but I couldn't turn and greet them.

The last of the fire balls hit home, bouncing off of my shield and disappearing into thin air. Momentarily forgetting our audience, I whooped, a sense of pride coursing through me. I'd done it. I had knocked the Fae Army General on his ass with my attack *and* withstood one of his. This whole powerful non-fae being thing was growing on me.

"May I announce King Ronan." Stubbe's nasally voice had not changed, still causing my hackles to rise.

Colin shot me a grin as he strode past, his hand held out in front of him.

I spun on my heel to watch as he clasped hands with King Ronan and dipped his chin to Colonel Stubbe in greeting.

The King was so much like his son, there was no denying the resemblance. They had the same dark almond colored skin and long honey blonde hair. It was only their eyes that differed King Ronan's were a dull gray—nothing like the deep mesmerizing blue of his sons. That must come from the Queen. King Ronan was also missing the warmth, the friendliness, that Lincoln radiated. It was hard to get a read on him beyond that.

"Your Majesty," he said, stepping back and bowing low. "What a pleasant surprise. Have you met Riley Emmett yet?"

He gestured toward me, and I moved forward, mimicking his bow and offering my hand to the monarch.

"Ah, yes, our most recent ascendant. Welcome, Riley. I trust you are settling in well?" Disinterest colored his tone, and he didn't wait for my response before continuing. "You've caused quite the stir here, young lady. The elders are in quite the uproar about your *unproven* heritage." He barely spared me a glance before turning back to Colin.

"That is why I'm here, General. You need to speak to them. Reassure them that this girl is no threat. That she is on our side, and you will personally ensure she remains so. I am at my wits end; General Hughes would have had this in hand by now." I bristled at his words; at the way he spoke to Colin and called me 'girl'.

He had no idea who I was or what I'd been through. How dare he judge me!

Colin shot me a look from the corner of his eye. A clear command not to respond. And he was right, I needed to be here. I couldn't risk that by losing my shit at one nasty comment. I bit down hard on my tongue, trying to rein in my temper. I could feel the crackling of fire on my skin as I struggled to keep myself from exploding.

The sound of Colin and King Ronan talking dulled, as though I was underwater, and I couldn't make out their words any longer as I fought tooth and nail to keep my power contained. Taking a couple of deep breaths, I felt the fire in my veins cool and slowly slink back to the well in my chest meant to contain it.

Sound returned to me in a flood as the King nodded at Colin and turned his attention back to me.

"Is there anything we can do to make your transition here any easier?" He asked. He was only asking because he had to, because it was good for his image. There was no way he truly cared how I was settling in or wanted to help. That didn't mean I couldn't take advantage of the question, though, right?

Before I'd even thought about what I was about to do, the words tumbled from my mouth. "The human communities are struggling, Majesty. They cannot grow enough food, and many go hungry every day. Whilst I understand now that exposure to magic is a risk to them, I feel there is more that your kind can do. You promised to heal the world after all."

Colin shot me a look of disapproval, his shock and displeasure written in the furrow of his brow and the thin set of his lips. He wasn't happy I'd made a request of the King. But why not? Why shouldn't I? They hadn't lived up to the promises they made when control of our lands was handed over to them. People were suffering. I had been one of those people.

It was the right thing to do.

"Our kind, you mean? You are one of us, Riley Emmett. In some way or another. There has never been any kind of power in this realm other than the arrogance of ordinary human beings. You are not from here. You are not one of them. You are one of us."

I lifted my chin, defiantly holding his gaze. He wanted me to break, to back down. I was not going to. His words held some semblance of truth. Deep down I knew that. But that didn't mean he could get away with letting innocent people struggle and hurt.

"That may be so," I was proud of how little my voice wavered as I held the King's steely stare. "But those people are hungry. They are scared and they need help. You have an abundance here. Surely there is some way to share that wealth without affecting their health."

He stared at me; the silence stretching between us until I was almost about to drop my eyes. Just before I did, he inclined his head ever so slightly. "Make a proposal through the official channels and I will consider it. Hold on to that fortitude, girl, you'll need it." He spun on his heel and strode quickly out of the room, Colonel Stubbe on his heels, shooting us what could only be a triumphant look.

I had to bite down on my tongue to hold my retort. He'd given me an opportunity at the very least—even if he'd called me girl again. What was that about, anyway? What did he mean when he told me to hold on to my fortitude?

"What was that?" I asked, turning to Colin as the door clicked shut behind the Colonel. "Hold on to your fortitude, you'll need it is an almost... threatening thing to say."

"I'm not sure, Riley." He said, scrubbing his face with one hand. "I don't know what to make of that whole interaction. Did you really have to taunt him on your first meeting?

"I wasn't taunting him." Colin wiggled an eyebrow at me. "Okay, maybe I did. It wasn't intentional. I just get so worked up over the inequality of it. Something needs to be done." I would fight tooth and nail to help my community.

"I'm not saying I disagree with you. Things need to change. We need to do more. It would probably be more effective if you followed the proper channels, though. Pushing him any more may make you an enemy of the King. He is pushing back against the elders on your behalf."

"It sounds like he just hand-balled that responsibility to you." I stepped into him, wrapping my arms around his waist and resting my head on his muscular chest, his body molding around my own as he embraced me back. I would take any comfort I could get right now. I didn't want to admit it, but I was unsettled by the King's words. It felt like a warning and a threat rolled into one.

"He did," Colin agreed, placing a soft kiss on my forehead. "I'll have to go see them this afternoon. But first, I'll take you back to the Academy."

CHAPTER TWENTY-EIGHT

Riley

"What am I supposed to do?" I asked, examining the sword I held in my outstretched hands. I looked up at Professor Flo from where I sat in a small armchair. She was perched on the edge of her desk in front of me, her foot tapping impatiently against the hardwood floor.

She'd been waiting for me when I'd returned to the academy, frantic and buzzing with an excited energy I couldn't quite decipher, and insisting I join her in her office. Resisting her had been futile. She'd all but dragged me back here. Colin had let her, too, just shaking his head, laughter dancing on his lips as he waved goodbye, off to deal with the Elders.

To convince them I was not a threat...

I sighed heavily. My mind was a whirlwind of thoughts and emotions. Was I a threat? Finding James was my highest priority.

The power I held would only help me achieve that goal, and I'd use it if I had to. Hurting others was not something I strived to do; it went against everything I stood for. But I'd already hurt others when I'd lost control.

No one really seemed worried about that—they treated it like it was a normal part of discovering your magic and your limitations. And maybe it was. I wouldn't know any better.

"Connect with it, Riley. Create a door in your mind and let it through. Strengthen the bond that started in class the other day."

"You mean when I almost killed Lincoln and filled a field with manicured wildflowers?"

She scoffs. "So dramatic, dear. He was far from dying. Minor head wound at most. And you healed him right away. No harm done. The flowers were a pleasant touch." She winked at me, her foot still tapping. "Now, try to connect."

Closing my eyes, I tried to do as she instructed. How was I supposed to open a door in my mind? A few long, silent seconds passed before I gave up again.

Blowing out a breath, I opened my eyes. "I don't know how to do this. It might help if I know why it's so important," I said, raising an eyebrow at her in question. She hadn't explained herself at all, too eager to dive right in.

"Oh, of course, I've gotten ahead of myself." She moved off her desk, plopping down in the seat beside me. "I found your bonding with that particular weapon extremely interesting, so I've been doing some research. Combined with how little we know of your own history; it seemed like something worth noting and looking into further. There isn't a lot of information on the sword available here. The texts I found repeated the same basic facts. Blessed by multiple goddesses, sucks the power—or soul in some iterations—out of those unworthy to wield it, has not bonded in hundreds of years. There was one text that mentioned that the sword held a message to relay to its bonded, once the connection was completed."

Stiffening, I dropped my gaze back to the sword in my hands. It had spoken to me in that otherworldly voice. Had said I might be the one it had been waiting for. Was it so far-fetched that it might have a message to convey? An agenda to fulfill? Nothing could really surprise me at this point. This week had completely turned my world and my beliefs on its head.

"What kind of message?" I asked, my voice low and as I turned the sword in my hands running a finger down the cold steel blade. The emeralds embedded in the dragonhead in place of eyes glittered in the late afternoon sun.

Why wasn't it talking to me now?

"I don't know." Professor Flo stood again, drawing my gaze to her, and began pacing as I studied her. It seemed like she could not stay still for too long. That excited, buzzing energy still radiated off of her. She wanted to know the answer, needed to solve the puzzle I had become to her. I had to hope her motivations for helping me were good. That she was truly on my side.

She hadn't done anything to make me think she wasn't, but my run in with King Ronan had my hackles raised.

"None of the texts I read go into detail about the message itself. They merely state that there is one to be passed along." Blowing out a breath, she sat again, burying her face in her hands. "I wish I had access to the libraries back home. I just know there's much more detailed information available. There has to be!"

"Just so I've got this straight—you want me to complete the connection with the sword so that it can deliver a message it has held on to for hundreds of years?" I scrubbed a hand over my eyes. A throbbing was beginning in my temples; the tension Colin had helped me release earlier building again.

Professor Flo nodded profusely. "Exactly."

"I'll try. Could you please get me some water? I'm feeling a little parched." I wasn't, but I needed a few minutes. Maybe without her frantic pacing, I'd be able to concentrate on the sword before me.

"Of course, dear. I'll run to the kitchens. I'll be back in a few minutes."

"Thank you." I said, watching as she crossed the room and pulled the door closed behind her, leaving me alone in the room.

As soon as she was gone, the energy surrounding me calmed. I took a deep breath, in and out. I repeated that a few times, calming my mind, before placing both hands on the sword and closing my eyes.

Intent and visualization seemed to be key parts of controlling and using magic. So much of it centered on what we wanted to achieve and picturing the result in our minds. Maybe if I pictured a door, or a thread, or some sort of connection to this magnificent creation in my lap, I could speak to it again.

A bridge! I would picture a bridge between myself and... Oh, I was already sick of calling it 'the sword'. Surely it had been named. Most weapons of this caliber were, weren't they? Or, if it possessed its own consciousness, it might have chosen a name for itself.

A familiar hissing voice filled my mind as the sword spoke, causing me to startle in my seat.

Siesoulae is my name, Blessed One.

"I'm Riley." There was something comforting about continuing to speak out loud, despite Siesoulae having a direct link to my mind. It felt... less invasive somehow?

I know who you are. You are who I've been waiting for these long, long years.

My blood was pounding in my ears as Siesoulae's magic began mixing with my own. The feeling was heady, intoxicating. I leaned back against my chair, tilting my face toward the ceiling, my eyes still closed, as I sank into the power buzzing through my very being.

"How do you know? What if this is some mistake?"

Your power matches what was spoken of. Were you not the one I've been waiting for, I would have consumed your soul.

A shudder runs through me at the certainty laced through those words.

Do not fear. I will not hurt you, gentle one. I submit myself to you. My power is yours to wield in order to fulfill your destiny. I have a message for you, a prophecy. Are you ready?

A prophecy? I had no use for a prophecy. I didn't need to know what the future held, or what seers had predicted hundreds of years ago. I didn't want it, didn't want any of this.

"No," My voice wavered, the sound barely audible in the silent room. "No, I'm not ready. I don't want your prophecy. I just want to find my brother." A tear slid down my cheek and I resisted the urge to wipe it away, keeping both hands upon Siesoulae to maintain the connection. Some small part of me wanted to know what else she had to say.

It will lead you to what you seek and more.

"It'll help me find James?"

Yes.

I sucked in a breath, my heart beating a frantic pace. I could not turn away now. If this prophecy could lead me to James, I would not refuse—I would beg to hear it if I had to. I would follow any path that promised to lead me to my brother.

"Go on then." The sound of the door opening sounded behind me, Professor Flo finally returning from the kitchens. Remaining still, I focused on that bridge in my mind, waiting for the prophecy Siesoulae had held on to for centuries.

A journey of peril. A plan gone awry.
Broken lands ruled upon a lie.

Time shan't heal as a curse holds fast.
Unknown lessons will be taught by the past.

Daughter of shadows holds the key,
Hope is lost 'til thy mother is free.

Souls will clash. Lives will be lost.
Contain the light no matter the cost.

CHAPTER TWENTY-NINE

Riley

"What do you think it means?" Bee asked for what must have been the thousandth time as we strolled along the main path leading toward the center of Danann. The day was mild, a warm briny breeze blowing my hair back from my face and keeping the sun from being too hot on our backs. "Journey of peril might refer to the crossing, that plan definitely went awry. Where is the lie though?" Frowning, she tilted her head to the side, considering her own question.

Broken Lands ruled upon a lie.

It could be referring to the promise the Fae made to heal our lands, though it hadn't really been a lie, Colin had said they'd been trying, all of their attempts failing despite their best efforts. Maybe it referred to something more sinister.

The entire prophecy had been a hot topic among Stefan and Bee since I'd recounted it after returning from Professor Flo's office the other night. They'd both spent the entire day yesterday trying to solve the damn thing—like a prophecy hundreds of years old could really be solved within a day of finally being shared. It had completely distracted me from earth wielding—I hadn't even been able to create a flower, despite filling a field of them unintentionally— and had taken all of my self-control not to constantly roll my eyes at them.

I was going to lose my damn mind if they kept at it.

"Can we just forget about it today, Bee? I can't work out what any of the damn thing means or how it will lead me to James. Or even what 'more' might mean." Buildings were taking form in the distance, and I quickened my pace, eager for my first tour of the Fae city. If you'd asked me a few weeks ago whether I'd be excited for a tour of Danann, I'd have laughed in your face. How quickly things change. "My brain might explode if I think about that damn riddle any longer. Let's just relax and enjoy our day off." Nudging her gently in the shoulder, I shot a small smile at her.

She was just trying to help. I knew that and I loved her for it. No one had ever accepted me as quickly and completely as Bee had. She'd quickly become like family to me. A break was overdue, though, and I really wanted to make the most of this day.

"Of course," Bee said, her face softening. "I'm sorry. Of course, you need a day off. It's easy to forget you haven't been with us forever." She laughed, linking her arm through mine and the sound was melodic, the notes dancing through the air and lightening the mood as we reached the outskirts of the city. "I'll drop it for the day. Let's go meet Amy."

Small, pale brick houses lined the streets, vines trailing up the walls and bright colorful flowers filling the gardens. Lots of Fae are milling about, catching up with friends, or heading toward the city, just like us. They looked just like the human's back home, but healthier, less stressed about surviving day to day.

The further we walked through the homes surrounding the city, the more I wondered whether James had lived nearby. Was one of these houses his? Had he been happy here? He'd seemed that way before his letters stopped coming. He'd seemed genuinely happy. What had happened to him?

"Earth to Riley," Bee said, snapping her fingers in front of my face. I blinked quickly, pulling myself back to the present and realizing we'd entered the city plaza.

The center of Danann was set out in a large semicircle, the flat edge of which ran along the beach, overlooking the ocean as it crashed upon the sand. The salt-tinged breeze was stronger here, chillier as it came in from the ocean. The whole space was lined with the same cobblestones that had been used for all the pathways I'd seen within the walls so far.

My eyes widened as I took in the shop fronts lining the boundary of the plaza. There were a couple of produce shops, some clothing stores, a store that looked like it sold furnishings and another that seemed to sell just knick knacks. The center of the space was filled with a mix of tables and benches, most which were full of fae, having completed their shopping for the day and taking a break or catching up with friends.

This was so much more than I had expected. This level of comfort—of wealth—could only be dreamt about back home. Anger burned through my veins and I clenched my fists as I felt the heat of my flame beginning to gather there. When would I gain control over this? My emotions were so volatile in this place, which was only making learning to control my power all that much harder.

I'd done as the King had requested and submitted a proposal. Well, I'd written one. Colin had promised to submit it on my behalf through the 'proper channels', whatever that meant. He'd said it would take time, but that didn't make the unjustness of the situation any easier to swallow.

It was beautiful, the way the sun shone across the space, reflecting off the water in front of us. It was easy to understand why so many wanted to ascend and move here. This had been the promise, this bustling, thriving space. Much better than the bleak reality back in Sommers.

A loud squeal from my left broke me out of the spell I'd fallen into and before I could so much as twist toward her, Amy was crashing into me, her arms wrapping around my body and squeezing tightly as she bounced up and down in excitement.

Her embrace was so strong, I struggled to suck in a breath, only just managing to choke out the words "Can't. Breathe."

Letting go, she stepped back, her hands grasping mine and holding them firmly.

"Sorry. Sorry. I'm just so damn excited to see you!" Her breathing is labored, like she sprinted across the plaza the moment she spotted us. Maybe she had.

"It's good to see you, too, Amy. You look great." Great was an understatement. She was positively radiant. Her bright yellow sundress sat just above her knee, showing off her slender frame and making her bright blue eyes pop. Her bright red hair was down today, loose waves framing her face, a couple of strands dancing in the cool ocean breeze.

"All thanks to you, Riley. I wouldn't even be here if it wasn't for you risking yourself and your own safety to help me. You'd met me only minutes before, and you still took it upon yourself to save my life. I am forever grateful."

A flush spread across my cheeks, and I shuffled my feet as she squeezed my hands again. In all honesty, I hadn't thought about what I was doing when I ran to her after the void creature ripped open her leg. Instinct had pushed me toward her, and I'd acted on autopilot. Her praise felt undeserved.

"Anyone in my shoes would have done the same," I said, dipping my chin and looking toward where Bee was standing back, waiting to be introduced. I dropped one of Amy's hands and waved Bee forward, glad to find something that would take the attention off me. "This is Bee, my roommate, and the sweetest person in this realm—possibly across all of them."

Bee shouldered me playfully as she extended her hand for Amy to shake. A smile spread across her face as they shook hands. "Nice to meet you," she said. "Riley here is clearly trying to deflect the attention from herself. She's not one to easily accept compliments and has already demanded a relaxing day." Her eyes danced with amusement as she shot me a grin. "Let's show her all Danann has to offer."

"Oh, yes! What have you got in mind?" Amy asked as my tablet vibrated in my pocket. Pulling it out, I could see a message from Garner. Amy and Bee chattered among themselves as a ringing sounded in my ears, drowning out the noise of the plaza as I hyper focused on the screen.

Garner had promised to send me James' address, but I hadn't heard from him. Until now. I'd been beginning to wonder if he'd decided against helping me. There was still a chance he had, and this was an apology message.

Holding my breath, my hands shaking—with fear or excitement, I wasn't sure—I swiped open the message.

> 32 North Street. I can meet you there in an hour if you'd like some company.

Blowing out a breath, I tried to decide if I wanted company. Going through James' belongings would be hard, emotional. My chest ached every time I thought of him. I missed him so damn much. It was happening more and more often the longer I spent in Danann, too.

Maybe having someone there would anchor me. It might keep me from becoming too emotional and help me focus on searching for some clue that maybe the Fae had missed.

I shot a quick text back, letting Garner know I'd meet him there, and looked up just in time to find Amy and Bee staring at me.

"So? What do you think?" Amy asked.

Grimacing a little, I asked, "About what?"

"Girl, you are so distracted today. What is going on? Better yet, which one was it?"

"Which one?" Amy asked, raising an eyebrow at Bee in question, and let out a groan. These two were thick as thieves already.

"Mmmmhmmm. Riley has her pick of Fae men at the moment."

"Oooh," Amy exclaimed, bouncing on her heels. "Colin was pretty sweet on her the night we met. Who else are you connecting with?"

"Stefan *and* Lincoln." Bee stretched out the and, making it seem like such a big deal and I rolled my eyes as Amy gasped, looking to me for confirmation.

Admitting defeat and realizing they weren't going to drop the subject, I nodded. "They're all so different, but I'm drawn to them all equally. It's an... experience."

Bee snorted loudly. The only person in the world who could do that and make it cute. Amy glanced at her, grinning, some emotion shining in her eyes as she studied Bee.

"It wasn't any of them, though. It was Garner. He gave me James' address and is going to meet me there in an hour to see if we can find anything."

"Alright," said Bee, her features taking on a more serious expression. We'd spent a lot of time talking about James, and she knew how important it was for me to try to uncover what had happened and where he was. I refused to believe he'd have left willingly, without telling me. But I also didn't want to consider the alternative. That he may be hurt or worse, dead.

"We should be able to find a dress for the dance tomorrow and grab that coffee before you have to meet him." She declared, looping her arm through mine again. To my surprise, Amy fell in on her other side, looping their arms together too as Bee led the way across the plaza to what was apparently the best dressmaker in Danann.

CHAPTER THIRTY

Riley

Feeling more relaxed than I had any right to, and grinning like a goddamn idiot after finding the perfect dress for tomorrow's dance, I left Bee and Amy to enjoy the rest of their coffee while I went to meet Garner.

The two of them had become fast friends, and I wondered if there might be a little something more flourishing there. Bee had been more flirtatious than I'd ever seen her. She wasn't going to escape my interrogation on that one tonight.

Following the directions Amy had scribbled down for me, I left the plaza and started down a side street. At the end, I'd turn left, and James' house should only be a few up.

The same light sandy brick covered in vines that I'd seen earlier made up the houses in this street too, the garden beds bright and inviting. It was quieter here, not another soul in sight. The only sound was the constant lapping of water on the shore. The beach couldn't be more than a street or two over. I let the relaxing sound wash over me as I walked, trying to calm my racing heart. A sense of unease plagued me, and I couldn't seem to shake it.

Would I find anything today? Would there be something the fae had missed when they searched through my brother's things? The idea that James had left, had joined the resistance without so much as a word of goodbye, didn't sit well with me. He'd never expressed any desire to join them and had openly berated some of their antics. Even if he had changed his mind, surely, I meant enough to him for some form of goodbye. Right?

A shadow flashed in my peripheral vision, and I spun on my heel, pushing my palms out in front of me, a shield of air bursting to life reflexively. Scanning the area, I tried to determine what had caused the change in light. There was nothing there. The streets were still empty; I was the only person here.

Putting it down to fried nerves, I dropped my shield and continued down the street. The hair on the back of my neck still stood on end and I couldn't shake the feeling I was being watched.

Maybe it wasn't anything sinister. It wasn't unreasonable that the Fae might watch a newcomer to their city. Wouldn't that be something Colin would have to order? He wouldn't do that, would he? Not after how our relationship had been blossoming.

Trying to ignore the ache in my chest at the thought of him doubting me, I turned the corner, immediately spotting Garner waiting for me a few houses down.

Blowing out a breath, relief washed through me, though my skin still tingled with an awareness of being watched. I still couldn't see anyone else, but I was still grateful not to be alone any longer.

"Hey," Garner said, from where he was leaning against the garden fence of a small house. "Are you ready for this?"

"I'm not sure," I answered truthfully, wringing my hands together. "I'm ready to find my brother, but going through his things feels..." Reaching Garner, I look past him, taking in the house that James had called a home.

It was one of the smaller houses on the street. All of them were small, really. I'd learned that not a lot of families had come across on the first crossing. Many had left their loved ones behind, preparing to cross when a permanent, safer way had been established.

That had never happened, so the need for large homes had been minimal. Many of the homes on this street looked as though they'd have two bedrooms at most. James likely had only one.

"Raw." Garner had moved to my side while I'd been staring at the house, and I jumped slightly at the sudden closeness of him. "Sorry," he said. "Let's go inside. The longer you wait out here, the harder it'll be."

"What if there's nothing in there, Garner? What if there's nothing to help me find him? I can't go in there and find nothing. He has to be okay. He has to be." A violent sob burst from my throat as I voiced my worst fears. I needed my brother back. I couldn't face a world where he didn't exist.

No one else had ever known me the way he did, had laughed at my silly quirks, or protected me from the worst of what the world had to offer. Though I was older now—a grown-ass woman and a powerful one at that, if the fae were right—I'd never not need him. James was my home.

"If you don't go in there, he's still gone," Garner said, his voice soft as he wrapped an arm around me, pulling me into his chest and holding me while I sobbed. "If you do, maybe he's not. You won't know until you face it, and maybe the not knowing is worse."

He continued rubbing my back in slow, soothing circles as I fought to pull myself together. Pulling back, I took a deep breath and swiped the tears from my cheeks.

"You're right. Let's do it."

He nodded and stepped forward, opening the small gate for me before leading the way up the small cobblestone path to the front door. He tried the brass handle, only to find it locked.

I'd come to learn that was a pretty unusual habit for the Fae. They seemed to have a low rate of criminality and trusted each other almost inexplicably.

Garner stopped over and lifted a small flowerpot by the front door, its contents still very much alive and blooming. It seemed the earth elementals still maintained the gardens, even though no one lived here anymore.

He pulled out a key, holding it up for me with a grin. A small laugh burst out of me at his celebration, despite the nerves racing through me at the thought of what we might find—or not find—inside those walls.

Lingering on the doorstep as Garner stepped inside, I took one last long look up and down the street. I still couldn't see anyone else, though the feeling of being watched had not eased. Shaking my head, I pushed the feeling to the back of my mind. There were too many other things for me to worry about today.

"Get your ass in here, Riley." Garner called.

"Coming." Blowing out a breath, I tried to brace myself for what was to come as I turned and crossed the threshold, pulling the door closed behind me.

Garner hadn't gone far. I found him lounging on a simple navy colored couch with cream colored throw cushions, his arm thrown over the side. There was a cream throw hung over the back on the couch, and a small wooden coffee table in place of it.

The other side of the room housed a small kitchen. There was no table, just a couple of stools pushed up against the counter. There was an empty wicker bowl in the middle of the counter, which might have held fresh fruit while James lived here. Next to it was a picture frame. The only item I could see in the room that might be personal. Everything else was simple, clean, but held no clue as to who resided here.

Crossing the room in a few steps, I grabbed the frame, turning it over in my hands to examine its contents.

A soft whimper escaped me as I saw myself staring back. Running my finger along the glass, I traced the edges of the picture. The photo was candid, my hair was blowing in a phantom wind, and I was laughing—at what, I couldn't tell you.

When had James taken this photo? How had he taken it? Our community hadn't possessed this kind of technology, so much of it was destroyed in the Last War. My hair seemed longer than it had been before James ascended and moved to Danann. How could that be?

"Garner?" There was no chance of hiding the tremble in my voice as I called his name.

He was off the sofa and by my side instantly, faster than I had expected.

Holding the photo frame in front of me, I gestured for him to take a look. "This photo isn't old. It's more recent than it should be. Like, after he moved here recently. How? Tell me how?"

Garner sighed heavily. "He snuck out once, to see you. Nearly had his head ripped off by his handler—the person assigned to be his buddy while he settled in. He told me you looked too happy to disturb, that he didn't want to turn your laughter into tears just for the sake of numbing his own pain at being separated. I didn't know he took this, though; he must have commissioned one of the cameras at the Academy."

Vines began to wrap themselves around my hands, winding their way up my arms as I shook, furious at my brother for the first time since he'd left me alone in Sommers. How could he be so goddam short-sighted? I'd been dying to see him, had begged and begged for him to visit or if I could visit him. The answer was always no. I'm too busy. You aren't allowed in Danann unless you've ascended. I'll come and see you soon. But he never did.

Balling my hands into fists, I slammed them down on the counter. My whole body trembled with rage that I'd been bottling up for the longest time. My heart had ached for him, missed him with every fiber of its being. He was the only family I had ever known. Why would he do this to me?

"How dare he? How dare he have the nerve to visit and not see me? That he can just up and leave me on my own, and then fucking disappear into the dead of the night?" My flames were burning inside me now, begging for release, the heat of them singing the vines still winding up my arms.

Snatching the frame from Garner's hands, I tossed it across the room. It smashed against the open doorway, leading to another room, glass flying everywhere upon impact.

Time slowed as I watched the glass shatter into a thousand tiny pieces, as the frame itself snapped at the corners, the photo of myself fluttering to the floor. I almost didn't see the other, smaller piece of paper floating down with it.

Rushing forward, I dodged Garner's arm as he reached for me, trying to halt me, stop me from whatever it was he thought I was about to do, and fell to my knees on the floor.

The shattered glass sliced into my knees and my shins, leaving tiny cuts all over my legs, but I didn't care. Didn't register the pain. My rage subsided, the charred vines around my arms retreating, leaving my hands clear as I reached for the note. It was folded so carefully, so familiar, in a way that turned the paper into its own envelope. The same way James had folded any note he'd ever left for me back home.

My heart was beating wildly against my rib cage as I carefully unfolded the page. This was it. The clue I'd been so eager to find. The thing that might lead me to James.

Riley,

Know I would never leave willingly. Everything I've done has been to protect you.

If you are reading this, I've failed. The Resistance has taken me, and they will use me to get to you.

I will find my way back. I promise. Give me time.

Don't come after me. Don't risk yourself. You are too important.

You hold the key, Riley.

Love you forever,

James

"I don't understand what he's talking about," I said, standing and handing the note to Garner. He's silent for a moment as he reads the words James has left me, his expression a mixture of concern and thoughtfulness.

"He always told me he didn't want you to come here, Riley. That you wouldn't be safe. I'm starting to think he knew a hell of a lot more than he ever let on."

"Me too." The realization that he'd kept something for me broke something deep inside of me. I ignored the pain, considering the note, and my brother's warning. "You hold the key. Why do I keep hearing about a goddamn key?"

Garner quirked an eyebrow, looking up at me. "What do you mean?"

"It's a long story," I said as I moved into the kitchen and rummaged through the cupboards. Pulling out a dustpan and making my way back to the shattered frame, I explained the prophecy to Garner as I cleaned up the mess I'd made.

"Maybe James was aware of the prophecy," Garner mused thoughtfully from where he'd plopped himself down on the couch. "Is there any chance you might be the daughter of shadows the prophecy refers to? That might explain what James means."

Taking a deep breath, I closed my eyes and reached down deep into my well of power, searching for the shadows I'd inadvertently used in my air tutoring session with Stefan. Once I summoned them, they flowed freely through my body, reaching my fingertips with ease. I let them flow out and wrap themselves around me, moving similar to that of a gentle wind twisting around my body.

Opening my eyes, I looked directly at him, searching for any hint that he might betray me and let this information fall into the wrong hands. James had trusted him, which meant I did too. When I didn't find any, I nodded.

"Yeah, I think Kala might be my father."

"Holy shit. That would make you a fucking demi-god."

CHAPTER THIRTY-ONE

Riley

"Cheers," Bee clinks her glass against mine from where she'd sat perched on the edge of the bathtub. Her smile was infectious, excited energy leaking from her in droves. "Gosh, I can't wait to dance the night away and just let loose."

Contrary to her bright, bubbly personality, Bee had worn a short black strapless dress to tonight's dance. Her short hair was pulled back from her face and pinned in an elegant knot at the back of her head, a few loose curls framing her face. Her green eyes were sparkling with excitement as she waited for me to finish getting ready.

"Mmmhmm, I bet you can't," I said, taking a small sip of faerie wine before placing my glass on the sink. The orange and strawberry flavor washed over my tongue, and I sighed, memories of my first taste at B station washing over me.

Leaning forward, I squinted into the mirror and lined my eyes with kohl. "Surely it has nothing to do with a certain someone agreeing to be your date?"

"It has everything to do with her, Riley. I can't believe we've never met before. I could kill Colin for not thinking to introduce us! I'm so glad you did. I..." Bee sighed contentedly, before catching my eye in the mirror and shooting a love-struck grin at me. "Thank you. I like her a lot. It's been a while since I've felt that way."

"Glad to be of service." Spinning to face her, blinking my lashes excessively. "How do I look?"

My dress was also strapless, though it was much longer than Bee's, the bottom of it just brushing the floor. The sage green silk hugged my curves in all the right places, a slit up the side coming almost to the very top of my thigh. The color really brought out the olive tone of my skin and made my hazel eyes seem more green than brown. A braid wrapped around the top of my head like a crown, the rest of it falling in soft waves down my back. The style was a nod to the way Lincoln had worn his own hair the day we'd met.

"Like a freaking goddess."

The words washed over me, sending an icy shiver down my spine, and I stiffened. I'd told Bee about the note from James that I'd discovered with Garner, the shadows I'd wielded when learning to control my air with Stefan, and that I suspected that I was somehow connected to Kala, the god of darkness and keeper of souls.

It wasn't much more than a week ago that I believed I was human. Processing all the new information and clues to my past and my power while also trying to figure out what the hell had happened to James was a lot. It was overwhelming and I needed to escape it for a little while.

"Sorry, Riley. I didn't mean... Let's not dwell on it. We *will* work out the prophecy. We'll find where The Resistance is keeping James and bring him home. And then we'll figure out your heritage. Let's enjoy tonight first."

Grinning at her, I let myself relax, rolling my shoulders in an attempt to let go of the stress I'd been carrying.

"Yes, let's go dance the night away." I winked at her while taking another sip of wine. The familiar warmth was spreading through my body, making me feel lightheaded and giddy already.

We left the bathroom and headed out of our room and down the hallway to the landing, where we'd agreed to meet Lincoln.

We moved through the double doors and my eyes found him instantly, his back to us as he leant against the balustrade and stared out at the ocean. It was dusk, the sun setting out over the ocean, the sky a kaleidoscope of colors.

It really was beautiful, and my heart ached at the thought that these lands were dying, that one day soon this view might not exist anymore.

My gaze didn't linger on the view for long, the man in front of me drawing my attention more completely than a pretty sunset could. He was wearing simple navy-blue slacks and a white shirt, and his long honey blonde hair was pulled back in a ponytail. I couldn't help but run my eyes over the lean muscles of his back as they flexed against his shirt.

My connection with Lincoln had been instant. The moment our eyes met, I'd felt a tug in my chest drawing him to me. It was an easy attraction. He was soft, kind, and gentle. Nothing like his father, King Ronan. I was more than eager to spend more time with him and explore the attraction between us. Maybe we really were mates.

Bee cleared her throat, giving me a knowing look as she stepped past me and made her way down the grand staircase. The dance was to be held in the dining room. Fae had been in and out all day as they transformed the space. First years had not been allowed in. It was, after all, a celebration of them, of their awakening and their introduction to the academy and learning to control their new powers.

Stefan had seemed to be in charge, barking orders at the older students and fae and offering me a quick kiss as he rushed around earlier today. He'd been very tightlipped about what to expect. I couldn't wait to see how the space looked. Imagining it as more than just a cafeteria was difficult.

Lincoln turned as Bee disappeared down the stairs, his eyes locking on me immediately. The world around us seemed to disappear as his navy eyes landed on my face, then trailed slowly down my body, lingering on the small swell of cleavage revealed by the bodice of my gown, tracing the lines of my waist and hips before raising back up to my face.

A wide grin broke across his face, those midnight eyes sparkling as he closed the distance between us.

"You look good enough to eat," he growled, a small squeak escaping me as he swept me into his arms and crushed his lips down on mine.

This kiss differed from our first. The passion, desire, and heat were all still present, but Lincoln moved slower, really taking his time to taste me. Sinking into him and wrapping my arms, I submitted to him, parting my lips as his tongue swiped across them.

His teeth nipped at my bottom lip, and I moaned, a rush of heat flooding to my core, making me want him, want more of this. His mouth was on my jaw, my neck, that sensitive spot near my ear. I dipped my head back, a whimper escaping me as a haze of lust wrapped itself around me.

Something in my chest was tugging, tightening, urging me closer to Lincoln. I couldn't think, couldn't see past my desire for him. The need to wrap myself around him and not let go was overwhelming.

"Let's skip the dance," I said, my voice husky and wanton. "Let's stay right here, just you and I. Get to know each other more."

A groan escaped him from where his lips met my neck. "I wish we could, Tyas, I really do." He placed a kiss on my collarbone, then straightened, cupping my jaw with one hand, while the other rested on my hip and his eyes searched mine. "I have to make an appearance. My father demands it. Maybe we can leave early?"

The fog of lust I'd been encased in cleared instantly at the mention of his father. How had I almost forgotten Lincoln was the Water Prince? Of course he had responsibilities and an expectation to appear at tonight's dance.

Pushing myself up onto my toes, I placed a gentle kiss on his soft tempting lips and smiled at him.

"Whatever this is," I said, gesturing between us. "It will keep. The pull I feel toward you—to Stefan and Colin as well—isn't going anywhere. We don't need to rush it. Let's go 'dance the night away' as Bee so elegantly put it."

"How did I get so lucky?" He voiced the question so low that I almost didn't hear him as he held my hand in his and led me downstairs.

It hadn't escaped my notice that he hadn't even balked at the mention of the connection I felt with Stefan and Colin, too.

My heart felt fuller than it had in the longest time. It really felt like I was finding my place, and my people. I just needed to find my brother, too.

⇒⟫⟩ ⟨⟨⟨⟵

Black silk curtains hung from every wall of the dining hall, encasing the room and transforming the space completely.

Vines wound their way up the curtains, blooming with flowers in white, pink, purple, and more. There were no lights on, instead extra chandeliers had been hung from the ceiling, hundreds of candles lighting the space with a flickering orange glow.

The floor had been cleared of the usual tables and chairs, seating instead placed off to one side, leaving most of the floor free to act as a dance floor. A makeshift stage had been set up against the far wall, a small band belting out the notes of a song I'd never heard before.

Students milled about, glasses in hand, many already on the dance floor, their bodies swaying to the music. I spotted Amy and Bee dancing together and grinned at them. They looked so happy together.

Bee looked up, catching my eye and waving me over. Tugging on Lincoln's hand, I led him over to the couple and fell in beside them.

I let the music flow through my body as I gyrated my hips to the beat the band was creating. The atmosphere was relaxed, heady, and I could feel myself loosening up.

Lincoln's hand grasped my hips as I let myself go, let the music take me where it would. He pulled me close to him, moving in time, our bodies fitting together snugly. I could feel every inch of him pressed against me and the overwhelming sense of lust I'd felt earlier reared back up. I pressed closer to him, bringing my mouth to his as we moved together on the dancefloor.

Heat pooled in my core, and I realized there was a very different type of dance I wanted to do with this man. That would have to wait. I'd just have to enjoy him like this for now.

And I did enjoy him. We danced like that for some time, our bodies pressed close, moving with the beat supplied by the music. The dance floor filled with bodies, all of them moving to the same beat, everyone enjoying themselves. I let go of everything that had been weighing me down. Stopped worrying about it for the moment. Whatever will be, will be. Tonight was about letting go.

A tap on my shoulder broke the trance I was in, and I peeled myself off of Lincoln, spinning around to find Stefan standing behind me, a massive grin on his face.

"May I cut in?" he asked.

Lincoln wrapped his hands around my waist and pressed a gentle kiss to my cheek. "I'll get us some drinks."

He was gone before I could say a word, and I immediately missed his touch, his presence. I watched him weaving through the crowd until he disappeared among the thrum of people, before turning back to Stefan.

"You look beautiful, little dove. Would you like to dance?" He held his hand out in offer. Stepping forward, I ignored his hand, moving right into his space and wrapping my arms around his waist and resting my head on his chest.

We hadn't seen much of each other since he'd begun teaching me to wield my air magic. Some part of me had been aching for him, and the strength of that ache surprised me.

Stefan wrapped his arms around me, pressing a soft kiss to the top of my head, swaying our bodies gently from side to side as the band began a slow song.

"I heard about your visit to James' house and his letter. How are you holding up?"

"Garner or Bee?" I asked, avoiding his question. My emotions were in turmoil. It was going to take time to process everything I'd learnt the last few days. Until I had, I couldn't be sure how I was feeling.

"Neither. Colin told me."

"Colin?" I asked, jerking my head back from his chest in surprise. "I haven't spoken to him. How did he find out?"

"He is the General, Riley," Stefan chuckled, amusement dancing in his silver eyes. "The man knows everything. He has eyes and ears everywhere."

Sighing heavily, I nodded and tucked myself back into Stefan's embrace as we continued moving to the gentle music.

It made sense that Colin would know something like that, and maybe it explained the eyes I'd felt on me in the city center yesterday. Didn't he trust me? Did he truly see me as a threat to his people? So much so that he had me watched?

Hurt and anger warred inside my chest. It was hard to tell which one might win this particular battle.

Stefan didn't press me for an answer. Seeming to understand that I didn't have one for him. He just held me as we danced through another song. We moved past Bee and Amy, the two of them locked in a similar embrace.

Good. It was nice to see this side of Bee. She'd been so full of life—vibrant and excited—since we'd returned from our day out yesterday. I couldn't be happier for her.

The song ended and Stefan stopped, loosening his hold on me, his hands drifting to my hips as he held me before him. "I better give you back to your date. He looks a little lonely over there." He inclined his head off to the side, where Lincoln indeed was standing alone, holding two glasses of faerie wine.

Lincoln's face was set in a soft smile as he watched us. He didn't look put out or frustrated that he'd had to share my time tonight. He looked... happy about it? As though he liked to see the connection building between Stefan and I.

They were close—had grown up like brothers. Maybe this could work. Maybe, just maybe, I could explore these feelings with both of them. Colin, too, if I were lucky.

Stefan's hand cupped my face, drawing my gaze back to him. Fuck, he was handsome. And the way he was looking at me made me feel all sorts of hot and bothered.

His thumb stroked my jaw as he lifted my face to his, pressing his lips to my own in a gentle, fleeting kiss.

"Lincoln claimed you for tonight, though he was kind enough to grant me this time. Spend tomorrow night with me, please?" His breath was warm on my lips, my body melting into his.

"Yes, of course." There was no way I could say no. I wanted to spend every spare minute I had with these men, exploring them, getting to know them on a deeper level—on a physical one, too.

"See you then," he said, placing another quick peck on my lips and nodding at someone over my shoulder.

I spun around to find Lincoln there, holding a glass of wine out to me.

"Want to get some air?"

"That sounds amazing." Whilst I'd thoroughly enjoyed dancing with both men, the heat and press of bodies was becoming a little claustrophobic. A short escape sounded refreshing.

CHAPTER THIRTY-TWO

Lincoln

The moon was hanging high in the sky as I led Riley out the back of the Academy house and toward the beach. The stars were shining brightly, bathing the world in a dim, romantic glow. They were beautiful. But they couldn't hold a candle to the woman on my arm.

Fuck, she was gorgeous. Absolute perfection. Not only was she sweet, kind, and powerful, she was an absolute stunner. Her sage green dress clung to her body, highlighting her curves and showing off the lovely olive tone of her skin. The desire to know her, inside and out, had been consuming me from the moment I'd laid eyes on her. I was convinced she was my mate–you couldn't tell me otherwise.

"Where are you taking me?" she asked, a note of laughter in her tone. "Have you made enough of an appearance, Prince?"

Surprised laughter bubbled out of my throat, and I stopped, spinning to face her. Her beauty floored me every time I saw her. Even after spending the last few hours holding her on the dance floor, that feeling hadn't diminished.

"I'm not sure I care Tyas. The whole 'Prince' thing doesn't appeal to me the way it should. The way you do tonight."

Winking at her, I gave her no other warning as I swept her off her feet and carried her down to the shore. There was a little patch of sand, hidden from prying eyes by large boulders, trees and bushes, only a short walk from the Academy, and I planned to make use of the privacy it offers.

Letting out a startled squeal, Riley didn't fight me, only settled her head in the space between my neck and shoulder, relaxing into my hold.

"You don't want to take your father's place as King of the water elementals one day?" she asked. Her breath was warm against my skin, the smell of orange blossoms—her smell—making me inhale deeply.

Silence fell between us, the only sound the gently crashing of the waves against the shore, as I considered her question.

She'd referred to my father as the King of the water elementals. She wasn't wrong. Back in Faerie, that is exactly what he was. He was one of four kings who, in combination, provided balance and leadership to the lands. Here on Earth, though? My father ruled alone and, over the last few years, had insisted he be addressed as King, without the water elemental label attached.

He was the only King here on earth, and without contact with those on Faerie, he could do as he pleased, command as he saw fit too, with no one else to answer to.

I wasn't sure that was a good thing. More and more, I felt as though he was making decisions that opposed his promise to return Earth to its former glory and allow the humans their land back. He had always been power hungry, and here on Earth his power was absolute.

"It's not that I don't want to take his place. I worry about what I will be left with when that day comes. And whether I'll be able to right his wrongs."

This fear was one I hadn't shared with anyone, not even Stefan, who I considered my brother despite our lack of blood ties. She brought it out in me, though. This honesty. One of many reasons I suspected she was my mate.

"What do you mean?" She pulled her face away from where she had nuzzled into my neck, her hazel eyes searching mine for an answer.

"I mean, fuck. I haven't told anyone this before, Riley." Blowing out a frustrated breath, I continued. "His actions don't align with helping your world to heal, with the promise we made to the humans. I fear what is to come. About how much longer the land and people will survive, whether we'll return home. The few that oppose him or raise any of these issues are quickly shut down, dealt with. He's even begun shutting the Elders out. I will have to challenge him, but I'm not ready. I've only just come into my power." The words sounded like excuses on my tongue.

Nodding gravely, she tore her eyes away from mine, staring out across the darkened sea.

"Before I came here, I hated your kind. Did you know that?" Her voice was low, almost a whisper, and I had to strain to hear her above the sounds of the ocean.

"No, I didn't."

"I was angry. I resented the lot of you. How could you live here, within your walls, and not care about what was happening outside of them?" We reached the alcove I'd been aiming for, and I moved inside the ring of trees and boulders. This alcove had been somewhat of a getaway for Stefan and I for sometime now, and we kept a stash of necessities in a small box hidden among the rocks. I placed Riley down softly on the sand, and grabbed a couple of blankets, laying one down on the sand and sitting down, gesturing for her to join me.

She scrambled closer, pulling her legs to her chest, the slit in her gown falling open and exposing the bare skin of her thigh, creamy in the rays of moonlight reaching us here. She wrapped her arms around her legs, still staring out at the ocean.

"I'm still not convinced enough is being done, but I can see that it's not all for a lack of trying." She turned to face me then, a grim look on her face. "I met your father the other day. I don't think he likes me, or what I represent. And I didn't much like him. If he's the reason my people are suffering, then I will stand against him."

Placing a hand on my chest, Riley twisted toward me, rising on her knees, her face level with my own.

"You and I might have only met recently, but my soul knows yours, Lincoln. Something deep down tells me you will do what's right, even if that means challenging your own kin. I'm sorry that the weight of that falls on you."

My soul knows yours.

My chest tightened and my pulse thumped erratically against my ribcage as those words sunk in. I couldn't think, couldn't breathe around the weight of them. She couldn't know what those four words meant. They were confirmation that I wasn't imagining this pull between us, that maybe—just maybe—she really was meant for me.

There were no words to describe how I felt in that moment. So, I did the only other thing I could do. I showed her. Lifting my hand, I cupped her face, my thumb tracing her jaw, then the soft flesh of her bottom lip, before I pressed my lips against hers.

She kissed me back, gently at first, the press of her lips against mine becoming more demanding as she wrapped her arms around my neck and leant back on her calves. We twisted, falling next to each other on the sand, hands roaming, exploring the other.

My fingers trailed lightly down her arm, her hip, as I broke our kiss and trailed feather light kisses across her jaw, her neck. She moaned as I pressed a kiss beneath her ear, my cock hardening instantly at the sound.

Pulling me closer to her, she cocked a leg over my waist, and I grasped the smooth skin of her thigh, tracing circles over the exposed skin as she rolled the both of us, until I was lying on my back, her straddling my waist. The heat of her core pressed against my erection, eliciting another soft moan from her lips.

Gyrating her hips, she ground her clit against my hard length, and I bit back the urge to rip that gorgeous gown from her body and take her immediately.

Trailing my fingers higher, I found her molten core, shoving her soaking panties aside and running a finger between her slick folds.

"Fuck, Riley, you're so wet. Is this for me, Tyas?" Dragging my fingers back up, I circled her clit once, twice, before finding her entry and pushing inside her.

"Yes," she whimpered, the need in her voice clear. "Fuck me, Lincoln."

Who was I to deny her when she asked so nicely?

"Tell me what you need, babe." There wasn't a chance in the world I'd deny her. My cock throbbed almost painfully in my pants as Riley gathered the hem of her dress and pulled it above her head. She was bare beneath, nothing but her small lace panties between us.

Reaching up, I cupped one of her small breasts in my palm before rolling her perfect pink nipple between my thumb and forefinger. She cried out, arching her back in pleasure and rocking herself against my hand. The need to be inside her, to feel her walls clamp around my dick as she came, took hold and I pulled my hand away, rolling us so that I was above her, bracing myself on one hand. Unbuckling my belt with the other, I dipped my head and sucked her peeked breast into my mouth, nibbling gently before letting it go and moving to the other.

Riley writhed beneath me and I tugged my suit pants down, unable to slow or wait any longer.

My erection burst free and, shoving her panties aside, I pressed against her entry, the wet heat of her against my tip almost sending me into a frenzy.

"Is this what you want, Riley? You want me inside you?"

"Please," she begged, and I was a goner.

Growling, I entered her slowly. Her pussy was so tight, her walls clamping down around me as I pushed myself inside of her. Her body trembled, so close already.

"So fucking responsive," I muttered as I seated myself fully inside her, giving her a moment to adjust to the full length of me. She was a goddamn picture beneath me.

"Lincoln," she whined, pushing her hips up in a clear demand for more.

Not needing any further encouragement, I moved, thrusting in and out of her in long, hard strokes. Riley met me thrust for thrust, raising her hips to meet mine.

"Fuck, babe. I'm not going to last long if you keep that up."

She smiled at me from beneath her lashes, her eyes dancing with lust and amusement as she brought her hand to her breasts and teased her own nipples as I continued pounding in and out of her.

Her moans and gasps of pleasure were almost enough to push me over the edge. Gritting my teeth, I reached down between us, gently teasing the small bundle of nerves before pinching it once.

"Lincoln," she cried out, her back arching as the walls of her pussy clamped down around me, her strength of her orgasm causing me to roar through my release.

Collapsing beside her, I'm careful not to crush her beneath me. Trailing my fingers gently up and down her arm, I watched as she slowly caught her breath. Pulling her into my arms, she rested her head on my chest, her hand pressed lightly above my heart.

We lay like that for a while before the peace is broken by a nasally voice calling for me from beyond the alcove, out on the sand.

"Prince Lincoln," Colonel Stubbe shouted from nearby. "Your father has requested you return home."

Of course he fucking did. Why I thought he'd allow me to enjoy myself tonight was beyond me. Wishful thinking.

"Shit," Riley cursed, her eyes widening as she scrambled to her knees, searching for her dress. "Why does this keep happening to me?"

Cocking an eyebrow, I looked at her questioningly as I located my pants and tugged them on, hopping on one leg as I pulled them up. Her soft giggle caused me to grin back at her.

"You'll have to explain that later. I'll make sure Colonel Stubbe doesn't find you." I leant down and pressed a quick peck against her lips as I buckled my belt, grateful I didn't have to fuss with shirt buttons given I never even took it off. I would have to fix that though. This girl deserved more than a frenzied tryst in the sand. Swearing to myself that I'd make it up to her, I continued. "Go find Stefan, enjoy the rest of the dance. I'll see you tomorrow."

"Ok, goodnight, Lincoln."

"Goodnight, Tyas." Ducking out of the alcove, I glanced back, committing the image of her face, flushed with a post-orgasm glow, smiling brightly at me to memory. I'd need it if I had to deal with Colonel Stubbe tonight.

CHAPTER THIRTY-THREE

Stefan

The current song ended, and I leant down, pressing a quick kiss to Bee's cheek as I excused myself and swung her back toward Amy. Both girls grinned at me, offering quick waves goodbye before turning back to each other and falling back into the music. The room had crowded in on me, the music too loud, the people too close. Fresh air. I needed some fresh air.

Pushing through the crowd, I made a beeline for the side door. The same one Riley and Lincoln had disappeared through some time ago. Honestly, I'd been surprised Lincoln hadn't stolen her away sooner, with the way she looked tonight. If she'd been my date, we wouldn't have made it to the dance at all.

The cool night air kissed my cheeks as I pushed through the door, moving to the side and leaning up against the Academy wall. Taking a deep breath, I tipped my head back toward the sky, closing my eyes and trying to focus on the calm night around me.

Sometimes, nights like tonight tested my control. When my senses were overwhelmed, it became harder to smother the unwanted presence inside my chest and it roused, lifting its head and peering around, waiting for an opportunity to strike.

That's exactly what it was doing now, assessing my strength, and determining whether this might be the time to attack and seize control of my body and mind. I didn't know what it was, whether it was some primal part of me, or a disease I'd been inflicted with.

Fuck, I hated this shit. Hated it with a goddam passion. Why was I cursed to battle another entity, one who tried to erase me the moment I let my guard drop? It was exhausting. I was exhausted.

"Stefan," Lincoln's voice carried on the night air, and I opened my eyes, searching for him. Spotting him approaching from the beach with Colonel Stubbe, I pushed off the wall and walked to meet him.

"Did Father call you home already?" It didn't surprise me, King Ronan often called Lincoln here, there, and anywhere whenever the fuck he pleased and for no fucking reason. It seemed a little early, though.

"Unfortunately," he confirmed, giving Colonel Stubbe, who was standing a few feet away, a dirty look. Stubbe just glared back at him, tapping his foot impatiently. That man was insufferable, though I probably would be too, if I were the King's errand boy.

"Where's Riley?" She'd left with Lincoln before but wasn't with him now.

"She's safe. In the nook. She said she'd come find you." Lincoln's voice was low, likely so that Colonel Stubbe couldn't hear. Neither of us trusted the sniveling bastard, and we weren't about to trust him with her safety. Lincoln had even gone so far as using our codeword for the little cove we'd discovered on the beach.

"I'll meet her. Good luck, brother." Lincoln nodded and followed Colonel Stubbe around the Academy, heading back toward the city and the Royal quarters. Once they were out of view and I was sure Colonel Stubbe wouldn't see where I was headed, I moved toward the beach, to where Lincoln had left Riley.

She should be safe there, but even as I thought it, something heavy settled in my gut, intuition warning me that something wasn't quite right. Quickening my pace, I stepped onto the sand, my body coiled to run to her, just as an explosion rocked the Academy behind me.

The force of it knocked me from my feet and I was thrown through the air, crashing onto the beach. Grateful for the soft landing, I sprung to my feet, eyes immediately locking on the academy building behind me.

My blood turned to ice in my veins at the scene before me, at the smoke pouring from the windows, the yells and cries of the Fae inside, fighting to get out. From the shadows around the building emerged what had to be at least a hundred hooded figures.

The Resistance. It had to be. The hooded outfits were their uniform. They'd been wearing them during the attack in the Dead Forest, too. How had they infiltrated the walls surrounding Danann? We had guards stationed day and night to prevent this from happening. Why were they attacking us now? Here? What did they want?

My stomach turned to lead, beads of sweat breaking out on my brow as fear flooded through my body.

Riley.

My heart beat almost painfully in my chest as I tore my gaze from the Academy, looking down the beach toward the nook where Lincoln had said he'd left her.

My ears rang, the sounds of screaming and fighting fading out around me as my focus shifted solely onto Riley. Getting to her, and then getting her to safety. Now. I had to get to her now.

Nothing was allowed to happen to her. I wouldn't let anything happen to her. She was the light to my darkness, the balance I'd been searching for my whole fucking life. They couldn't have her.

I couldn't see her. She wasn't on the beach, which must mean she was still inside the nook. Pushing up from the ground, I ran, my feet slipping on the soft sand as I tried to close the distance between us.

"Stefan!" A voice yelled from behind me, anger and fear lacing it in equal parts. I didn't need to turn to know that voice, to know Colin—General Brand—was behind me. He'd fallen just as hard for Riley. Of course he was here, searching for her, too.

"This way," I shouted at him, without so much as looking in his direction. Colin could follow me, he'd catch up, I couldn't slow for a moment. The alcove came into view, or at least the trees and rocks surrounding it did. Not daring to slow, I only pushed harder as I felt Colin catching up with me. We'd make it. We'd find her. We had to.

Muscles tensing, every inch of my body recoiling, I roared in horror as at least a dozen hooded figures leapt out of the trees, converging on the alcove.

No. Fuck, no.

They were too far for my air to hit them. My magic had never failed me before, but it couldn't help me now. When it felt like I needed it most.

Colin's roar echoed my own, the sound full of warning. Both to Riley, for her to get the fuck out of there, and to the fuckers clearly attempting to take her.

The fucking creature inside of me lifted its head again, its ears perking up in response to the General's roar, sniffing at the air like it too recognized the sense of impending doom. Smoke from the explosion surrounded us, filling the night air, urging me forward, and I pumped my limbs as hard and fast as I could.

Just a little closer and I'd be able to fight. Stop those people from taking my girl.

There was no time to smother the beast inside, to push it down, and ensure I had control of myself. To make sure I grasped that control and held it in an iron tight grip.

Riley was all I could focus on. Just a little further.

More hooded figures leapt from the trees surrounding the alcove, turning to face us as we raced toward them. They were going to stand their ground. Fuck if I'd let them get away with this.

Pushing my hands in front of me as I ran, I gathered my air, let it flow through my veins, and built into a crescendo in my palms. I was going to knock these fuckers out of my path. They would not keep me from my girl.

Colin was by my side now, and we were closing in. I could see his flames dancing in his palms. Good. He was ready.

"On three," he shouted, panting hard as we ran. Nodding my agreement, I pulled more and more power from my core, readying myself. I'd drain every last drop of magic inside of me if it would save her. My little dove, my sunshine.

"Three. Two. One—"

Boom. Boom. Boom. Boom. Boom.

A series of explosions rang out across the night, the ground beneath my feet rocking violently as sand flew through the air.

Something hard slammed into me, throwing me to the ground, shock and alarm causing me to release my air attack into the skies. The weight of whatever had knocked me down—Colin, I realized quickly—knocked the wind from my lungs, stunning me for a long second.

Scrambling out from under him, I tried desperately to get my bearings. Fire and smoke surrounded me, Fae and Resistance members fighting all around me. I tried to ignore the crumpled figures spotted around the grounds. I could think of them later. Riley needed me.

Locating the alcove, I realized in horror that it was no longer surrounded. A group of figures was further out, sprinting for the outer wall of Danann. In the moonlight, I glimpsed curly blonde hair hanging over the shoulder of one man at the center of the group.

Icy rage filled me. If they'd hurt her—

My inner beast flexed his paws, releasing large, sharp claws from where they'd been retracted and scraped them across the cage I'd built around him in my mind long ago.

The agony was instantaneous, and I fell to my knees, grasping my head as bright white stars stained my vision. My breathing quickened as he repeated the motion, striking harder this time, pain causing me to curl in on myself.

This agony was like nothing I'd ever felt before. It filled every space inside my mind, leaving me no room to focus on anything else. Push it down. Push it down. But I couldn't.

As he swung his claws back and struck a third time, the crippling pain of it causing me to curve in on myself in the sand, I realized he'd never fought me like this. My cage had never been enough. Whatever he was, whatever he wanted from me, he'd been biding his time until he could take it.

White hot blinding pain spread through my body as the beast seized control. The crack of my bones and the raw, otherworldly scream tearing from my throat were the only sounds I could hear despite the fighting taking place all around me.

As darkness took over and became all I knew, it became clear that this time was different. The beast, soul, demon inside of me was not just taking control of my mind. He was taking control of my body.

Maybe I'd finally learn exactly what had plagued me all these years.

CHAPTER THIRTY-FOUR

Riley

Lingering in the alcove long after Lincoln left, I stared out the small entrance to the ocean, and the star-studded night sky beyond. The air was crisp against my still naked skin, but I reveled in it. I felt alive tonight.

I couldn't believe I'd only been here for just over a week. Danann already felt like home.

Back in Sommers, I'd had James and Sarie. But that was it. The friends I'd made here, the *connections* I'd formed were those unbreakable bonds of family. Wrapping my arms around myself, I smiled up at the night sky. Fate was a funny thing. I'd never have expected mine to lay here.

There was still so much work to do before I'd be at peace, finding James at the top of that list. Then I guess I'd have to figure out this damn prophecy. But for now, at this moment, I felt content.

A faint boom sounded from the Academy grounds, and I straightened with surprise, tilting my head and listening closer. Shouts followed soon after, together with a crackling sound that made the well of magic inside me crackle in return.

Something was wrong. Fuck.

Pushing to my knees, I scrambled in the sand for my gown, trying to pull it over my head in such a rush that I twisted myself within it. Wrestling with the silken fabric, I eventually pulled it off again and untangled it.

My heart was beating erratically in my chest as I pushed to my feet, trying to keep my hands from trembling as I tried again to pull on this fucking dress.

Some serious shit was happening, and I was struggling with a fucking dress.

Fuck.

What if my men were hurt? I had to get out there and help.

Twin roars sounded from down the beach at the same time shadows danced in the moonlight filtering through the cave opening. Shimmying into the dress, I frantically hitched it up around my waist and over my breasts, twisting toward the entry, ready to run.

Boom. Boom. Boom. Boom. Boom.

The ground shook violently with the explosions as I twisted toward the door and I lost my balance, falling forward.

Before I could blink, a black, hooded figure was before me, one arm wrapping around my waist, catching my weight against me.

"Sorry, love. Nothing personal." The only warning I had before something hard crashed into the side of my head and the world went dark.

Someone was knocking on the door.

Knock. Knock. Knock.

Groaning, I tried to roll, quickly realizing I wasn't able to move, both hands chained behind me where my back pressed against a hard, cold wall.

My eyes flew open, and I found myself in complete darkness. The movement made me realize no one had been knocking. The noise was a throbbing pain emanating from the side of my head where I'd been struck and knocked unconscious.

Panic grew inside me, my chest constricting and my heart beating furiously in my chest as memories slowly came back to me. Keeping still, trying not to alert anyone that I was awake, I tried to piece together where the fuck I was.

Quick glimpses came back to me.

Of dancing with Stefan and talking with Lincoln on the beach. Of Colonel Stubbe calling him away.

An explosion and the sounds of fire and of men roaring. My men, I think. Roaring for me.

Fuck. We'd been attacked.

I'd been taken.

Fear had me calling on that well of power inside me, hoping I could somehow break free of the chains around my wrist. The power flowed to my hands, and fizzled out, unable to escape.

"What the fuck?" I muttered aloud. There went any pretense that I was yet to awaken.

Next to me in the darkness, another set of chains rattled, followed by a sharp intake of breath. Stiffening, I strained my eyes in the gloom, trying to pinpoint where the movement had come from, who might be in here with me. I couldn't see a fucking thing. Fuck.

"Riley? You're awake?"

I froze, the voice one I'd recognize anywhere. One I'd been dying to hear since he'd left and ascended to Danann a long two years ago.

Tears slid down my cheeks as I turned toward the voice, needing to know if it was him. If he were real and not a figment of my imagination. Had the knock to my head rattled me that hard?

"James?" I asked. If he were here with me, then...

"Yeah, it's me, sis."

The Resistance had me.

About the Author

Raised in regional Australia, Roxy Leigh much prefers the kangaroo covered hills on the way to school pick up than the hustle bustle of the city.

You can usually find Roxy with her nose buried in a book, more often than not a fantasy or dark romance.

Writing a novel has always been a dream of hers, one that she is now making a reality!

When not off in a fantasy world, you can find Roxy playing survival RPG's with her husband, crafting or baking with her daughters, and spending entirely too much time watching bad reality TV.

www.instagram.com/authorroxyleigh

Roxy's Raunchy Readers – Facebook Group

Newsletter – http://subscribepage.io/WfgGoN

Also By

Wand to read more by Roxy Leigh?

Black Swan

Fairy Tales Reloaded: Happily Ever After

I am Octavia Hendrix, sole heir to my Fathers empire.
At least, that's what I thought.
Right up until my father, Liam Hendrix, ripped the rug out
from under my feet and demanded I marry a man of his choos-
ing. A man he sees fit to step into his shoes and rule over the
Hendrix Mafia.
A role I've always coveted.

Dean Lawson is my childhood best friend, my protector, and the love of my life. After he hurt me when we were younger, I swore never to get too close and give him that chance again.

Now he's my 'fiance'.

I refuse to be a broodmare, to marry someone so that they can take everything I've always wanted.

I've got to get away. Start fresh somewhere else.

If only it were that easy...

Octavia and Dean's story is a contemporary mafia Swan Princess retelling. It contains some steamy scenes and some darker themes such as kidnapping and SA (attempted). Please review the trigger warnings before proceeding.

Tasting You

Sweet Somethings II

There's never a bad time to receive a gift—especially a sexy one. Why limit them to holidays, anniversaries, or birthdays? You deserve to be spoiled 'just because' with sexy lingerie, toys, roleplay, videos, and so much more. After all, the best gifts are the ones that...keep you cumming.

Let us spoil you. Fourteen days of unbound pleasure await you on these pages. Pick as many gifts as you'd like, and read to your heart—and body's—content. Let these talented erotica writers take you on a journey to new pleasures.

Sweet Somethings II is a sexy collection of short and quick reads that will bring you lots of spicy moments, passion, love, foreplay, and fun! Of course, sit back, relax—with a drink, and maybe a vibe or toy—and enjoy!

Remember, alcohol and toys are optional, steam and sexiness are required.

Acknowledgements

Writing has always been a dream of mine, one I pushed to the side in favor of 'serious' careers. Oh how I regret that now. There is nothing wrong with following your passion, and I will forever be grateful I followed mine in the end!

I couldn't have done this without the love and support of my family. Mum, thank you for reading every thing I write, even when it's awkward. I love you.

A big thank you to Jess, Ashley, and Shana. You have been my cheerleaders from the beginning and I am thankful for you every single day.

A big shout out to Meg and the Baby Authors Support Group. If Meg hadn't adopted me and helped me find my people within the bookish community, I'm not sure I would have gotten this far.

And lastly, to Ellie Lukas. There is no way I could have done this without you! The love and encouragement you give me does not go unnoticed. I am a better writer, a better person, for having met you. I am forever thankful to have you by my side on this journey.

Thank you.

Made in the USA
Las Vegas, NV
13 December 2023

82688988R00215